HENRY'S TATTOO

HENRY'S TATTOO

A Novel

Michael Cronin

ISBN: 978-1-7324388-0-4

For Ellen

ONE

JUNE 3–8, 2013 (1)

After work during his first week in Philadelphia, Henry Knudsen patrolled the residential streets near Rittenhouse Square, looking for a studio apartment. He sought a quiet place within walking distance to work and close to where his beloved Gwynneth planned to move in a month, into her aunt and uncle's home in Antique Row, on Clinton Street, near Eleventh.

He first scouted west of the square, but the high-rises on Nineteenth and Twentieth Streets formed noisy urban canyons and were expensive. So he looked east, nearer City Hall. But there, the streets seemed even noisier and the apartments just as pricey.

On his third and fourth days of hunting, he looked south of the square and was captivated by the low-rise townhouses in the federal style lining the narrow streets. Their flat brick facades, symmetric rows of windows, and semicircular fanlights over the front doors presented a more pleasing ambience than the Philadelphia high-rises, and reminded him of the sundry designs of residential structures in the Dupont Circle neighborhood of Washington, DC, where he'd lived the previous six years.

Staff in the delis and coffee shops he patronized south of Rittenhouse Square seemed friendlier and more informative than the folks he'd encountered in DC. The bakery and café employees he asked about rentals knew the neighborhood and shared their ideas with him. A young barista at Plenty Café on Spruce Street told him over breakfast, "Try down on Pine or Waverly." She pointed with her thumb over her shoulder, south along Sixteenth Street. "We see signs for rents there once in a while."

Then, on Friday, June 7, in a polygonal bay window on Pine Street, he espied a neat, handwritten sign, "Apt for rent #2." Below the gray-painted bay window frames, three wooden planters held magenta petunias. Sprays of English ivy cascaded down to the sidewalk from the planter boxes. Above the bay window and front door, three stories of plain flat red bricks were balanced with pairs of window frames whose lintels, painted dark red, made a subtle complement to the bricks.

He climbed five well-worn white marble stairs, stepped into the shallow portico, and pressed the buzzer for number 2. A dark-skinned black man in his fifties, about as tall as Henry's six feet two inches, loomed in the two large glass center panels of the polished-wood front door. His white short-sleeved T-shirt and creased wool charcoal trousers displayed a trim and muscular torso.

As the man pulled the door open, raking late-afternoon sunlight shone on his face. "Help you?" he asked.

Henry gasped with a sharp inhale at the sight of a pistol in the man's side holster but, keeping his eyes from the gun, he made eye contact with the man and asked, "Is that your sign? For rent —"

The man saw Henry's gape and interrupted him. "Yes, that's my sign, and this Glock Gen4 is my duty pistol. I'm Detective Martin Perez, Pennsylvania State —"

"Ah," Henry said, regaining his composure. *That's a relief,* he thought. *If it's true.*

"Police. Just got off work, and here, I'm the landlord. If you want to see the studio —"

"Yes," Henry said.

In reply, the black man swung the door toward him and invited Henry inside with a sweep of a right arm adorned with a faded replica of an eagle, globe, and anchor. It was the tattoo of a young marine recruit, Henry guessed.

2

Martin turned around and said, "Third floor," with the overtone of a drill sergeant's order. Despite having just met the man and seen he was armed Henry's sense was that he could be trusted. He kept up with Martin's brisk two-at-a-time pace up two flights of stairs. Neither man was out of breath when they reached the studio's entryway.

"Rent is nine fifty a month if you qualify," he said, turning the doorknob and pushing open the latched but unlocked apartment door. Henry stepped over the threshold and walked in.

The place was tiny, but its varnished broad-plank wood floor was immaculate. Walls painted beige reached to the twelve-foot tin ceiling. Light poured into the studio through two eight-pane windows, each two feet by six feet. The windows faced into a deep garden below them and up to the twin glass art deco spires of the Liberty Place skyscrapers six blocks north. The glass in the windowpanes was spotless. Lined umber faux-linen drapes hung from traverse dowels almost to the floor. The baseboards behind the drapes were free of dust.

Henry turned back toward the Pullman kitchen and reached down for the refrigerator handle. "Do I qualify to open the fridge?"

Martin smiled and nodded. "Sure. New in town?"

Henry did not answer the question. He opened the small refrigerator. Its racks were clean and empty. "What's included in —"

"Heat and electric. We're air-conditioned. Wired for Wi-Fi and cable. You need parking?"

"No," Henry said. "How many in the building?"

"Eight units. Seven rentals. I'm the live-in owner, bursar, and maintenance crew. One tenant on the first floor, three on the second, two up here, and this vacancy."

"How big is this studio?"

Martin said, "It's small, about four hundred square feet."

Henry answered Martin's earlier query. "Just transferred from DC to the home office of ACI, a small consulting firm. I'm at the Warwick and looking for my own place."

He paused, then said, "What I've seen of your house is in excellent condition."

"I keep it that way, but it was in good shape when I bought it in the eighties. I was still in the corps, based in Quantico and the Pentagon."

"In Virginia," Henry said.

Martin stared at Henry, unsure what he meant by his comment. "Right," he said. "And the banks here wouldn't loan me a dime to buy in this area. But the Marine Corps credit union wasn't into redlining, so I got a mortgage on this place based on my work history, account balances, and credit rating."

Henry appreciated Martin's personal details.

In 1999, when he was sixteen, Henry asked his father why the run-down areas in Hempstead, NY, their hometown, were racially segregated. Lars Knudsen explained to his son how in the 1930s and '40s, banks rated certain districts for credit risk. On city maps, rich areas were outlined in blue and green, marginal ones in yellow, and high-risk ones in red. "Banks didn't loan money to the mostly black residents in the high-risk areas. Housing stock inside red lines deteriorated as middle-class blacks moved out. Banks claim redlining isn't a racist practice. It's just financial reality. Risk management, they call it." Henry was well aware that redlining persisted well into the twenty-first century.

Martin continued. "My parents lived here till they passed in the late nineties. I'm here solo now. Philadelphia's been home all fifty-six years."

They returned to the first floor. "Mail and packages are delivered here." He pointed to an alcove with a narrow English walnut sideboard. Two small oak-framed mirrors on the wall flanked eight wooden cubbies, each four inches by four inches, painted red. A wastebasket and blue recycle tub sat beneath the cubbies.

"Deposit?" Henry asked.

"One month's rent if you sign a lease. Three months if you don't. Three-month minimum."

Henry had seen dozens of places online and visited twenty others during his search for an apartment. Most were dumps. A few of the gloomiest studios in high-rise buildings were smaller, rented for twice as much as this one, and added lease application fees and charges for activities, storage, and utilities. This studio on Pine Street offered easy walks to work, the subway, Saint John the Evangelist Catholic Church, and Gwynneth's future home.

"It's quiet," Martin said. "I'm two floors right below. We both face the rear garden."

"Good. I have a practice of tattoo before ten at —"

Martin stiffened. "We don't want you blowing any bugle late at night."

Henry shook his head. "No. The music's on my phone."

Studying Henry's countenance, Martin asked, "You're military?"

"No. As a Boy Scout I heard tattoo for years at summer camp. Now it helps me settle down at the end of the day. Haven't found a church offering compline."

Martin gazed at Henry. In twenty years, he'd had many consultants as reliable tenants, though he couldn't recall one who'd mentioned tattoo *or* compline. Here was young man who knew both. A trace of admiration eased his scrutiny. And the inquisitive twenty-five or thirty-year-old consultant seemed to know about redlining.

Henry returned Martin's eye contact, but his thoughts focused on the small studio apartment on the third floor. *Many good signals,* he told himself. *I'm OK with a twelve-month lease.* Gwynneth was set to move into her aunt and uncle's place on June 30. Her teaching contract at Drexel University ran one year.

Martin asked, "You'll be working full-time here?"

Henry exhaled and said, "Yes. Full-time. I'll take it."

Martin said, "Be right back." He returned shortly with a lease form, placed it on the sideboard, and wrote, in a blank space on its second page, "Pending verification of employment and credit rating." Henry initialed the addendum and signed it. Martin took it down the hall.

Moments later, Henry stood in the mailroom glancing at his copy of the lease as Martin examined Henry's check.

While Martin assessed his new tenant's broad shoulders, ruddy good looks, short blond haircut, and business-casual attire, Henry asked him, "Can you let me move in tomorrow?"

Martin blinked. "*Tomorrow?* You got a moving truck double-parked at the Warwick?"

"No. I can get a bed, floor lamp, and kitchen table delivered tomorrow. And I'll move a few things I have in an office storeroom."

"What's *a few things?*" Martin asked.

"Five boxes and a suitcase. They'll fit in a cab. You'll be here?"

"All morning," Martin said, "verifying your information. If it checks out and you move in on the eighth, I'll calculate a seven-day credit you can take when you pay the July rent."

Henry smiled and nodded. *Fair enough.*

Martin said, "You're working at ACI?"

"Yes. It's a consulting firm, started here by two guys —"

"Which two guys?" It was the pointed question of a police detective.

"Andre Morneau, the *A* in ACI, met Dave Carmichael, the *C* in ACI, about twenty years ago. They formed their own —"

"They incorporated. The *I* in ACI."

Henry said, "Yes, that's right. Now there are forty-plus employees here and six or seven each in Boston, New York, and Washington."

"They're from here?"

"Carmichael's from Philadelphia. He went to Cheyney State and Penn. Andre studied at Carnegie Mellon in Pittsburgh. He moved here in the nineties."

"And you work with these two?"

Henry said, "No. I work with a principal, Carmen Stanhope. Banking work."

Martin nodded and changed the subject back to Henry's moving in. "No books?"

"One dictionary. A Kindle. With the lease I can get a library card. That'll cover me."

Martin smiled at Henry's brief summary of how he met his reading needs.

Saturday morning, Henry carried his boxes and a suitcase to the third floor of 1589 Pine Street. At noon, two young Latinos delivered a double bed and frame and three flat boxes containing parts for a floor lamp, kitchen table, and two chairs.

Martin Perez bellowed at them, "*Mira las paredes en esas escaleras estrechas.*" The two men paused to show they were taking care to watch the walls on the narrow staircase.

The deliverymen assembled the bedframe, unpacked the box spring and mattress, and set them on the frame. They used Allen wrenches and screwdrivers to put together the square wooden table, small ladder-back chairs, and the lamp. It took them just fifteen minutes. Henry tipped each of them ten dollars and then put the linens and his quilt on his new bed.

TWO

JUNE 3–8, 2013 (2)

In December 2012, Henry Knudsen and Gwynneth Trevor met at the program for the homeless at Saint Matthew's Cathedral in Washington, DC, where Henry was a parishioner and Gwynneth, on sabbatical from the Roman Catholic Church, was a volunteer. They grew close. In the spring of 2013, Gwynneth accepted a promotion to conduct research and teach biochemistry in Philadelphia. When she asked him about moving, he got transferred there. Henry proposed that they each ask and answer two questions: *How do we feel about one another?* and *Can we commit to one another?*

Their discernment practices did not give them clarity on the queries. They resolved it would suit them to move to Philadelphia and live apart, just as they had in Washington.

Most nights in June 2013, at home in Washington, with a seventy-page lemon-yellow spiral-bound notebook open on a table in front of her, Gwynneth posed the two questions and awaited insights about them. At first she was frustrated at what seemed to her an arid exercise, but she was gratified at her patience when she persevered, even when no insights presented themselves.

In the meantime, she conducted biochemistry research at George Washington University. She imagined what she would take with her to Philadelphia and what she would leave behind after two years in Washington. She accepted her mother's invitation to be home in the Bronx for Father's Day.

Early Saturday June 8, she sent Henry a text message. "Off to NY for Father's Day. Join me?"

Minutes later, he accepted and asked about a present. "How about a full-size replica of the last 34 oz. Louisville Slugger Babe Ruth ordered from Hillerich & Bradsby?" Gwynneth had told Henry that Cedric Trevor raised all four of his children to be both Roman Catholic and fans of the New York Yankees. She said the bat would be fine.

She continued to ask herself the two questions and to record her thoughts, unconcerned that the thoughts were puzzling or inconsistent from one day to the next. One evening she wrote, "It's a mistake to make any commitment to Henry, despite my affection for him." Another evening she wrote, "Marry him?" She did not understand either the words or the question mark. Yet she continued to register her thoughts out of esteem for the discernment process and her confidence in herself.

And she was intrigued but not distressed to write down replies to queries she hadn't posed. "I'm not waiting to have a baby" was one. It arose with a jangling stridency, and it persisted. Another question grew out of her years of helping her three brothers run their landscaping enterprise. "When are you going to fortify your business experience with formal education?"

Later on Saturday June 8, she called Henry. "A while back you told me your old boss assigned you case histories in business management. You read and discussed them. You and Wainwright."

"Yes," he said.

"Do you still have the management case histories?"

"Yes."

"Would it be OK for me to take a look at them?"

"Sure," he said. "We can discuss one next weekend."

Later that evening, Gwynneth was confused by an unsolicited thought to put her queries about Henry in the negative. She posed one. *Do I have contempt for Henry's behavior or traits?* The answer was no, even though he was a practicing Catholic and she was not. She'd never slept with a better lover. He was one of the very few men she knew who listened to her.

Her second question ran, *What's keeping me from committing to him?* And her answer was *Fear. Last winter some of his wisecracks were mean. And in the seven months we've known each other we've both been on our best behavior.*

Then, on reflection, she told herself, *He may not be perfect but I'm fond of him and can commit to him. He's struggling to live a principled life. He respects me. My view is he can be trusted.*

That same Saturday evening, Henry's first night at 1589 Pine Street, he tended to his toilette, then sat on his zabuton, his back resting on the wall between the apartment windows, its curtains open to the clear and quiet Philadelphia night. He listened to a fifty-second recording of tattoo and felt himself calm down even as the bugle call's musical discordancy assaulted his auditory system.

When the recording ended, he recited aloud the traditional monastic compline psalms, numbers four, ninety-one, and one thirty-four. He was careful to pronounce each word and to pause at the end of every recalled line to keep from racing through them.

Next, in a traditional examination of conscience, he posed two questions. *Am I living my life according to the Gospel? How am I showing gratitude for the guidance of the holy spirit in my daily life?* He was glad to have moved from ACI's offices in Washington to Philadelphia and to be working full-time with Carmen Stanhope, for whom he'd worked in February 2013 on a banking project.

He dictated into the "Tattoo 2013" notes file on his phone: "We're lucky to be learning the banking business and how to market our services."

His examen continued with two questions he'd been posing to himself for ten weeks: *How do I feel about Gwynneth?* and *Can I commit to her?* He discerned each question as it affected his life purpose, spiritual path, vocation, family, stewardship, and body.

The answer he heard was *I adore her and can commit to her.*

After his examen, he ended his twenty-minute tattoo with *Peace. Be still*, a prayer suggested by his parish priest in Washington, DC. He turned off and removed the Bluetooth earbuds, set the alarm on his phone, put both in a basket on the kitchen table, and went to bed.

THREE
JUNE 9–10

Sunday, June 9, Henry set out for the eight thirty Mass at Saint John. He wore a tan lightweight parka, dark-brown khakis, and a plain light-blue baseball cap. Martin was at the front door, wearing an inky-dark navy suit and wrestling with an umbrella.

"Good morning," said Henry.

"You're up early," said Martin Perez.

"Me?" Henry teased.

"Off to Mass at Saint John," said Martin Perez.

"You're a parishioner there?"

"Yes," Martin began. "And I go —"

"That's where I'm headed," Henry interrupted. "OK to walk with you?"

On their way home from Mass, they stopped for coffee and something to eat at the Metropolitan Bakery on Nineteenth Street.

They ordered.

"Biscuit-and-egg sandwich and a small cappuccino," said Martin.

"French tarragon chicken salad and a Rocket Roast." In his nine days in Philadelphia, Henry had acquired a yen for Greenstreet Coffee's espresso.

They sat. They ate.

"Next week they read *Ulysses* aloud on Delancey Street, a few blocks west of here," Martin said.

"The whole eight hundred pages? Aloud?"

"Yes. Every word. Readers come from all over the world. Every year."

"Gonna miss it," Henry said. "Going to New York for Father's Day."

"Maybe next year," said Martin. "Meantime, can I ask you about your tattoo?"

Henry nodded.

"Were you a monastic? Is that where you —"

"No," Henry interrupted. "My tattoo is a deliberate time for psalms and quiet at day's end, not the traditional military call to quarters. The bugle call is not a lullaby. It's weird enough —"

Martin laughed. During his years as a marine, he'd heard the discordant strains of tattoo hundreds of times.

Henry continued. "And jarring enough to separate me from the rest of my day. It runs less than a minute."

"A minute can be a long time," Martin said.

Henry, recalling he was chatting with a state police detective, regarded the older man's poignant observation. It had a ring of profound experiences. Being underwater? Listening to the screams of casualties from a violent car crash? Confronting savage punks?

"It's grating some nights, but it's not as bad as reveille," Henry said.

"Oh," said Martin with a smile. "I know. Is that what you use to wake up?"

"No. Not in the morning."

"Morning is when they play it," Martin said. "Reveille."

"Some days I need wake-up calls all day long to live according to the Gospel."

They ate and drank, easy with the long gaps that fell into their conversation.

"I use tattoo in place of the bell used to call monastics to prayer."

Martin asked, "You've heard that bell?"

Henry paused before replying, wanting to avoid a lengthy aside. "In Berryville, Virginia, past the Blue Ridge on the Shenandoah

River, the Trappists offer individual retreats. Monks are called to prayer five times a day by a bell. Guests can join them." Henry hesitated. He'd responded to the question but didn't want to hijack the conversation.

When Martin made it clear he was interested and listening, Henry continued. "Benedictines have a guest house at their monastery in Collegeville, Minnesota. They use a bell, too."

Martin asked, "You've been there? Collegeville?"

"Yes. Anyone may join those monks too, five times a day. In monasteries, the compline rite varies from place to place. The monasteries schedule the hours —"

"The Divine Office."

"And compline can be brief or lengthy. It's short and early in Berryville, later and longer in Collegeville. The abbot decides at each monastery."

"So you've created your own compline or tattoo, and it starts with a bugle call?" Martin asked.

"Right, followed by psalms and —"

Martin cut in. "Four, ninety-one, and one thirty-four."

"Yes. Then an examination of conscience. And a concluding prayer."

"Devout practice, Henry."

"It helps to live a life in keeping with the Gospel. And heed the *Code of Canon Law.*"

"How long've you been doing this?" Martin asked.

"A few weeks. Started in DC when I knew I was moving here, so I'd have some continuity at the end of the day."

After a pause, Martin changed the subject. "At Saint John this morning, you were examining the June bulletin. Looking for anything special?"

Henry shrugged. "Bible study. Or a reading group."

Martin nodded. He didn't want to make unsolicited suggestions. But he asked, "Did you find one?"

"No. Maybe Saint John's young adult Christians are on vacation —"

"They call themselves Jack's YACs. Sometimes it's spelled as one word."

Henry nodded, unsure what to make of the group's bizarre-sounding name.

Martin said, "About Bible study? I *do* know of a group, but it's not at Saint John."

Henry looked at the older man, thankful for his calm demeanor. Their conversation was more open and richer than he'd expected during a stop after Mass. *Maybe we're becoming friends*, Henry thought.

"There's a seminary," Martin said.

"Many universities in town," Henry said. He was not exuberant about studying the Bible in an academic setting and thought Martin should know this about him.

"The one I'm recommending isn't at a university."

Henry waited.

"You're not old enough to know this, but before we had *los hedonistas* in the sixties, we had the beatniks. Some of our best artists. Some still around."

"Beat nix? Anti-drummers?" Henry asked.

"No. Followers of the beatitudes. They rebelled against rich parents or no parents and the button-down ways of the fifties. They lived in the Village in New York, the Mission District in San Francisco, and a few here on South Street back when it was part garment district and part black ghetto. Some beats were painters and writers and sculptors. They drank wine, smoked reefer, and advocated peace and a simple life. Most were white. One is still here, running a floating street seminary."

As Henry set down his white china espresso cup and sat up straight on his stool, Martin could see he was paying some heed.

"You interested in any of this?"

"Yes," Henry said. "Not so much in the history lesson. Yes to what's going on now. What's a floating street seminary?"

"Armando Beluga is seventy-five or eighty. His groups meet in Francisville, Fairmount, and Spring Garden churches and rec centers. Sometimes in the underground concourses —"

"Are those rough areas?" Henry interrupted.

Martin said, "In Francisville, near Eastern State Penitentiary, there's a coffee shop called Mugshots."

Henry smiled. "Francisville. So is that where Armando teaches now?"

Martin shrugged and shook his head. "Don't know. Try Sister Nicki. She might know."

At Saint John, Henry had learned that Sister Nicki ran UniPhil, a coalition of interlocking organizations that housed homeless people, provided them with medical care and education, and mentored those who qualified for jobs and could show up for them. Nicki's key assistant was Sister Anne, a former bond dealer at Fidelity who served as UniPhil's CFO. Both were Benedictine nuns who drew no salaries.

Sister Nicki's organization had contracts with the city and state to do outreach services no one else wanted to do. They responded to police or anonymous alerts about souls who were passed out or puking or freezing in the streets. Staff drove a used van all hours of the night, hunted down their suffering human prey, and brought them to shelters for evaluation.

And they were living out radical Christian testimonies. Their successful housing programs, for example, accepted everyone, including homeless men and women with serious mental disabilities.

During lunchtime the next day, Henry found the website for UniPhil and its staff listing. He called the number for Nicki's assistant. She answered.

"Tamia Burke, Sister Nicki's office."

"Hi, Tamia. Martin Perez at Saint John said you might know how to contact Armando Beluga. Henry Knudsen calling."

Tamia paused and then in a pleasant tone said, "Armando is hard to keep up with, isn't he? Just a sec, Henry."

He listened for almost a minute to the soft pulse of a telephone on hold.

"Hey, Henry. Sorry to keep you waiting. Here's Armando's cell phone number. Ready?"

"Yes," said Henry, his index finger poised to tap in the number. She gave it to him. He repeated it back to her.

"Right. And that's it for today, Henry?"

"Yes," he said. "Thanks. Can I use your name if I reach Armando?"

"Sure, but you'll get further if you tell him you got his number from Sister Nicki's office."

He called Armando, who also answered. "Hi. Henry Knudsen calling. Sister Nicki's office gave me your number. Calling to ask about your study group."

"In eight days, we'll be at Holy Family. Two ten North Eighteenth, below Vine. Six thirty till about nine o'clock. We're studying the parables of the prodigal son and the talents."

"That'll be Tuesday, June eighteenth," Henry said. "Is there any —"

"For the first meeting, just bring yourself," said Armando.

FOUR

JUNE 15

O n Saturday morning, Gwynneth took an early train from
Washington to Thirtieth Street Station. Henry was waiting for
her. At nine o'clock he recognized her tall, chic presence stepping
off the escalator onto the marble floor of the station's concourse.

Gwynneth's café-au-lait countenance, framed by a bob haircut,
complemented her trim figure. She wore a long-sleeved fuchsia
pullover tucked into tan dungarees, two-toned pink sneakers, no
jewelry, and no make-up.

From near the information kiosk, he called her name. She went
to him, and, dropping her bags at his feet, raised herself on tiptoes
to embrace him and accept his kiss. "You look ravishing," he said.

Without releasing the kiss, she said, "Oh, man, I'm glad to be
holding you. Been too long."

After their impassioned coupling, he shepherded them to the
taxi stand.

At his place they undressed each other and let their desire
lead them through intense and deliberate lovemaking to a sweaty
collapse.

Later, under his umbrella, they walked in the rain through
Rittenhouse Square to Nuts to You, already one of Henry's favorite
local shops, where they bought dried fruit and shelled nuts to bring
to the Father's Day fête.

Back in his studio apartment, they called to arrange early dinner
at Fork with Aunt Maria and Uncle Bennie. Then, Henry showed

her the case histories. They filled two notebooks. Each had a three-inch spine and weighed two pounds.

Gwynneth opened a binder on his kitchen table. "This is a great deal of material," she said.

He nodded in agreement. "It took us a couple of years to study all of it."

Saturday afternoon, she sat at his kitchen table reading the history and study questions about the BP Deepwater Horizon disaster of 2010. Henry sat on his zabuton, his back against the wall, reading Teju Cole's novella about life in Nigeria, *Every Day Is for the Thief.*

After poring over the material for an hour, she interrupted his reading to ask, "Critical troubles hit when the brilliant macho men in charge didn't talk to one another. Is that what you say about this? Or communication worsened as they built an organization with too many parts? Or cowboys abused their own equipment and cut corners on safety? Then managers assigned four rookies to key positions at the same critical time?"

"Wainwright didn't mention those factors in the crisis."

"Ah," said Gwynneth, "but that's when the crisis developed, according to the case history."

"We focused on the catalysts for the Macondo blowout and how three firms communicated and managed the cleanup," Henry said.

"You reviewed the lies they told while they were putting out the fires and have been repeating for three years?" she said.

"We talked about the falsehoods Halliburton issued. Lots of blame to go around."

"So, eleven men were killed, and BP is back in business."

There was a pause in the discussion. He waited, then looked up from his zabuton and asked, "What did you make of the study questions?"

"They were intriguing. But there's another matter."

Henry waited for her to continue. After a few moments, Gwynneth said, "My mother had her four children before she was twenty-eight."

Henry nodded, recalling without a prompt he'd be thirty years old in October and Gwynneth would be twenty-eight in November.

"It's on my mind, Henry, and I want you to know it. I've asked in my discernment practice how I feel about you and whether I can commit to you. This came up instead. 'I'm not waiting to have a baby.' And I asked about your management case studies because I need some formal education in business. That's coming up, too."

He nodded, aware his discernment practice had made it clear he was fond of her and comfortable committing to be her loving partner. He was at peace with her not waiting to have a baby and happy that it might be their baby.

They went to dinner at Fork with Aunt Maria and Uncle Bennie. Walking home from dinner, Gwynneth said, "This discernment practice has pointed out a weird vacuum here, Henry."

To show her he was listening, he said, "Hmm. Weird?"

"It's weird to me. We know about each other's families and our academic, professional, and religious pasts, but we haven't spoken about our romantic pasts."

In reply, Henry nodded and cupped her elbow as they crossed Thirteenth Street.

"My mentors say it might be better to leave it that way. Do you have any thoughts about it? Sharing our romantic pasts?"

Henry knew Gwynneth was in regular telephone contact with his sister, Gabriella, who could've mentioned some of his past to her. He said, "My questions would be 'Is there value in it?' and 'If there *is* value, then how might it help us now?'"

She said, "Good questions. Not sure."

"I don't have any secrets. Would it help you to know I was pressed to cosign a lease so two of us could live together? That I resisted and then said no? That it caused a tiff that turned into a loud fight inside the leasing office of an apartment tower in Crystal City and ended cold and nasty outside in a parking lot in Northern Virginia near National Airport? You want to hear about that sort of —"

She cut in to repeat her diffident reply. "Not *sure*, Henry."

To clarify his willingness to discuss it, he said, "I'm OK with clearing the old record by saying 'Before Gwynneth, these affairs didn't work out' and put energy into being as strong as we can be. But I'm also OK with our sharing our pasts if you think it might help us."

She said, "I had a one-year affair with a colleague when I taught biochemistry at Columbia."

Henry was listening and watching her countenance and the turning traffic as they walked across the eight wide lanes of Broad Street.

"We broke up during Pre-Cana counseling."

His quizzical look overpowered his attempt to maintain dispassionate body language.

She responded to his expression and his spike of heightened attentiveness. "Yeah, right. For members of the Church who plan to marry. I agreed to it." She cursed and shrugged.

"When the betrothal disintegrated, *everything* disintegrated. Sex. Cooking. Paying the cell phone bill. Scheduling anything. It got *ugly*. My friends told me to leave him at once. 'Hard to do when we're living together,' I said."

Henry felt Gwynneth was containing a fury. *She's telling me something that's important to her, and I need to listen.*

After a pause, Gwynneth cited her Merry Godmother, an internal spiritual guide who'd spoken to her since her years at Fordham, where she'd met women who were outraged that they weren't worthy to engage in Church governance or serve as priests. "Some of us are OK with it, and some of us are not OK with it," she'd told Henry. "So it stands."

Continuing with her account, she said, "Merry Godmother told me, *Sleep on the couch. Get out of here when it makes sense for you, but don't panic. Be patient.*"

Gwynneth said, "So as for you and me, Henry, our bruises have made us cautious in affairs of the heart. Here we are — you, a practicing Roman Catholic, trying to live your life according to the Gospel, and me, a refugee on sabbatical from a Church I see as hypocritical. And despite our serious religious differences, you and

I are listening to one other. We agree we're devoted to one another. When we see what we agree on, our disagreements look puny. Is that where we are?"

"Yes," he said, "and so far, we're at peace with it." He paused a moment, then added, "And I'm glad we're hot and together and goin' upstairs here."

She squeezed his hand in agreement. They climbed the steps at 1589 Pine Street and went to bed.

FIVE

JUNE 16

E arly the next day, Father's Day, Henry drove them to the Bronx. In the passenger seat of the rented car, she reviewed the case and study questions for the BP oil disaster of 2010. But it was too bumpy on the New Jersey Turnpike to concentrate on her reading.

She asked him, "What's Carmen Stanhope got you working on?"

"Technology and management of banking online and with mobile phones, and trends in the US and in Africa."

"Africa?"

"Mobile telephony has gotten big real fast in Kenya and Nigeria. In a few weeks, I'll make a presentation on the growth in banking by cell telephone in Africa."

"How would that work?" she asked.

"Same as in other countries where it's working," he said.

"In the US?"

"No," he said. "The US is seventh worldwide in the percentage of customers who bank by cell telephone."

"Seventh? Who's first?"

"South Korea. It's changing fast. In Kenya, usage doubled in 2010, and almost forty percent of the population uses short message service for bank transactions. But SMS technology isn't as secure —"

Gwynneth cut in. "So they're getting you up to speed. In banking."

"Yes," he said. "Meeting colleagues. Examining factors that encourage banking by cell phone. I'll discuss them in my presentation."

"Because customers using telephones can transact business without a teller," she added.

"Right," he said. "And it's more secure than cash. And faster. *And* can build a solid customer base."

Their discussion of payment technologies was punctuated when they edged through the turnpike and George Washington Bridge tollgates in the E-Z Pass lanes. As they sped up the Deegan, Henry added, "Stanhope is mentoring me about cultivating clients. She wants to hear how that's going every week."

She said, "And you're OK working for boneheads who generated the worst financial crisis in eighty years?"

Before he could answer she added, "And got bonuses for their stupidity and greed?"

"We're aware of our client's past behavior," he said.

She did not pile on but didn't completely change the subject. In a softer tone, she asked, "So, you remember telling me when the Gospel became important to you?"

Henry was unsettled by what seemed to be a sharp change in the direction of their conversation, but he trusted her sincerity, so he began an answer. "Yes. It was—"

She cut in. "And you said it was when you were eight years old, after talking with your thirteen-year-old sister, Gabriella—"

He nodded and said, "I remember—"

She again spoke over his interruption without raising her voice. He stopped talking so he could hear her.

"And Gab said the catechism was rules for behaving in church and the Gospel was guidance for behaving in the real world?"

He nodded.

"And that's when the Gospel became important to you? Twenty or so years ago?"

He turned to her, still nodding, less exasperated than curious about why she was replaying a conversation from a few months earlier.

"How do you reconcile your commitment to the Gospel with working for bankers and oil company tycoons? Isn't that throwing pearls before swine?"

She settled back in the passenger seat, as if to tell him her question had been asked and she would not interrupt his reply.

"It's a struggle," he began. "I don't have the power to reform the banks, but I *can* work with allies in the financial world to make their commercial systems work for everyone, not just the rich. My goal is to see it—"

She blurted out an interruption. "Right. Use your eyes to see. Matthew seven, one verse before not throwing pearls before swine."

He nodded, appreciative of her command of the Gospel. "Yes," he said. "Yes, that's right. Expanding services to the underserved is the focus of our work in Africa."

Gwynneth did not deride his use of *underserved,* a euphemism for poor people the banks had frozen out of their systems. And she respected his answer because it sounded as if he'd given the difficult issue some thought.

In her family home in the Bronx, while helping prepare dinner in the massive kitchen that afternoon, Gwynneth asked her mother, "How did you and Papa decide when to have your children?"

From his chair in the living room, Henry acknowledged Cedric Trevor's thanks for the bat. He overheard some of Sonia's answers, *sotto voce*, in Spanish. "We wanted children. I was ready to quit teaching high school chemistry and wanted to stay home. It's the custom of our family in Puerto Rico. Your father made enough money. So we did it."

Henry could not hear all of Gwynneth's reply, but he did hear Sonia say, in English, "You...could've started...if you'd married Cramer. The chemistry..."

The sound of water running in the kitchen sink combined with the clatter of pot lids on the stovetop obscured much of Gwynneth's answer. And the two women lowered their voices from time to time, so Henry missed much of what Sonia or Gwynneth said. He did hear Gwynneth say, with some emphasis, "Man of *integrity*, Mama…and he listens to me."

In the living room, Cedric Trevor sat with his three grown sons and Henry. He thanked his children and Henry for their gifts of books, a rain jacket, and the bat. He slid the baseball bat out of its long box and read the label burned into the bat's barrel. The new wood smelled fresh to him, but even though he smiled as he gripped the smooth bat handle, he didn't know what to do with it.

Gerry, his youngest son, relieved him of it, put it back in its box, and leaned it against the side of his father's chair. "Luis and Ramón want to steal your bat, Papa. Keep your eyes on it."

Cedric Trevor smiled and said, "*No seas chismoso.*" But after his paternal chiding of his son not to gossip about his older brothers, Cedric let Gerry slide the bat under his chair, out of sight.

Henry and Gwynneth left the Bronx for Philadelphia before seven o'clock. After crossing the George Washington Bridge and surviving I-95's rough road connecting them to the New Jersey Turnpike, Gwynneth asked, "Henry? How do you relate family and spiritual path?"

Henry was not sure he understood her query. "Hard to say," he said. "Every family and every family member's spiritual path is different."

But Gwynneth was not interested in every family. She wanted Henry to talk about her and *her* family, so she said, "Can we make this less theoretical? You have a spiritual path, and so do I. You have a family, and so do I."

Henry merged into the cars-only lanes of the New Jersey Turnpike, heading south. She waited for him to respond, but he didn't. She figured he might be concentrating on navigating the turnpike's heavy Sunday evening traffic or avoiding the glare of the setting sun.

He didn't respond because he wasn't sure what she was asking.

Gwynneth wanted him to say something about his visit to see her family. She followed up, trying to pry an answer from him. "Here's an empirical question. After today's visit, can you say something about your and my spiritual path and your and my family?"

"Yes," he said. "First impressions after this one brief visit?"

She was disappointed in his reply and said, "Henry, that sounds a little too cagey."

Tension invaded the car. He heard her frustration and made his silent prayer. *Peace. Be still.* Then he reached for her hand. She clasped it in hers. "I'm not sure about your question. I'm as devoted to you as ever. That's not going to change. Maybe we should start there?"

Gwynneth was glad to hear his solemn response. The heaviness of confusion and a potential argument seeped out of the car as they flew by Newark Airport.

Henry said, "I'm glad we're talking about our respective spiritual paths. We haven't done it in a while. Right?"

"Right," she said.

"And family. Is that your family in the Bronx or mine in New York and Virginia? Or are you asking something else? Do your parents expect you to date a PhD or a New Yorker or a dark-skinned Nuyorican? Or are you and I forming a family? Not sure here."

She turned her head to the right, watching without focus four lanes of cars and trucks speeding south on the turnpike's parallel roadway. She whispered a soft curse. It ricocheted off the glass onto her cheek. Henry did not hear it.

She said, "Oh, man, Henry, my question is vague. I thought it was clear, but I see it isn't."

Gwynneth didn't follow up, so after a long pause, Henry said, "Yes, well, the word *family* is as complex as the phrase *spiritual path*."

"Right," she said. "Can I have some time to rephrase it?"

"Sure," he said. They drove on in silence for a few miles. Gwynneth opened the BP case history but stopped trying to read the study questions in the dim twilight. She put her arm on his thigh and let

29

her hand curl over his knee and said, "Everyone in my family told me you're an all-star, Henry. They were impressed with you. Not as much as I am, but close."

Henry appreciated hearing the report. He nodded but said nothing.

"Oh, man," Gwynneth said. "I'm beat from traveling all weekend." She moved toward him in her seat and laid her head on his shoulder and upper arm. "Can I just rest here for a while?"

"Oh, yes," he said as she fell asleep.

An hour later, Henry awakened her. "Gwynneth?"

"Mm-nn?"

"We're at Thirtieth Street Station."

She stirred and saw they were parked at the intercity bus stops near the terminal. They gathered her two small bags and soon found the track for her train to Washington.

Henry returned the car to the Avis night drop-off and, after a nine-block walk, got home by nine thirty. Gwynneth arrived at her home at eleven.

SIX

JUNE 18

After work on Tuesday, June 18, Henry, his parka slung over his shoulder, joined several hundred other pedestrians on Eighteenth Street walking from work to the train station, subway, or nearby bus stops. After crossing Market Street, he passed the one-story Arch Street Presbyterian Church. At 160 years old, even with its verdigris-coffered dome, it was dwarfed by its adjacent neighbor, the five-year-old, 974-foot-tall Comcast Tower.

Three blocks later, beyond the Ben Franklin Parkway, at the south side of the Holy Family Center Church, an open wrought-iron gate beckoned him into a wide alleyway, still wet from an afternoon rain. He followed a woman down a well-used stairway that led to an open door.

As he reached the bottom of the stairs, a gentle voice asked, "Henry?"

"Yes. Armando?" Henry answered. Before him stood a short, thin white man leaning on a gnarled wood cane.

"Yes. We're in here," said Armando, tapping a doorjamb with the side of his cane's rubber ferrule.

Henry followed Armando into a small classroom. Fifteen padded folding chairs were arranged in a semicircle, its open side facing a single chair and small table. Armando sat in this chair and rested his cane on the tabletop. Henry sat in one of the two unoccupied chairs.

"Let's get started," Armando said, closing his eyes while raising and relaxing his shoulders. The others joined him in the quiet. A latecomer slipped into the vacant chair. After two minutes, Armando broke the silence.

"Welcome, everyone. We have a newcomer — Henry Knudsen." He looked at Henry as if inviting him to speak.

Henry said, "Henry Knudsen. New in town. Heard about you through the Jacksyacs group at Saint John. Glad to be here."

A few in the group said, "Welcome."

Henry scanned the faces in the semicircle to return every greeting. The group was young but otherwise diverse. Three were unkempt enough to be street people. Seven were people of color. Henry was relieved not to be sitting in a white yuppie Bible study group.

Armando said, "Last time, we began our discussion of the parable of the prodigal son."

Henry had struggled with the well-loved story of an impetuous youth who claimed his inheritance, lost it all on riotous living, returned home broke, and was welcomed by his father. It had been celebrated by many generations of artists. Henry had initial difficulty reconciling the tale of a clueless father who showed little appreciation for the loyal service of his older son and facile disregard for the irresponsible behavior of his younger son. After a deeper look, Henry saw the parable as a reminder to welcome back into the church all sinners who repent.

Armando continued, "Jasmine pointed out Pope John Paul II in his second encyclical in 1980 instructed us to be rich in mercy. As was the prodigal son's father." By his look, Armando invited the young black woman to amplify her earlier remarks.

Jasmine accepted his offer. She said, "And later, in his apostolic exhortation, John Paul reminded us the Church's mission of reconciliation is God's initiative." As she finished speaking Henry glanced at her. She was an attractive dark-skinned woman. Her business suit and sturdy hiking shoes suggested she'd walked from work to the Holy Family Center Church.

"Yes, that's right, Jasmine," said Armando. "Other comments?"

A man sitting next to Henry, who appeared to need a haircut, shower, and a clean shirt, said, "Hey, it's fine to show mercy and reconcile with a wastrel. But that's not what happens in this parable. The wastrel is welcomed, not just forgiven by a self-centered father who's glad the bum is back home."

Armando said, "Thank you, Thomas. You mentioned those ideas last time."

A black man wearing a business suit said, "Well, those *are* good points, Armando. Many say this parable tells us to welcome back repentant sinners. But does it? A rich kid has a tantrum and takes off with his inheritance. It doesn't work out, so here he is, back in his rich home, asking for a free ride. And his father is not just OK with it. He's *elated*. Where is Pope John XXIII's commitment to the poor? That seems to be lost in this story."

By his nodding, Armando welcomed the insight. "In our group we give these biblical narratives a close reading."

His look at the group invited comments. No one spoke. He looked at Henry, who paused, then said, "The parable emphasizes the prodigal son's easy return to a fat life on his father's estate. It took me a while to see that, as a Christian, I'm supposed to welcome all returning souls, no matter why they strayed. But forgiving rich punks for squandering their money is hard. It's a high standard."

Armando waited for others to respond to Henry's remark. When no one spoke up, he said, "All right. Let's move on, speaking of high standards, to the parable of the talents. Who can tell us about that story?"

Jasmine, the woman who'd spoken earlier, said, "There are two basic stories. In Matthew 25, a man gave to three of his servants, five, two, and one bags of gold based on their ability, and went away. When the man returned, he asked for an accounting. He applauded and rewarded the ones who'd turned five talents into ten and two into four but rebuked the one who'd buried his talent in the ground and who'd said to the man, 'You reaped where you didn't plant, so now have what belongs to you.' In reply, the man called the servant wicked and lazy, took away the talent, and gave it to the servant with ten. The moral is the rich get richer without working for it and whatever the poor may have will be taken away from them.

"In Luke 19," the woman continued, "details are different but the moral is the same. Both versions of the parable of the talents praise as trustworthy those doubling the master's money and rebuke as wicked those who don't."

She paused, then added, "This the voice of Jesus? And both versions seem to distort the Gospel message to serve the poor. We're directed to amass unearned wealth for the benefit of the wealthy?"

"Thank you Jasmine." Then, speaking to the group, asked, "What do we make of these two versions of the parable of the talents?"

Henry was curious why Armando hadn't challenged Jasmine about her claim the parable seemed to distort the Gospel message not to pile up wealth. As the discussion continued, Henry weighed the parable's meaning. As his career was on an upward track, did the Gospel require him to continue earning more for himself and his managers?

Just before nine o'clock, the discussion ended. Armando spoke with Henry while others stowed the folding chairs and departed.

"Next month we'll begin our study of the preferential option for the poor."

Henry said, "And it'll be here? Is there registration? Are there fees?"

"It'll be somewhere else. Call me to verify time and place. Read the encyclicals online. And there's no registration or fee."

Henry had more questions, but it was late, and Armando looked tired. They left the church in fading twilight. Armando walked eastward through the alley, and Henry west toward Eighteenth Street.

As he passed through the wrought-iron gate, Henry noticed in front of him a massive black high-country Silverado, double-parked even though there were many parking places on Eighteenth Street between the few Prius and Ford Focus sedans. As he reached the sidewalk, Henry had the impression something was amiss when all four crew-cab doors flew open at once and were left ajar. Before he sensed any danger, four skinheads jumped out of the Silverado and punched Henry's chest and back, knocking him to the sidewalk. He landed on his right forearm and skidded to a stop. When he scrambled to get up, two assailants kicked him in the ribs. Another grunted as he beat Henry in the arm and shoulder with a heavy cudgel. Henry was knocked onto his side by the blows. He heard his work ID, building pass, and house keys fall out of his parka onto the sidewalk. He protected his head with his forearms, hands clasped at his crown.

The skinheads cursed his retarded, liberal, socialist ways and spat on him. All but one piled back into the Silverado, leaving Henry on the sidewalk. The lingering attacker stood over him, brandishing a jingling metallic weapon. "Here's a little souvenir for your forehead," he said.

Henry did not want a souvenir. He crabbed away as the attacker's hand and keys slapped at him, scraping the side of his head. The attacker cursed him. In the confusion and panic, Henry heard the sound of a metal bundle fall onto the sidewalk. He also felt a dull, warm pain in his right knee. Then he heard the attacker grunt and cry out in a fury. "Agh. My cursed hand. You made me cut my cursed *hand*."

Henry was terrified by the murderous rage in the man's voice. *Oh man, if those guys get out of that pickup, I'm in big trouble.*

He rose to his hands and knees and sought to escape from the howling man but did not get far. The enraged attacker pounced on him, and with one knee on the sidewalk, held Henry's parka to keep him from moving as he pummeled him. Then he delivered three open-handed blows to Henry's chest, grunting and cursing with each blow. "Socialist." Unh. "Liberal." Unh. "N-lover." Unh.

The blows stung his chest and made him dizzy and hot and afraid. *This is not good*, Henry thought. *Turn the other cheek cannot be what I'm supposed to do here.* He recalled the bandaged image of another mugging victim, Mike Doyle, his boss when he'd worked on Capitol Hill. *That was six years ago,* he thought. *Why is Mike coming to mind now?*

The next sound he heard was the blast of the pickup's horn. One of the attacker's confederates screamed, "Get in, or we're leaving youse. *Now.*" They called him Mick or Rick or Dick. In response, the attacker suspended his assault. Seconds later, Henry heard a car door slam shut. The vehicle sped north toward Vine Street, leaving him on the sidewalk, battered and disoriented.

He rose to his feet and tried to steady himself against a parking meter. His legs and arms were shaking. He retrieved his iPhone from an inside pocket of his parka and turned on its flashlight. He aimed its beam at the sidewalk, looking for his ID and keys, but his arms and hands shook so hard the beam jumped erratically. He did see a few drops of red blood oozing into the concrete.

His quaking hands moved the light beam away from the blood-stains. To still his hands, he took a breath and exhaled, yet his hands convulsed. Then, the beam fell on a bundle of keys, a keyless pod, a lead skull, some plastic tabs, and a red Koosh ball. It lay just a few feet away, near a baseball bat. The skull lent an air of doom to the bundle. He picked it up by the Koosh ball and dropped it into a pocket of his parka.

Henry took another deep breath. His brain and his limbs seemed to work, but he couldn't stop shaking. And he still needed to find his own keys and ID.

He turned his flashlight to the sidewalk again and shuddered at the sight of the baseball bat. It was stained with oil and carried deep scratches, as if it had been stored on a garage floor. Under his parka's sleeve, his left shoulder and upper arm throbbed. *Maybe it's bad,* he reckoned. *But could've been lethal if the bat had connected with my head.*

He spotted and retrieved his ID, pass, and keys, then started homeward. He finished his one-mile trudge well after nine o'clock. Inside the front door, he stopped to examine himself in a foyer mirror. His ear was red but not bleeding. Spots of blood and dirt dotted his shirt and tie where his assailant had clobbered him. His right trouser was ripped and hanging open at the knee. His parka was missing a Velcro tab, and the sleeve was scraped but not ripped where he'd skidded on the sidewalk. Ignoring his mail, he started upstairs to his apartment. His torso throbbed, and his right patella ached and felt hot. Standing in the feeble glare of the bathroom's CFL lights, he started to bend down to remove his shoes and socks. Sharp pain in his chest forced him to stop.

He wriggled out of his parka, stepped from the bathroom into the walk-in closet, and hung it on a peg. He used his feet to pry off his shoes and left them on the closet floor. Back in the bathroom, with the mirror guiding him, he loosened his cravat, removed it, and draped it on the vanity. He was glad to have removed the tie, but he did not feel well. *My stomach's unhappy*, he thought. *Because I haven't eaten. Or because I'm going to throw up.*

Henry shed the rest of his clothes except his socks. He could not endure the wicked pain of bending over to remove them. Even the slight moves of bending and twisting to remove his shirt had caused fierce pains in his ribs.

Back in the closet, he took a pair of workout shorts and a sweatshirt from a drawer. When he tried to step into the shorts, the stabbing pang in his ribs stopped him. He dropped both garments back into the drawer, coughed, and then picked up his cell phone and called Martin.

"Henry? Gettin' late here, Henry. You calling from Los Angeles?"

"No. I'm here. Listen, I got mugged about a half hour ago. Beat up. Maybe I need first aid or —"

Martin's tone changed from casual to serious. "Where?"

"Outside the Holy Family Center Church, after Armando Beluga's seminar."

"And you're home now?"

"Yeah. Walked home."

"Walked," Martin repeated. "From Eighteenth and Vine. So your legs aren't broken."

"It feels like I'm shaking all over," Henry said. "I can't explain it."

"Yeah," Martin said. You're a white civilian who's never been beaten in the street, Martin did not add, but said, "Be right up."

Henry, clad in his socks and boxer shorts, walked out of the closet, through the short hallway into his living area, and sat on the edge of his bed. He set the alarm on his phone for 7:00 a.m. and put it in airplane mode to disable incoming calls and texts. The piercing ache in his ribs was aggravated when he stood up to set the phone in a basket on the nearby kitchen table. The pain subsided when he sat on the bed but returned with a vengeance when he lay down. It was not the pain of a stubbed toe. It was the pain of an ice pick into his side. He forswore rising for tattoo.

Less than a minute later, Martin used his passkey to let himself in and winced at the bloodstained shirt and tie on the bathroom sink. He took a chair from the small dining table, where Henry's cell phone, keys, wallet, and work ID lanyard sat in a small wicker basket. He pulled the chair near Henry's bed and sat in it.

Lying on his back, Henry mumbled, "Thanks for checking in." His voice trailed off and then resumed. "Got smacked around out there. Three of 'em. Maybe four."

Martin said, "I'm going to take your pulse here, Henry. Can you let me have your wrist?"

As he spoke, Henry extracted his arm from beneath the quilt on his bed. He said, "This arm and shoulder hurt. Baseball bat."

Martin cradled Henry's forearm and let the wrist fall toward him, then calculated the pulse. At eighty beats per minute, it was elevated but not alarming.

Martin walked away from Henry's bed and made a call. "My new tenant got mugged." He paused and then said, "He's a little disoriented."

Martin, answering a few questions, said, "He's home. Walked over a mile to get here."

Pause.

"Eighty."

Pause.

"No. It's cool and dry. Skin color is normal." Martin paused. "Normal…you know, for a white guy."

Pause.

"Doesn't smell drunk. Don't know if he started with the Bolivian marching powder tonight, but I'd guess he didn't."

Pause.

"My assessment? He'll be all right here and worse if he has to sit in a plastic chair in your ER for three hours. What's *your* assessment?"

Pause.

"Don't know. There's blood smeared on his shirt and some on his tie, but no cuts or bruises on his face. Maybe somebody else's blood."

After a longer pause, Martin said, "Thanks."

He returned to Henry's bedside. "All right," Martin whispered into the silence. "I'm turning out your light." Martin switched off the floor lamp. "Get some rest."

Henry opened his eyes and said, "Martin. Keys."

"Right here in your basket, with your wallet and —"

Henry, still prone, shook his head and said, "Not mine. *His* keys."

"OK, Henry."

"In my parka."

Martin left the bedside. He turned on the light in the walk-in closet and saw Henry's parka hanging on a peg. He tapped one of the pockets. Its heft told him something was in it.

Martin retreated into Henry's Pullman kitchen. In the cabinet under the sink, he found a small box of plastic bags. He took one, and as he returned to the closet, put the plastic bag over his hand as if it were a bizarre parody of a thin mitten. Reaching into the coat pocket, he wrapped the bag around the bundle and pulled it out.

In the muted light, Martin made out a large steel ring with a red Koosh ball, keys for padlocks, a keyless pod for a Toyota Tacoma, and a small jackknife. On a smaller ring looped through the larger one were three plastic loyalty tabs for two stores and the Free Library of Philadelphia along with a miniature lead skull.

Martin whispered, "How you feeling now, Henry?"

Henry had fallen asleep.

"Taking these keys, Henry. Call you tomorrow." Martin turned off the hallway light and pulled the door closed. It locked itself with a soft click.

The morning after his mugging, Henry rolled out of bed at 7:00 a.m. in response to his cell phone alarm. The pain in his ribs jolted him as he reached to quiet its carillon. The pain lingered after he'd turned it off.

As he arose, he recalled the previous night's mugging and Martin's coming to see him. While showering, he continued to experience sudden and unexpected discomfort in his ribs when he reached for his soap, shampooed his hair, cleaned his underarms, and dried his neck — movements he'd always made with ease. The pain was sharper when he shaved and even more unpleasant when he twisted his torso to slide his arm into his shirtsleeve.

On his walk to work, he stopped at Dunkin' Donuts for a large, black, dark-roast coffee. In his office at eight thirty, he took his phone out of airplane mode. Martin had sent a text message at eight that morning.

"Hey, Henry. You OK?"

Henry replied, "Yes. At work. See you tonight."

SEVEN

JUNE 19, 9:00 A.M.

M ost Wednesday mornings, Detective Captains Martin Perez and Ronald Sweeney worked out of the medical examiner's office, located west of the Schuylkill River among several other ugly concrete buildings on South University Avenue. There, they managed a database of several hundred cases of evidence analyzed by the ME for state police investigators and dozens of small Pennsylvania police departments. Afternoons, they resumed their investigations in Philadelphia and area counties.

On Wednesday, June 19, in their shared office, Martin emptied the plastic bag he'd taken from Henry's apartment. Before transferring its contents to an evidence pouch, he took photos to record the bar code numbers for the drug store and library tabs, then called and left messages for a contact in a drugstore chain and one at the Free Library of Philadelphia.

He took the evidence pouch to the lab upstairs from his office and asked about a DNA test. The lab director looked up from her work and said, "Leave it all right there, Martin. It'll be four, five days...next Monday the earliest."

When he got back to the office, Sweeney put aside a case file and said, "Your IT guy from the library called."

Martin rang back. The chief information technology officer at the Philadelphia Free Library system told him the number was for an account issued to a Heinrich Gerhardt at the Chestnut Hill branch on Germantown Avenue. He gave the home address on the account.

"I've sent this info to you in a text for your records," he added. "The card was used at Chestnut Hill and also a mile south of there at the Lovett Memorial Branch on Germantown Avenue."

Martin's contact at the drug chain confirmed the account holder's name was Gerhardt, but without an official police request, he couldn't say any more.

Martin said, "We have a lead."

"You got a statement from your witness?" Sweeney asked.

"No." They both knew they needed a signed statement from Henry, the victim and only known witness, in order to request a warrant for the assailant's arrest.

Sweeney said, "We can investigate this one. There've been eight similar assaults in the city in the past few weeks and no other leads."

"OK. Let's do it," said Martin.

As Sweeney drove their unmarked unit out of West Philadelphia up the Schuylkill Expressway, he said, "Not many investigations take us into Chestnut Hill. When we're north of the art museum, we're in Strawberry Mansion or Allegheny West and on full alert."

"Why is that?" Martin asked.

Sweeney snapped his head to the right to face Martin, his face awash in disbelief at the question, before shifting his focus to the road in front of him. "You're asking —"

"Until 1950, they sold strawberries and cream to wealthy homeowners in Strawberry Mansion."

Sweeney barked is response. "No. No cursed way."

"Yes," Martin insisted. "And now it's the highest-crime area in the city, and a newborn's life expectancy there is twenty years less than a kid born in Chestnut Hill, only a few minutes north."

Sweeney cursed again. "So what happened?"

"Are you following this conversation? You say we're on full alert in Strawberry Mansion, one of the poorest regions in the city. And when I ask 'Why is that?' you glare at me."

Sweeney defended himself. "I did. Because it was a stupid question. Everybody knows what happened in —"

Martin cut in. "You *don't* know what happened. You just *asked* me what happened, so we agree you have no cursed *clue* what happened. Right?"

Sweeney said, "I know what happened."

"Oh. OK. What happened?"

Sweeney exhaled. "OK. First, this is my view."

"OK, thanks. That clears it up."

"You remember when we met, when you told me why you joined the state police?"

Martin said, "Yes. We were impressed by how Pennsylvania responded to the coal miners' strike in 1902."

"Your parents told you —"

Martin cut in. "Local police departments were bought off by the mine owners. So the governor created a state police force that reported to him, not the coal mine owners."

"That's what you were *told*," Sweeney said. "That's *your* uninformed view. It's why you think Governor Pennypacker was the savior. But in Scranton, in the mines, we saw the state police mauling mine workers. They were as bad as the private Coal and Iron Police. They didn't stop beating mine workers until the 1930s, when cars on the highways got the state police out of the strikebreaking business. They moved on to licensing and registering cars and ticketing speeders. There are two viewpoints here: one in the city and wrong — yours — and one in mining country and right — mine."

Martin waited as Sweeney took the Lincoln Drive exit and crossed the Schuylkill before saying, "By the 1920s, Pennsylvania's state police training was a model for other states. And I wanted to work for this one."

"For strikebreakers."

"When I applied to join the state police in the 1970s, my application was rejected. When I applied in the 1990s, they looked at my qualifications and accepted me. That's how I got here."

Sweeney said, "OK, so they changed, and you changed. You were a better applicant."

Martin cursed. "That's hogwash, and you know it. In the 1970s, all my qualifications were the same as yours. Except one. You were white."

Sweeney nodded. "Yeah. Right. They were a little old-fashioned back in the seventies."

"Is that what they were?"

"About not taking married applicants or women, they were old fashioned. About you, racism could've been a factor."

Sweeney drove up Lincoln Drive toward the address south of the Morris Arboretum near Wissahickon Valley Park, a mansion on Crefeld Street. Sweeney drove past it and then turned around and coasted to a stop two car lengths from its driveway. It had taken them a half hour to reach the soaring glass-and-stone mansion after leaving the ragged gray concrete structure housing the medical examiner's offices.

Sweeney looked in the rearview mirror and, with the car still idling, said, "OK. We have two viewpoints about the Pennsylvania State Police. And we have two viewpoints about Strawberry Mansion. I see it as the most dangerous precinct in the city. You see it as what?"

Martin said, "Another workshop for blockbusting, redlining, city disinvestment, and municipal neglect."

Sweeney said, "All right. Maybe you and I share that one. What beatniks did to help the turnaround in South Street in the sixties, artists are doing now in Strawberry Mansion."

"And how did house prices drop from three hundred thousand to forty thousand dollars for thirteen-room —"

Sweeney broke in. "All right. We agree. Blockbusting realtors and redlining banks."

Martin said, "Helped by city neglect. Now, a few pioneers are moving in and getting their heads cracked open. But it *is* safer than it was."

Sweeney turned off the engine, as if to suspend the discussion of how good neighborhoods become bad ones and give him an opening to change the subject. "Was Crefeld the developer who built these travesties?"

"No," Martin said. "Crefeld is a town in western Germany. The German Quakers who settled here three hundred years ago came from there."

"And the new wave architects?"

"Locals from the salons on Market Street."

There were no sidewalks on Crefeld, so they walked in the street. Mansions set on four-acre lots were obscured by hundred-foot-long stretches of nine-foot-tall wrought-iron fencing, mature hardwood trees, and low walls made of deep-gray Pennsylvania fieldstone.

Martin and Sweeney entered the mansion's grounds along a gravel driveway.

The mansion's front door was crafted of dark-brown wood inlaid with lighter wood depicting two local wildflowers: wild radish and sheep sorrel. The exterior surface of the door might be a masterpiece. There was no visible lock or keyhole in its facade.

Martin pressed the lighted circular doorbell. In response, the harpsichord and allegro moderato strings for the first movement of the Third Brandenburg Concerto sounded within. The lilt of its energetic strings alerted anyone within earshot that someone was at the front door.

"Whoa. Johann Sebastian Bach announces visitors," commented Sweeney. "Now *that's* a doorbell."

Thirty seconds later, a woman swung open the door, and as she did, the concerto recording stopped. The woman, dressed in a crisp beige suit and stout black shoes, could have held the senior staff position of housekeeper.

"Welcome to the Gerhardt residence," she said.

Martin said, "Is Heinrich Gerhardt at home?"

"He is at home. Is he expecting you?"

"No. Detective Martin Perez, Pennsylvania State Police. My partner," he said with a tilt of his head, "Detective Ronald Sweeney." Martin removed a leather case from the inside pocket of his suit coat and flipped it open. She looked for a moment, first at his shield, then at his photo identification, and then at Martin's face to verify the photo belonged to the man in front of her. She did the same with Sweeney's shield and photo.

Satisfied, the housekeeper said, "You may come in. I'll see if he is available."

A polished welcome, Martin Perez reckoned.

They crossed the threshold and stepped onto a pristine black-and-white checkerboard-patterned marble floor. It was as wide as the mansion's fifty-foot front and half as deep. The floor was lighted from the sides by clerestories and from the back by two fifteen-by-four-foot opaque cathedral windows. Inside, behind and to the right of an arced, unpainted wooden staircase, Martin could see a cavernous closet. There was no furniture in the foyer.

In two minutes, a twenty- to twenty-five-year-old young man followed the woman down the curving staircase. He towered over the housekeeper as they descended. When they reached the bottom step, he said to them, "I'll be right with you."

They watched him retreat. He was at least six feet four inches tall in his bare feet and a lean, muscular two hundred pounds or more. He wore a polo shirt and woolen trousers.

The young man disappeared into the sun-filled cavern behind and to the left of the staircase. They overheard him talking on the telephone.

A minute later, he reappeared and asked Martin, "May I ask what this is concerning?"

A bulky mass of gauze and adhesive tape serving as a bandage on the man's right hand caught Martin's attention. A small patch of dark red suggested the bandage had stopped some bleeding.

"Cut yourself?" he asked. "Maybe on Eighteenth Street last night?"

The man did not take Martin's lure. He said, "What's this concerning?"

Martin said, "Even if it just happened last night…you should see a doctor about it. Don't want any infection to —"

The young man interrupted him. "I've called my mother. She's a lawyer downtown and says I don't have to talk to either one of you."

"Just a few questions?" Martin asked.

"I must ask you to leave now," said the young man. He spun around and walked up the stairs.

"We'll be on our way, then," Martin said to the departing man's wake.

The housekeeper reappeared and opened the door for them. Handing her his business card, Martin said, "Thank you for your cordial hospitality. If he wants his keys back, he can call me next week. The crime lab will be finished with them by Thursday."

The woman accepted the card without smiling or nodding. Martin and Sweeney pocketed their identification cases and walked back to the street.

EIGHT

JUNE 19, 9:00 P.M.

The night after the mugging, Martin greeted Henry in the mail area at 1589 Pine Street.

"You said you're OK?" Martin asked.

"I'm moving all right," Henry replied.

"Can we talk for a few minutes?"

"Sure," said Henry. "Now?"

"Are you up to it?"

Henry agreed. "Upstairs OK? I need something to eat."

"It can wait —"

"No," Henry said. "If you're all right with my having some —"

"Fine," said Martin.

They climbed the two flights of stairs. In Henry's studio apartment, Martin sat at the kitchen table. From a cabinet, Henry took mason jars with almonds, pistachios, apricots, and black mission figs — loot from Nuts to You. He put the jars on the table in front of Martin and then filled a tall glass with water from the nearby tap. He picked out nuts and fruits from the jars at random and ate them, one or two at a time, as he stood there, leaning against the countertop, facing Martin.

"You don't want to sit?" Martin asked.

"No," Henry said. "Ribs hurt when I get up." He pointed to the jars and added, "Help yourself." He drank most of his glass of water and refilled it.

Martin thought Henry might have a few broken ribs. One treatment was rest. Another was to be twenty-nine years old. Henry would be fine in few weeks.

After a pause, Martin said, "Off the record? I talked to one of the guys who assaulted you."

Henry reached for a fig, pinching off its hard stem and flicking it into the trash. He took a bite and then popped the rest of it into his mouth. Martin regarded Henry's eating the fig in silence as his approval to continue. Henry raised his vertical index finger to his lips, his signal that he'd honor Martin's request to keep their conversation private.

"Young guy —"

Henry cut in. "White guy." In less than two weeks, Henry had heard Martin identify as black any neighbors, parishioners, or street artists who were African American. If he didn't identify someone as to race or darkness of skin, it meant the guy was white.

"Correct," Martin said, lapsing into a professional police monotone. "White male, twenty-two years old, no visible scars or tattoos, living at home in a Chestnut Hill mansion with at least one parent. At this point, he is uncooperative."

"How can you tell that?" Henry asked.

Martin snorted at the question. "How about he wouldn't talk to me? That's the first clue someone's uncooperative."

Henry held up both hands in ersatz surrender, then took a fat apricot from its jar. He used the side of the apricot to wipe a smear of fig dreck off the tip of his index finger. Martin had never witnessed such a maneuver but suppressed a smile of admiration for its practicality.

Martin followed up. "If you sign a report I've drafted, we'd have a witness —"

"Who is this guy? Why did he —"

Martin was calm in his reply. "I do not know, Henry. He wouldn't talk to me. I can't ask him anything unless we can arrest him and —"

"Can I talk to him?"

"You?" Martin was incredulous. "Why would he talk to *you*?"

"Because I want to talk to *him*." It was as clear as it could be to Henry.

"OK. Look. Henry. We don't run classes for do-it-yourself police work. We do have programs for compensating victims, though, and one for emotional support of crime victims."

"Victims? I'm not a *victim*. I just want to *talk* to the guy. Who is he, and where does he live?" Henry took two almonds from a different mason jar and tossed them into his mouth as if to emphasize the reasonableness of his question.

Martin contained his sputtering. He resumed a police officer's professional monotone. "There are procedures for what happens when an assault occurs. Or an assault with a deadly —"

Henry interrupted him. "Oh, man, *that* didn't happen."

Martin hardened his tone. "Uh…Henry? *You* don't decide that." He avoided pointing at Henry's chest but spoke in the tone of an adult explaining dodge ball to a kindergartener. "You told me one of the three or four assailants hit you with a baseball bat. Right?"

Henry nodded.

"When that happens, an assault with a deadly weapon has occurred. Even if they didn't spread your brains on the sidewalk."

Henry shook his head. "I don't know, Martin. I don't know about all this. Arresting someone. All I want to do is talk to him."

Confused at what he deemed Henry's callow responses to his routine request for a report, Martin stood up. "I hear you. My business here is concluded." He started for the door.

Henry heard the anger and frustration but barged ahead with a bold question. He introduced the query with an admission. "Martin, I should've asked when we were downstairs."

Martin turned and glared at him.

"This isn't a good time to ask you for a favor, but can you help me? Can you loan me an armchair or rocker for a few days?"

Martin was stunned at the brazen request.

Henry gave his rationale. "The pain of getting in and out of bed with these ribs...." He shrugged, shook his head, then added, "It's too much. I need to sleep upright, and these little wooden chairs at the kitchen table are too flimsy for me."

During his years as an officer in the US Marines and a police detective, Martin had had his share of bruised ribs and broken bones. His compassion for Henry's discomfort changed his silent scowl to an empathetic nod. He didn't speak, but on his way out, he left the door open.

In a few minutes, Henry heard him climbing the stairs at a slow, steady pace. Martin reentered the apartment a bit winded, holding by its sides a tan upholstered chair with a high back and wide pine arms. He set it down near the kitchen table.

Henry said, "Martin...thank you. I couldn't've carried that chair up here, and it's gonna help me get some sleep tonight with a lot less pain."

Martin nodded in recognition of Henry's sincerity, but he did not speak. When he left Henry's apartment a second time, he closed the door behind him.

The next night, they greeted one another in the mail area at 1589 Pine Street.

"That was righteous, Martin, carrying that chair up two flights for me last night."

Martin nodded but said nothing.

Henry added a sly crack about Martin's generosity by thanking him, *en español fluido*, for not damaging the walls on the narrow staircase when he'd brought the chair upstairs.

Martin was glad to know Henry spoke Spanish but wasn't amused by the young man's bilingual wit. He respected Henry's brass but did not smile.

Henry addressed their contentious issue. He asked, "You gonna evict me for what I said last night?"

"No," Martin said. "Can't do that. Stupidity is not prohibited in your lease."

Henry curled his lips into a pout, but his feelings weren't hurt. He sensed amity in Martin's remarks, as if they'd grown out of a spirit of affection, not bitterness. Hoping he was right about Martin's sally, he said nothing as he flipped his two pieces of third-class junk mail into the blue plastic recycling basket.

Henry said, "So you're not gonna evict me...but you are mad at me."

Martin shook his head and then in a soft voice said, "We have different perspectives on what happened."

Henry nodded. "You may see this every day. It's happened to me only once."

"That's part of it."

"What else?"

Martin raised his eyebrows and took another breath. "Well, I'm about twice your age. I've seen a lot more of this kind of thing than you have. That's one thing. Another is you haven't been a first re-sponder to a police call or fought in combat in a real war. So you haven't seen broken and bloodied bodies lying in the street after an assault. Or heard the desert squish with the sound of blood-soaked sand wherever you stepped."

Henry nodded again. Compared to Martin Perez, he was younger and less seasoned. And while it was true he'd seen union organizers and priests shot in the streets when he was in the Peace Corps in the early years of the century, he knew his limited experience did not refute Martin's point.

He said, "That's right, Martin. You're right."

The mood in the mail area became less hostile. Henry recalled Martin had been kind to him and generous with his time, and he knew what he'd said the night before had not been well received.

"Another difference." Martin stopped. "You've never seen your uncle dragged out of his house by four white guys and lynched in his own neighborhood. Then doused in kerosene and set on fire. So there's no way you can remember the stench and my aunt Marian's howling with grief."

Henry faintly gasped at the intimacy of the black man's horrifying narrative.

Martin continued. "You read *To Kill a Mockingbird* in high school, so you think you know all about it. But you've never seen your family gathered at the home for the wake and no one says one word about going to the police.

"No one went to the police when that happened, because the police never did anything. And if you pressed the issue, police and the four men would come back and see that you paid for what they called stirrin' up trouble."

Henry kept his eyes fixed on Martin's countenance and heard the power in his soft voice.

Martin continued. "That wasn't two hundred years ago, Henry. Or one hundred. It was forty-six years ago. I was ten. Visiting my aunt and uncle in North Carolina during school vacation.

"So when there are police who *are* willing to investigate an assault, it's confusing when a victim doesn't want to hold attackers to account. I can live with it, Henry, but it is puzzling. Do you understand what I'm saying here?"

Henry said, "Yes. Yes, I do. And I have deep respect for you, Martin. But I'm not Emmett Till, and these guys aren't the Klan, and this is Pennsylvania, not —"

Martin cut in without raising his voice or hardening his tone. "I know where we are, Henry. I just want you to know how our perspectives are different."

Henry shook his head and looked at the varnished floor. He felt his adversarial tone had sounded clumsy. He said, "This is happening too fast for me, Martin. I'm sorry I've said things that upset you." Then, after a pause, he said, "And can I say something else?"

Martin made relaxed eye contact with Henry and said, "Go ahead."

"I know police work is hard and dangerous and thankless. My uncle Stanley was a police officer in New York for twenty-five years. And I know I'm late telling you this."

Martin seemed willing to listen.

"If I could talk to this guy, maybe he'd stop flogging strangers. But arresting him and that whole drill? Talking to him might line up with what the Gospel tells us. To love our enemies."

Henry took a breath. "Maybe it'd help us if you told me why you became a detective."

"Us?"

"Me."

Martin shrugged and shook his head as if in confusion at the suggestion. But he answered, "I wanted to work for justice in the streets and in the barracks. I could do both by being an excellent state police detective.

"That was a little naive. I forgot that to be a force for justice in the barracks, you have to get hired. That was not going to happen for a black man in the 1970s. It was just the way the world was. By the 1990s, some things had changed."

"So you got hired then?"

Martin said, "Yes. At thirty-nine I was one of the oldest cadets they'd ever admitted. It's worked out, but not the way I planned."

Henry was glad Martin could see he was listening.

"My partner and I are tech savvy. We're trusted to manage hundreds of evidence files for the state police and eighty small-town police departments in the state. Helping to solve more cases than other detectives isn't going to change the world or the state police, but I'm glad to be doing it."

Henry waited for Martin to continue his narrative.

"I've had to set aside my idealistic career goals in policing. But it can be satisfying, helping to make citizens' lives safer. Even if some don't want to be helped."

Henry said, "Martin, if my ribs weren't screaming, I'd give you a hug to consecrate our temporary cease-fire."

"All right, Henry. Maybe you're right. Maybe we understand one another. Consider yourself hugged."

Henry went upstairs, hung up his clothes, took an aspirin, and got into his sweats. Wrapping his quilt over his shoulders and around his knees, he coaxed his long limbs into Martin's armchair, did his tattoo, and slept.

NINE

JUNE 19–24

When settling into Martin's chair on Wednesday and the following three nights, Henry followed his tattoo routine. After playing the recording of the bugle call and reciting the three compline psalms, he began his examination of conscience with two questions. The first was *How do I feel about Gwynneth Trevor?* He was certain of his devotion to her. Modifying a passage from the Book of Ruth, he concluded, *I will go where she goes.*

The answer to the second, *Can I commit to her?* was also certain. It was yes, even as it had deepened when Gwynneth told him her mother had had all her children before she was twenty-eight. "It's on my mind," she'd added. His answer was yes even when he modified the question so it ran, *Can I commit to Gwynneth by fathering our baby?* Those four words, *by fathering our baby*, clarified and simplified his commitment.

So, as he ended his Wednesday night tattoo, Henry was clear he was both committed to Gwynneth and to fathering their baby. But he knew when he felt such clarity about his decisions, it was important to discuss them with his beloved sister, Gabriella, who had a way of pointing out in a tender and loving way when Henry was being impetuous. He vowed to call Gab soon.

Next night, he understood that their hot sex and tender afterplay generated in him robust, earthy feelings for Gwynneth, adding passion to his judicious regard for her. And the passion was essential. When deciding on a commitment to her, it was too risky to rely on objective measures, pass/fail grades calculated by some abstract emotional algebra.

Changing life circumstances would affect rational concerns, such as familial, professional, financial, intellectual, and physical relations. But he was glad the human passion he'd felt and she'd demonstrated in bed needed to be as monumental as it was, and honored.

During his tattoo on Friday night, he revisited the parable of the talents. Ought it impact his career decisions? His bright future at ACI seemed to beckon to him: *if you continue to be faithful in small matters, your joyful masters will give you more authority.* And while he believed he wanted freedom to succeed at his ACI business, he was revolted by the thought of doubling his money, for himself or others. He felt a hunger and thirst for a different goal. But was searching for a principled and simple life in business so naïve it was heedless of reality? He did not know.

Saturday night he resolved to let the matter lie fallow. And, at last able to sleep lying down, on Sunday morning he returned Martin's chair before they left together for early Mass at Saint John.

His left humerus still ached from shoulder to elbow. When he moved in the shower or twisted his torso reaching for a pencil or saltshaker, his ribs stung with the same intensity as five days earlier. When Stanhope asked about his awkward gait, he told her about the June 18 beating. She encouraged him to see a physician if his condition worsened.

At noon on Monday, June 24, Henry set out from his office to call Gab. He walked along the narrow urban strip of Sansom Street to the corner of Twentieth Street and stood outside the buzz of the Capogiro Gelato shop. When he reached Gab, he updated her about the trip to New York to meet Gwynneth's family and mentioned but gave no details about the physical damage the assault had inflicted on him.

During the call, Gab told him their oldest, Laura, wanted to visit Philadelphia and that sons Lukas and Kevin were looking forward to the end of their school years.

Then Gab asked, "Can you say more about your trip to New York?"

"Gwynneth said everyone in her family thinks I'm an all-star. And she talked with her mother about having kids."

Gab asked, "Having kids?"

"The day before we drove to New York, Gwynneth told me she's not waiting to have kids. I'm sure this'll come up again."

Gab was silent for a few moments then asked, "How are you feeling about that?"

"Fine. I think I'd be OK to be part of it."

"You were sorting out your feelings about her, and now you're thinking of starting a family with her? That's a big shift, Henry."

"So is it brash to say I welcome having our baby? Am I missing something here?"

Gab said, "Don't know, Henry. When will you see her next?"

"When she moves here. Saturday, the twenty-ninth, I drive to DC in a rental car, and we drive back here."

"OK. Look, Henry, I'm gonna need a little time to think about this. Can we talk Thursday or Friday?"

"Sure. I'll call you around noon. Friday?"

Gab said, "Friday's OK." Then she added, "Henry, you have a discernment practice, and you know you don't need any answers until you move Gwynneth and her stuff from DC to Philadelphia. That's almost a week."

After a short pause, Gabriella continued. "You sound as if you're being patient. Deciding to have a baby is colossal compared to whether to move or change jobs. But your holy spirit can handle it. Stay out of its way. And be patient."

He was surprised by the openness of his sister's counsel. Gab's belief system rejected any notion of a Christian trinity, but she seemed to know the strong power of Henry's holy spirit was a force in his life.

"And Henry? I'm in a little jam here. Gwynneth is talking to me about when I had our kids. We talk twice a week. Some of what you're saying isn't news to me."

Gratified at her candor, Henry said, "Thanks, Gab. I'm also wrestling with whether it's possible to succeed in business while living according to the Gospel."

"You're dealing with some heavy issues, Henry. Most folks are glad to be keeping their heads above water. Good idea to take your time before making decisions that affect your future. And Gwynneth's and a baby's future."

"Talk to you Friday, Gab."

TEN

JUNE 24–27

After Monday's conversation with Gab and later, during his tattoo, Henry appreciated his sister's respect for the power of his holy spirit. But his mind wandered off to the meaning of the parable of the talents and its impact on his career. He went to bed.

On Tuesday, June 25, he resumed his tattoo by listening to the jarring music of the bugle call and reciting the compline psalms. Pacified, he sought to consider the parable of the talents during his examination of conscience. But his mind generated thoughts about pursuing formal business education. He didn't miss working for James Wainwright in ACI's Washington office, but he did miss their weekly reading and discussion of management case studies. What was he doing to create such opportunities for himself in Philadelphia? No ideas for management studies came to him.

On Wednesday evening, June 26, after listening to the tattoo recording, he understood he was delighted about the certainty of his devotion to Gwynneth and giddy at the thought of fathering *their* baby. His happiness crowded out thoughts of business education. He ended with his customary prayer and benediction. *Peace. Be still.*

On Thursday, Henry's tattoo began as usual with the one-minute musical recording. When it ended, he repeated his gratitude for everything. Then, aware he'd vowed to write down his thoughts, he reached for his phone to activate the Notes app.

Before his hand touched the phone, an instruction arose in his mind, a voice without audio, saying, *Imagine yourself in paradise, Henry. Tell me what you see.*

He was awed by the directness and challenging power of the new and unexpected instruction. The same voice-without-audio issued a follow up comment: *Stop wandering in the thick woods of your own confusion. Start in the clearing where you want to be.*

He recorded the new query and his reply. "My view of paradise: we're opening the door to our house in Antique Row. We are together, with at least one toddler. Gwynneth is expecting a baby. When Gwynneth and I are together and raising children, that'll be paradise."

He went to bed happy and refreshed.

ELEVEN

JUNE 28–29

On Friday, Henry called Gab at noon to resume their conversation about having children.

Gabriella asked, "Anything new come up this week in your tattoo?"

"Oh, yes." He told her of the rephrased query about *our* baby, not of *a* baby, the passion he felt for her, and new words directing him to envision paradise and describe what he saw.

"It sounds as if the holy spirit gave your discernment practice quite a boost."

Gab paused then asked, "And can you tell me what you saw?"

He described the image of Gwynneth, pregnant, standing with a toddler, in front of their home. "It came unbidden, after I remembered your suggestions. Don't rush. Be patient."

Gab said, "You said it came out of your discernment. During your tattoo."

He said, "Right. So I must be the source."

Gab was in awe of Henry's question about a vision of paradise, stunned at the clarity of his answer, and impressed with his humble admission of its origin. She repeated his answer to herself but did not ask him what he made of it.

Early Saturday, June 29, Henry drove a rental car to DC. There, he and Gwynneth bid adieu to Caroline Washington and May Kim, her housemates for two years. They loaded her stuff into the car and embarked for Philadelphia.

When they pulled away, May said, "She told us he opens car doors for her. Did you see it then?"

"Yes," Caroline said. "Nice touch."

"No, it's more than that. It's an act of love. He does it every time."

"They rent cars only a few times a year, May. He doesn't do it —"

May cursed when she interrupted. "Every taxi, every car, every time. It's a tender act of affection and respect."

Caroline paused. "Good point."

May said, "And she's told us for months that he gives her everything she wants in bed. Every time."

The two women nodded at their appreciation for Henry's ways, and went back into the house.

As Henry navigated the curves in Rock Creek Parkway, Gwynneth said, "In Philadelphia, Lincoln Drive meanders by Wissahickon Creek, and that flows into the Schuylkill. In DC, this parkway follows the winding course of Rock Creek, a tributary of the Potomac River."

He recalled that Gwynneth had spent 2009 and 2010 at Penn, where she first worked with Hildegard Zimmer. "Worth checking out?" he asked.

"Yes," she said. "We'd rent a car to explore the fifty miles of hiking trails in the parks off Lincoln Drive."

Henry said, "Wissahickon Creek sounds as if it wasn't named by William Penn."

"No. It's the Lenni Lenape word for catfish. We use their words for lots of places. They don't mind. All their survivors were marched off to Oklahoma long ago."

"By William Penn?" asked Henry. "He had a reputation for fair dealing with the Delaware Indians."

"Penn died in 1718. By 1737, his heirs had cheated the Lenni Lenape…" Gwynneth let her voice trail off for a moment. "It's an ugly legacy. Can we leave it at that for now?"

Henry nodded his agreement. They were solemn and quiet as they crossed the Anacostia River on the Pennsylvania Avenue Bridge and then headed north on local freeways to Interstate 95 through Baltimore.

Still in Maryland, as they approached the Susquehanna River, Gwynneth said, "Henry." She paused. He nodded to show he was listening.

"Something has come up in my discernment exercise. My journal has a month of entries. I asked how I feel about you and whether I'm able to commit to you. But in the silence, I've been hearing answers to a question I didn't ask." She paused as they sped under the electronic tollgate in Perryville.

As the pause lingered, Henry spoke up. "Right. We've talked about this. It happens."

"I am past committed to you, Henry. I trust you. I respect you. I want to be with you, and it doesn't seem helpful to put those sentiments in words. That's where I am."

Henry nodded. "Yes. I'm getting something similar during tattoo."

"Tattoo?" Gwynneth asked.

"It's deliberate time for psalms and quiet at the end of the day. I started it last month."

He went on. "We can talk about it any time, but we don't have to wait until we get to Philadelphia to finish the conversation you started."

"Good," she said. "Because I want to say now that my mother had her first child at twenty-one and her fourth at twenty-seven. We talked about it during the Father's Day visit."

Henry nodded. "I overheard some of what you and your mother said on Father's Day."

She did not ask him what he'd heard. She said, "I'm not waiting to have children. The details are fuzzy, but the message is clear. I'm not waiting. And it's in my journal in my own handwriting. It's not about age-related risk factors. I'm just going to have children, and I'm not waiting."

They approached a large sign announcing a rest area six miles ahead. He gestured toward it, a silent query asking whether she wanted to stop.

Gwynneth shook her head. "So I'm not waiting to have children," she repeated. "I want you to be the child's father, Henry. I don't want the independence of a 'single mother by choice.' I don't want an anonymous donor father, and I don't want to pay an agency thirty thousand dollars for IVF. Just our baby. We can manage the details, as you call them, if we have accord on The Six."

"The Six?" Henry asked.

"That's what I'm calling them," Gwynneth said. "The factors we consider in discerning how we feel about one another and committing to one another. The Six we talked about in Washington. One's life purpose, spiritual path, vocation, family, stewardship, and body."

Henry nodded.

"You've said that when we're discerning an issue, if we have agreement on those six, most other issues are details we can manage."

"Right."

"So on the matter of having a baby, or even two babies, if we have agreement on The Six, we can manage the other issues, the details that come with having children. You still believe that?"

"Yes, I do," he said.

"OK. Well, many serious matters arise with having children. Marriage, for example, or where we'd live. Child care, parenting, finances, pediatricians, and schooling. Relations with the in-laws and outlaws and employers and neighbors and the government —"

"Right," he said, cutting in. "Serious matters."

"Well...good," Gwynneth said. "They're important for any parents. And we're leaving out how we make a living and who's gonna fight the insurance companies."

She paused, glanced at him, and then asked, "You agree those are *details* we can manage?"

He was nodding in agreement as he listened, but his eyes were watching the road ahead and the rearview mirrors.

"You agree?" she asked again.

"Yes, but The Six, as you call them, have limits. I created them to add some rational thought to my decision-making. Because in affairs of the heart, I relied on emotions."

"That's why they're called affairs of the heart, Henry. But I don't want my emotions managing some matters."

"Right," he said. "Because in *my* affairs of the heart my decisions were impassioned and the results were not good. I needed a better way."

She waited for him to continue.

"And today, it feels as if my passion for you has overwhelmed me." His voice rose as he added, "And it feels wonderful."

She said, "Are you consulting the Gospel?"

He shook his head. "No. There's no guidance for me in the Gospel about my passion for you. And The Six are just an untested system for making decisions. They sound flat and technical and cold. That's not what's going on with me. My passion for you is running hot, and my commitment to you is decided."

He took a breath, then continued. "And we can talk about them but we don't need accord on The Six. On stewardship, for example. I'm conservative in some financial matters and willing to take risks in some others. We haven't talked about this at *all*."

"Is that a problem?" she asked.

"No," he said. "It's just an example. And we need to talk about money but right now I don't want another calm discussion about money or anything else. You need to know about my burning affection for you. We have calm discussions about other stuff some other time."

"Right," she said, waiting for him to continue. But she was thrilled to hear his words and the power in his voice.

"OK, so let me ask you, how are you making your decisions here?"

"Long story," she said. "I'm sitting in the silence and journaling about our questions. How I feel about you and whether I can commit to you. But I haven't thought much about how we'd address stewardship. It's more than agreeing on a budget. And I'm talking to Caroline and May and Gab."

They were quiet for a moment.

"It does feel a bit…" Henry's voice trailed off. Then he asked, "Is it rash to decide this in the car before we get to Delaware?"

"I don't know," she said. "What's coming up for you? Besides Delaware."

He nodded and smiled, glad at her question. "During tattoo? After the compline psalms? An examination of conscience."

"I remember the Catholic tradition," she said.

"I've talked to Gab. She knows about my tattoo practice and says I'm gonna be all right."

Gwynneth said, "I'm talking to Gab too, Henry. I want you to know that's going on."

After a minute, he asked, "So…do we have accord here? Or a disconnect? In tattoo, I'm verifying my deep feelings for you and adding that my commitment includes fathering our baby. Where does that leave us?"

"We have accord. I couldn't have our baby without genuine trust in you. And your sister's been magnificent, Henry."

He said, "She told me the two of you have been talking. Just not what about. And she tells me, 'Don't overthink your affection for Gwynneth.'"

They were quiet for a moment, appreciating the support of Henry's sister. The rental car sailed up a rise in the interstate roadway, passing the Our Lady of the Highways Monastery.

After a long pause, he said, "In my own place in Philadelphia, knowing you'd be here soon, I've imagined us in the city. The image includes three of us. Maybe more."

He took his eyes off the road to glance at her. Had she been upset or appreciative of his candor? He couldn't tell, because when he'd said, "Three of us," she'd smiled and turned away from him, staring out the rental car window.

But she was neither interested in the lush green roadside nor upset. She was feeling the rush of an emotional smorgasbord of jubilation and relief and excitement.

He added, "If we're true and we have accord that we want to start an untraditional family, all the details you mentioned will sort themselves out. Or we'll sort them out. We're doing well here."

Gwynneth turned to him, nodded, and then said, "And how does that make you feel?"

"Excited. And how do you see it?"

"Yes. The same," said Gwynneth. "Excited. Happy. Getting my confidence from talking with Gab. She's been an angel, Henry... and my mother, and May and Caroline. Despite the unknowns, I'm ready."

Then he asked, "We start now? Is it today?"

"Yes."

"And we can wait until we get to my place on Pine Street? We don't need to stop at a motel?"

She smiled. "We have time."

After a pause she asked, "You told me when we talked on the phone Wednesday night you'd caught a few bumps and scrapes. You want to say anything more about it?"

"No," he said. "Not much to tell." Everything but his ribs and shoulder were healing from his run-in nine days earlier.

Gwynneth waited to see if he'd say more. They sat for a minute in the quiet hiss of the Ford Fusion's air-conditioning fan and then glided under the Delaware toll transponder in the E-Z Pass express lane.

Henry said, "So we'll conceive a baby, and then there'll be a pregnancy. The child will be born. Details will rain down on us. We'll work them out. *We* means you and me and our families. That's where we are?"

"Yes," she said. "That's where we are."

"I thought this might be a fun trip," he said, "but this is hilarious. We'll remember this conversation. We can say, 'Oh, yes, having the baby. We talked about it in the car.'"

When they arrived at his place in the early afternoon, Henry showed her the small room off the foyer where he picked up his mail. Just then, Martin came into the house, carrying groceries in four white-and-red plastic bags from the Acme supermarket at South and Tenth.

Henry said, "Martin, this is my beloved, Gwynneth Trevor. She's moving into her aunt and uncle's place on Clinton Street today."

Martin looked pleased to see her tawny coloration and Latino features. He looked at Henry with a smile and then, with a respectful nod, greeted Gwynneth, "*Senorita.*"

Martin asked Henry, "Gwynneth has my cell phone number?"

Henry nodded. "Yes, both your cell and home."

To Gwynneth, Martin said, "Any problems getting in here, just call or text."

Gwynneth thanked him in Spanish for his offer and for his kindness after Henry was assaulted. "*Gracias por su oferta y por su amabilidad después de que Henry fue asaltado.*"

Martin's body language expressed appreciation for her sentiment, but he was subdued. He and Henry were still in conflict about the mugging.

Yet, moved by Henry's intimate introduction of Gwynneth as his beloved, Martin said to Henry, "You want to borrow back the upholstered chair for a few months?"

Henry was touched by the generous offer. "Yes, Martin, and thanks. It'll be a comfortable option for Gwynneth when she visits."

Henry and Gwynneth climbed the stairs to his studio apartment. Inside, she put her bags in the walk-in closet and they steered each other to the bed.

After their time together, he said, "This may be out of sequence but —"

She sighed as she cut in, "Oh, man, Henry, you —"

He interrupted her by cupping her chin in his hand. "I've missed you. I'm glad you're moving to Philadelphia. I'm glad you're lying in this bed with me."

In reply she put her hand on his naked belly and laughed as she said, "Yeah. I got your message."

He smiled as his hand glided along her tawny thigh, stopping at her hip. He said, "Can I ask you a personal question?"

She pushed his hand away and said with false seriousness, "Yeah, look, Henry just because we're paired up here doesn't mean you can ask me any question you feel —"

But she could not keep a straight face and they both laughed. He put his hand back on her hip and said, "Have you been avoiding the sun? You're a little pale here."

"Funny, Henry," she said. But her tone was playful as she rolled onto her back and sighed. "You are one funny and beautiful man."

Afterward, they drove to her aunt Maria and uncle Bennie Irizarry's place, where they took fifteen minutes to carry Gwynneth's stuff upstairs. Before going off for dinner, they sat for an hour in heavy brown-leather chairs. Maria served a platter of mango slices, and Bennie made them three rum and Cokes. Gwynneth drank water.

The Irizarrys said they were glad Gwynneth was staying with them and wanted to support her new career in Philadelphia. "Let us know how we can help," they said.

They sipped their drinks and chatted for an hour. Then Gwynneth, Henry, Maria, and Bennie walked to Mixto Restaurante, five minutes away on Pine Street, for an early dinner.

At Mixto, they ordered. The food came. They ate. The check came. They paid it.

After walking back to Maria and Bennie's, they bid one another adios. Gwynneth joined her aunt and uncle in her new place on Clinton Street. Henry returned the rental car to Avis on Sixth Street and then walked home.

Upstairs at 1589 Pine Street, Martin's chair sat in front of Henry's apartment door. He carried it inside and set it near his kitchen table.

Gwynneth and Henry were both moved in. They were now residents of Philadelphia.

TWELVE

JULY 6–7

At dusk on Saturday, July 6, Henry and Gwynneth walked ten blocks from her place on Clinton Street to Spruce Street Harbor Park, an ingenious architectural melding of grass, trees, floating gardens, hanging lights, and a boardwalk beside the Delaware River.

From the park, they strolled along the river up Columbus Boulevard, watching fireworks explode against the night sky over Penn's Landing, a block to the north.

On their walk back to Gwynneth's place, she said, "Those might've been the baby's first fireworks."

Henry was unsure what she meant. But later, lying in bed next to her, he said, "We missed the July Fourth fireworks on Thursday."

Gwynneth said, "Some of the fireworks were in bed last night. Friday. We didn't miss those."

He said, "At Penn's Landing tonight, you said those might've been the baby's first fireworks. How do you know we have a baby?"

"I don't have any data to support it. Maybe it's just my hope for a miracle."

"Compared to that miracle, almost nothing else is important."

Gwynneth rolled off her back on top of him and said, "You're important." She let her hand rest on his pale, white shoulder. She mused about the contrast between her darker café-au-lait skin.

She asked, "We're both from New York but living in Philadelphia. Will the baby be a New Yorker?"

He looked at her and said, "Plenty of time to sort that out."

Then, remembering the damage from the recent mugging, she slid off his torso and lay next to him. "So," she said, "your ribs have recovered?"

"No. It'll be a while before all the pain is gone. They still send me a little jab when I'm twisting or getting into bed or up from a chair."

"I thought you did OK tonight."

He nuzzled her neck and said, "I just have to be careful. I did interview a doctor who takes my insurance. We're going to do a full physical in September."

"September? That's the earliest —"

"Yes," he cut in. "They're booked until then. But all broken ribs heal in time."

Gwynneth said, "My mother is dark skinned. And so is my brother Gerry. My other brothers and I are lighter and about the same color. But we never mention it. We're just Nuyoricans."

He said, "Your father's skin is similar to mine."

"Yeah. Two fine white men, you and my dad."

The next morning, after Henry went to early Mass at Saint John, he and Gwynneth walked together from Clinton Street eight blocks to the Italian Market. As they turned the corner off South Street onto Ninth, Gwynneth stopped them. She pointed to a sign in a bicycle shop. It read, "We Cheat Everyone and Pass the Savings On to You."

"Let's remember this," she said. "If we decide to get bikes, we should look here."

They passed Di Bruno's and Claudio's, Italian grocery stores crowded with customers lining their narrow aisles.

Henry said, "I need to tell you something. It's a little on the heavy side. But I need to tell you."

"So tell me."

He exhaled. "Martin."

"Martin. Your landlord?"

He nodded. "Well, yeah…but he's not just my landlord. Even when we argue, he's more a friend and counselor. But we've had a tiff about the mugging. We disagree about prosecuting the assailants, as he calls them."

"The guys who tried to kill you."

Henry thought that was overstating matters. He shrugged and said, "Martin Perez asked me to sign a report about the assault."

Mindful of his commitment to living his life by the Gospel, she said, "Right. And you want to turn the other cheek."

He reckoned Gwynneth's two statements were authentic, but he felt they were facile oversimplifications. Yet he asked himself, *Why are her words so troublesome to you?* He did not know. *Maybe because she's right?* He did not know.

His conscience, the one he examined every night at tattoo, observed in a calm voice without audio, *Put aside the words for now. Ask during your tattoo why the words are troubling.*

Henry felt he should have spoken to Gwynneth in June about the disagreement with Martin. *How can you say you trust Gwynneth and keep to yourself something as important as this?*

But Gwynneth did not appear to be vexed about the delay. "That's it?" she asked.

"No. I was thinking about why I waited to tell you about our beef."

"All right. And this has been going on for how long?"

"Three weeks. But this is just a part of it. He says he knows who did it. I want you to know we're discussing it. Martin and me. And we're not approaching resolution."

She nodded, taking in the information.

After crossing Carpenter Street, Henry asked, "Need anything in the market besides a stockpot?"

"No," she said, "but I want to look around. Just not in the bakeries."

They continued south on Ninth Street and up two concrete steps to the landing in front of Fante's Kitchen Shop's red-trimmed glass-paneled door. Inside, a manager directed them to the rear of the store, where they climbed a short flight of stairs.

At the top of the stairs, commandeering six aisles of kitchen appliances, gadgets, and multicolored cookware, a fiftyish and trim black woman wearing a plain green T-shirt and tan slacks greeted them. "Can I help you this morning?"

Gwynneth said, "We need a pot for pasta that's big enough to make paella for a crowd."

The woman nodded, guided them along a narrow aisle containing tall shelves of pots and pans, and stopped. She pointed to a three-gallon stainless-steel stockpot. "This All-Clad is our best seller. It's a classic and stylish enough to bring to the table for serving. It's three fifty."

The woman went a few steps farther and rested her hand and manicured nails on a cherry-red enamel stockpot. "This one is ten quarts, just as versatile. The handles stay cool. Here…" The woman removed it from the shelf and held it out for Gwynneth, who took it. "Some cooks think the enamel and steel make it too heavy. But you're tall and strong. Is it —"

"It's fine," Gwynneth said. She handed it back to the woman.

"This one's eighty dollars. We also have it in green and what the French call flame." Then, lowering her voice and looking behind her to check for eavesdroppers, she said, "But I say it's orange."

Gwynneth laughed. Henry took a step toward her and nestled his hip against her side. He considered offering to contribute half the cost of the All-Clad but said nothing. For now, this was Gwynneth's transaction to manage.

With a calm sweep of her hand, the woman added, "If you decide this pot doesn't work for you or you'd rather have the All-Clad, you can return it."

Satisfied with the woman's knowledge and relaxed explanations of the advantages of the two stockpots, Gwynneth said, "I'll take the red enamel-and-steel one."

"Good. We'll send it downstairs. You can pick it up at the cashier."

On their way to the checkout, Gwynneth stopped to look at displays of silicone hot pads. A short dark-skinned Mediterranean woman staffing the area told her, "The Vremi here come in a set of four, two square and two round. These are twelve dollars but on sale now for eight. Are you familiar with them?" The woman was in her late sixties or early seventies. She wore a tricolor T-shirt resembling the green, white, and red Italian flag and was just as trim as her colleague they'd spoken with upstairs.

"No," Gwynneth said.

"You can use them as trivets or potholders. I also use mine for opening stubborn jars with these old paws." She held up a gnarled hand to emphasize her point.

Gwynneth needed potholders but wasn't sure she wanted the Vremi.

The woman was in no hurry to close an eight-dollar purchase, but she did add, "They're dishwasher safe, if you have a dishwasher. Besides the tall blond guy here, I mean."

Gwynneth smiled at the woman's comment. "Thanks," she said, picking up a set of four.

On the way through the narrow aisles of the crowded shop toward the cashier, she asked, "So, Henry, are all the salespeople in Philadelphia this cordial? And knowledgeable?"

"Don't know," he said. "Been here just a month myself. They do know about what they're selling in here. In Nuts to You, where they carry a thousand SKUs, even the new kids on staff seem to know where everything is."

"What about the church?"

"Yes. Cordial, enlightened, and committed Christians."

"And you're volunteering at a homeless ministry there?"

"No. At a different church, serving lunch, first and third Wednesdays."

At the cashier, she paid for the kitchenware and accepted Henry's offer to carry the pot and pads.

To let him know her sojourn in the Italian Market was over, she started up Ninth Street. At Bainbridge Street and again at South Street, she was impressed by the presence of the urban murals they saw painted onto the flat concrete facades of some of the residential and commercial buildings.

"Lots of urban murals in this part of Philadelphia," she remarked.

"Yes. Almost four thousand artistic creations have been painted since the 1980s," he said. "I've seen fifty or so of the two thousand still in public view."

"Nice they can afford these drab and uninspired —"

Henry cut in. "It doesn't claim to be great art. But it has saved millions and added to the art scene here."

Gwynneth felt informed but not rebuked by his interruption. "How's that?"

"In the 1980s, the city was locking up the graffiti artists, who sprayed the city nonstop. Now, some of those guys are on the Rec Department payroll, working with professionals from museums and galleries. Some grumble that the murals are dull and lifeless. But nobody's campaigning for the return of the graffiti."

As they turned onto South Street, he asked, "Is this more information than —"

"No. Go on."

"In Philadelphia, most think murals are a smarter investment than spending millions to remove graffiti."

She nodded. "Smarter if it's working, Henry."

On South between Tenth and Eleventh Streets, they passed a multistory mixed-media and sculpture installation. She frowned at its garishness but said nothing.

Henry saw her frown. He smiled and said, "Jacksyacs told me —"

She shook her head. "Jack's what?"

"It's the young adult Christians at Saint John. Saint John the Evangelist Church. Young —"

"Ah. Jack's YACs. Got it."

"They told me about this place. Zagar's Magic Garden. Isaiah Zagar has installed dozens of outdoor mosaics in the neighborhood."

"What do you make of it?" she asked.

He paused. "In 1968, geniuses in this city wanted to pave South Street with a superhighway to connect the interstate on the Delaware River to the interstate on the Schuylkill River. Three miles."

She looked askance at him.

"It's true. In the 1960s South Street was a black commercial area and garment district. Real estate values nosedived while geniuses dithered over superhighway plans. Businesses and residents moved out. It became a dangerous area. Artists including Zagar moved in for the low rents and opened studios. He bought lots for this and other installations. Sculpture replaced vermin. Forty-five years later, Whole Foods and Acme are selling groceries and high-end produce across the street. Most locals see it as an upgrade."

Gwynneth nodded. "You've learned a lot about Philadelphia in a month, Henry. Learned anything about yourself?"

"I feel the same, but this city has more vitality than Washington. That could be a catalyst for change."

They turned up Eleventh Street. As they crossed Pine Street, Gwynneth pointed to a storefront sign that read Baria Antiques. "That's Uncle Bennie and Aunt Maria's store. Closed today."

He nodded, glad to know the antique store's location. Then, resuming their conversation he said, "Time with you seems to have more vitality too."

To show her appreciation for what he'd said, Gwynneth slipped her arm around his waist, careful not to aggravate his ribs or dislodge the stockpot.

After a moment he said, "I've done some drawings of federal townhouses south of Rittenhouse Square, and some ruins in —"

Gwynneth interrupted him. "Drawings? Ruins?"

"Concrete and stone remnants of the Cliff House. A mansion with a long history. It fell apart when vandals and arsonists tore it up in the 1970s and '80s."

"That's new, Henry. How long have you been making drawings?"

"A month. How a pencil drawing evolves —"

She cut in again. "And that's how you're learning about yourself here in Philadelphia? When you see what your internal artist produces —"

He interrupted her with a shrug. "Maybe. Too early to tell. Haven't done any drawing since high school. But the story of the Cliff House is a sad tale, and it's right in front of us. What's left of the Cliff House is less than two miles from the art museum. I enjoy standing near it and seeing what the pencil draws."

Gwynneth was both thrilled and confounded by their conversation. She would not have imagined Henry drawing. He'd never hinted at having any interest in it.

As they neared her home, Merry Godmother said, "*You can ask him how this vitality he mentioned is playing out at work and in this city. Keep asking him what he's learning about himself. And you might ask yourself the same question.*"

At 1110 Clinton, she unpacked the pot and removed labels from the four silicone pads. He broke down the cardboard box, put it in the recycle bin on his way out, and walked home.

THIRTEEN
JULY 8–AUGUST 14

On July 8, early in his second month at ACI in Philadelphia, Henry negotiated $2 million in new work on risk assessment, to begin in the fall with a banking client.

On Wednesday, July 10, Carmichael knocked on the doorjamb of his office.

"Good job on the new business with the bank," he said. "We expected them to pare the level of effort."

Henry said, "They know our full update on best practices could save them a fortune."

"You showed good strategic thinking," Carmichael said.

Henry nodded. "Thank you."

"We get these materials here from time to time," Carmichael went on, holding up some glossy trifolds. "Wharton brochures. Any interest?"

"Yes," Henry said. "After I recover from moving twice last month."

Carmichael laughed. "We'd consider supporting a Lauder scholarship." He took three steps into Henry's work space, set the brochures on the desk, and departed.

Henry blinked at the information. The Lauder was the nickname of a challenging two-year MBA program coupled with a degree in languages and international studies at Wharton, the graduate business school at Penn. Tuition and expenses were higher than at schools he'd investigated when he lived in Washington. Annual costs at Wharton ran to $200,000.

That night at home, Henry reviewed the materials. He tempered Carmichael's vote of confidence by ending his tattoo with a prayer to decide soon on the Lauder opportunity.

Thursday morning, he went to Carmichael, thanked him, and said, "Maybe this could work next year? Many of their programs start next week —"

Carmichael broke in. "Henry, one Lauder program starts next month. The application deadline is Monday, July 15, four days from today. Are you interested or not?" He sounded annoyed at Henry's narrow-minded reaction to the scholarship offer.

Henry left unanswered a flurry of imagined questions. *What about the baby? What about Gwynneth? Or studying with Armando? What about yadda and bada boop?* But after hearing the irritation in Carmichael's tone, he shook off the questions.

To Carmichael, Henry gave a bolder answer, "Yes. I have a strong —"

Carmichael nodded and interrupted. "Good. Complete the on-line application tonight and check in with me early tomorrow."

A week later, Stanhope asked Andre, "Henry is thinking about Wharton?"

"No," Andre said. "He's decided. He'll be at the Lauder."

"That happened fast."

Andre said, "After talking to Henry's clients in Washington, Carmichael is sure he's gonna be an all-star. When he spots one, he thinks of ways to keep them. Same as with you."

Stanhope tilted her head and shrugged in accord. She'd commuted to Temple from South Philly to earn her BA after her three children were in elementary school. By 2011, she'd excelled for five years at ACI in managing projects and developing new business. To show their appreciation, Carmichael and Andre had offered to support her at an MBA program at Wharton.

She was gratified by the gesture, in part because she felt valued, and also because ACI could be stingy with its compensation. But she declined. It was not on her agenda to revisit the demands of balancing family responsibilities, full-time work, and part-time university studies.

So Carmichael and Andre awarded her a five-figure bonus. Carmen, her husband, and their three kids went to Tuscany, Rome, and Sorrento for a month before school started in 2012.

Andre added, "He's looking at the joint MBA and International Studies program."

"Lauder is a tough regimen, even with his fluent Spanish," she said.

Andre shook his head. "His language? Chinese. Mandarin."

Stanhope was amazed to hear Andre's update. "That's cursed impressive," she said, loud enough for Andre to raise his eyebrows in faux shock. "Strong guy, eh?"

"Yes," Andre said.

Henry's strength, charisma, humility, or all three traits combined had also impressed senior officers at the client bank. During a banking conference held from July 16 to 19 at the Philadelphia Convention Center, Henry had presented a poster session on how ACI identified opportunities for delivering profitable cell phone-based financial services to underserved populations in emerging markets in Africa.

He showed that demand for these services in a few African countries was high and rising. One strategy for market entry was to partner with local banks, expand the customer base five- to tenfold, and collect below-market fees for transactions.

This wasn't just an idea. In the previous decade, UK banks partnering with African banks earned high returns on their investment in cell phone-based financial services. In Kenya, fifty percent of banking customers managed money by remote access. It was easier and much safer than transacting business in cash.

And the opportunity was at hand. Most US banks were conducting research, scheduling focus groups, and offering free symposia to finance ministers on ways to improve access to financial services in emerging markets such as Africa. It was the response of bankers whose underwriters voiced caution about doing business in foreign countries, and whose senior officers were wary about competing with expanding Chinese investments there.

Broad Street Bank officers knew this about their business. But after listening to Henry, they knew if they seized the initiative, they could be gaining a credible commercial presence in Africa and making money on banking services within a year.

Roused by Henry's presentation, two Broad Street Bank officers made a persuasive pitch to their board. They opened discussions with ACI and on August 9 contracted for $10 million of ACI's services to initiate and expand banking services in Botswana and South Africa.

Michael Larson, a junior associate who'd worked with Henry at ACI in Washington, was transferred to Philadelphia to join the project staff. Stanhope and Henry negotiated subcontracts with vendors in Africa. They postponed hiring a senior associate until they had a firm starting date for the project.

Broad Street Bank's Susan Hazari and Henry were assigned the job of reviewing the terms of the $10 million contract. On Monday, August 12, after a lunchtime outing, Henry noticed Susan exiting from the Acorn Club, the country's oldest club for women. She was by herself, looking pensive, and poised to cross Sydenham Street. She wore a light-blue wool suit and a lighter-blue blouse. He considered leaving her to her thoughts but decided to greet her.

"Hey, Susan," he said. "Henry Knudsen from —"

She interrupted him. "I remember you, Henry." Her steady gaze emphasized that she recognized him, and her smile told him she wasn't irate at his offer to identify himself. She added, "And we're meeting Wednesday morning in our offices."

He said, "Yes, that's right. Wednesday, the fourteenth."

Henry had not recalled that Susan was tall. Today she wore high heels, and their eyes met at the same height.

"Warm afternoon," she said. "Running an errand?"

Tiny pierced earrings gave her earlobes a hint of blue, lighter than her suit, darker than her blouse. They might've been selected to match her ensemble and short blond hair.

Henry said, "Quick look at the sculptures at Gallery One, down on Broad —"

"Yes," she cut in. "On the lower level in Hamilton Hall. Anything interesting there?"

While accommodating the interruption, Henry took a deliberate breath as a picaresque thought challenged him. *You don't pay this close attention to Gwynneth's earrings. Why are you staring at hers?* Henry's ripostes were prompt. *Gwynneth doesn't wear earrings,* and *Peace. Be still.*

Then he canted his head to one side and said, "Yes. Ceramic marine sculptures. A blue-and-white ten-foot shark jarred me."

"We did some of that in school," she said.

"Ceramic sculptures?" he said.

She nodded.

"Where was that?"

"Prescott," she said without expression.

"Ah."

She stared at him. "You've heard of it?"

"Yes," in an economics seminar. In the 1960s, the Ford Foundation asked Prescott to prepare students for a changing world, in the tradition of congregational schools committed to it. Grinnell and Pomona and —"

She stared at him and then tilted her head as she interrupted him. "And Colorado and Oberlin and Harvard."

He said, "Our professor pointed out that Prescott was founded in Arizona in the late 1960s, at the dawn of the modern era, when mobile telephones weighed fourteen pounds."

They both laughed.

"See you Wednesday, Henry."

"Good," he said. "At nine fifteen at the bank."

They separated. Henry suppressed an urge to look behind him to watch her gait and carriage, to see if she were as trim from afar as she seemed when they spoke face to face. *Is she a member of the Acorn Club? Or just having lunch with a member?* There had been no mention of the club when he'd read her online profile. He stanched the queries and returned to his office.

Wednesday morning at seven thirty, Henry sat in his office reviewing materials for his nine-fifteen meeting with Susan Hazari. He scanned the scope of work, budget, and schedule.

ACI used initial meetings with clients to verify their schedule, clarify lines of communication, and gauge where their point of contact, Susan, fit in the bank hierarchy and power structure.

Later, as he sat across her desk from her, he reminded himself that his first report on the bank work assignment would be to provide Stanhope and Andre his assessment of Susan's position in the bank. So he asked, "You've been here five years now?" Then he waited.

The personal question startled her. She hesitated, then said, "It's been a ride."

"A *ride?*"

"New officers here pass through an orientation. It's a one-year hazing gauntlet for all of us — men, women, MBA hotshots, internal recruits, everybody. You have to shine in all your team-project work and avoid negativity."

"How many in your cohort?"

"Twelve," she said. "I was puzzled that our essentials weren't excellence in computer science and finance. But we all had those. They wanted us to be trusted teammates and not grumble. Grumbling got three of us sacked the first month."

"Benedict forbade grumbling fifteen hundred years ago." The comment was out of Henry's mouth before he knew it.

Susan looked at Henry. "In Benedict's *Rule*."

"Yes."

It was nine twenty-five. They had not looked at the agenda.

After a moment, Henry said, "You got through your orientation year."

She canted her head and said, "Yes. My mentor was a random draw, but she's the key to my success here so far. And it had little to do with her expertise in equity and debt markets."

As Henry listened, he recalled how his first mentor at ACI, James Wainwright, had evolved into a foe. Now his mentor was Carmen Stanhope, a savvy adviser for two others at ACI. He hadn't chosen either one.

At nine thirty, Susan picked up her tablet and said, "Agenda. Shall we? Are you still looking at a December or January start date?"

Henry said, "We have flexibility. Either is fine with us."

"I'll let you know next week what works for us," Susan said. "I want to ask about your project staff."

Henry described Michael Larson's work as a junior associate in Washington and his transfer August 5 to Philadelphia.

"So, he's working out for you?"

Henry said, "Yes. He's strong. One of our best associates."

Susan asked, "But you still have a vacancy on your team?"

Henry said, "Yes, we have a few candidates and a month or two to decide. We'll let you know when we've made a hire."

"Not grumbling about it, Henry," Susan said. "And by the way," she added, "I don't hear many references to Saint Benedict at this bank."

Henry nodded but said no more. They wrapped up their meeting before ten o'clock.

Back at the office, Henry told Stanhope and then Andre what little he'd heard from Susan Hazari about her place in the bank's power structure.

Andre asked, "This was your first face-to-face encounter with Susan Hazari?"

"No," Henry said. "The second. We chatted for a couple of minutes Monday. Around one o'clock, she was leaving the Acorn Club. I was coming back from a lunchtime visit to Gallery One on Broad."

Henry paused. By saying nothing, Andre invited him to continue.

"She asked about Gallery One. There's a show of abstract ceramic sculptures. And she did some sculpture in college."

Andre asked, "What was she doing at the Acorn Club?"

"She didn't say. That was it on Monday."

"Nothing else?"

Henry blinked at the reply. In his view, it was irrelevant that on Monday he'd thought Susan was an attractive woman. But he did give Andre a summary of their exchange about Prescott College and Saint Benedict. Andre had not heard of Prescott.

After a pause, Andre asked, "And today you discussed what?"

"We chatted for ten or fifteen minutes before getting to the agenda," Henry replied. "Ms. Hazari says all the Broad Street execs know local and global banking. They're aware there's a vacancy on our project team. And in their corporate culture, the key traits of successful executives are being good teammates and not grumbling."

"Good report," Andre said. "It isn't written in ACI's employee handbook, but we aren't fond of grumbling either."

Henry smiled and nodded.

Andre said, "OK. Stay with it."

FOURTEEN

SUMMER 2013

I n the summer of 2013, Martin Perez and Ronald Sweeney cel-
ebrated over sixteen years as partners in the Pennsylvania State
Police. They were assigned to the criminal investigation section.
Their barracks were at the Philadelphia station on Belmont Avenue.

Perez was a six-foot-two-inch-tall, muscular, dark-skinned black
man who'd grown up in Philadelphia and served twenty-one deco-
rated years in the US Marines. A maverick, he'd entered as a private
and retired in 1996 as a major. He'd earned a BA in 1992 in chemistry at George Mason University while working in intelligence at the
Pentagon and an MA in 1994 in mathematics at the University of
Maryland as he served as a marine cryptologic analyst at Fort Meade.
At thirty-nine, one year under the age limit, he applied in the spring
of 1996 to the Pennsylvania State Police and was accepted. After his
twenty-seven-week training course in Hershey in September 1996,
he graduated second in his class of twenty in February 1997.

At six feet tall, Ronald Sweeney, a broad-shouldered white man,
was shorter than Perez. His rugged features included a square jaw
and acne scars on both high cheekbones. He wore his full head of
light-brown hair as short as he had at West Scranton High School,
where he'd won varsity letters both in martial arts and as a striker
on the soccer team. A strabismus in his left eye gave the appearance
he was not paying attention to what was in front of him.

Born in 1972, Sweeney had grown up fatherless in a trailer park
near Scranton. When he graduated in 1991, the anthracite coal

mines were closing. Local job prospects were few. He made his way to Harrisburg, where he worked for Catholic Charities, drove for Burlington Air Freight and Brinks, hustled as a barback, and studied at community colleges before applying to the state police academy. A brilliant underachiever, Sweeney made honor grades in college and had historically high scores on the police aptitude tests. He began his training in Hershey in September 1995 and graduated number one in his class of nineteen in February 1996.

In his first year as a trooper, Sweeney's partner had oriented him to the operations of both the patrol and criminal investigation sections. But late in 1996, his partner came under suspicion of taking bribes to protect an interstate prostitution ring operating at a rest area on the Pennsylvania Turnpike near Harrisburg. Sweeney was not involved, but when his partner was arrested, he had a sudden need for a new one. Martin, fresh out of the academy in February 1997, was paired with him. It was unusual to couple Sweeney with any rookie, but Martin was seen as a mature presence, and the assignment was deemed temporary.

On paper, the differences in experience, race, and age made them an odd pair. Moreover, Sweeney was uneasy, because at Catholic Charities, in the freight business, and at Brinks, all his supervisors and most of his colleagues had been white. And his morale was low. He was embarrassed not to have sniffed out his crooked partner's corrupt ways throughout 1996. Martin, unaware of Sweeney's chagrin, was fine with a younger partner.

One of their first assignments was a plainclothes stakeout at a service plaza fifty miles east of Harrisburg, where a motorcycle gang sold meth to truckers and high school kids. They were to establish positions and observe activity in the food court of the South Midway Service Plaza by ten and get out by noon or before.

Their orders were to keep their eyes open and mouths shut and, if they saw drug deals going down, to remember as many details as they could about the parties and to confront no one.

Sweeney got settled in the food court at ten. Martin was stationed outside the video game arcade, using one eye to aim his light gun at cartoon zombies in *The House of the Dead* and the other to watch Sweeney.

Two goons spotted Sweeney as he sat in an orange plastic chair welded to a yellow table, nursing a coffee. He looked out of place, because even at coffee-break time, few customers hung out at any of the turnpike's service plazas.

They approached him. One challenged Sweeney. "Having trouble finishing your coffee?"

Sweeney, in T-shirt, dungarees, and heavy boots, said, "It's paid for. Why doncha mind your own cursed business?"

The goons didn't appreciate his answer. They came closer. The taller one, at six feet five inches tall and 280 pounds, could've played tight end for the Pittsburgh Steelers. He grabbed Sweeney by the T-shirt and yanked him out of his seat, knocking his coffee onto the greasy concrete floor. He stood Sweeney up in front of him.

Sweeney was alarmed at the man's heft, strength, and quickness. To distract him, he waved his arms and screamed, "*Hey*. Whatcha *doin'*?"

To create another distraction, Martin slapped the glass screen of *The House of the Dead*. No one looked in his direction. All eyes in the place were on Sweeney.

The hooligan grabbed for Sweeney's throat. Keeping his composure, Sweeney recalled that a stomp might be an apt response.

The stomp, *fumikomi geri* in Japanese, was one Sweeney had performed to earn his brown belt at West Scranton High. He'd had to stomp through a two-by-four with his bare foot. It occurred to him that his attacker might stop choking him if he crushed his instep.

So, as his throat was being mashed by the goon's hand, Sweeney managed to squeak, "Awwkhh," then, with one heavy boot, he stomped down hard with all his weight on the thug's left motorcycle boot, just above the ankle. The fierce blow snapped off the ends of both bones in his attacker's lower leg.

The lug screamed as he let go of Sweeney's throat and fell to the floor, howling in pain. The bruiser's partner started around the chair and table, intending to restrain Sweeney.

Martin, seeking to help his partner, barreled across the food court, bellowing, "Medical emergency here. Hey. A man needs a *medic*. Someone call 911." Martin's hollering brought a small crowd to the fracas.

Sweeney, scared but reassured that Martin was standing near him, bent over the injured man, trying to look as if he were administering first aid. His charade made little difference, since Sweeney was hidden from view, squatting down behind the yellow and orange plastic furniture. Martin was the only one who could see him.

The fallen bruiser's sidekick was unable to reach and subdue Sweeney before he hit the fallen man with a swift *taisho zuki*. The punch landed on the side of the lug's head with the force of a crowbar, popping his skull onto the concrete floor. It made the sound of a breaking eggshell. The man stopped shrieking.

The hood's partner was now frozen in place. Martin joined restaurant workers who had formed a small crowd in the area occupied by Sweeney and the fallen, silent man. As Sweeney stood up, Martin roared, "Somebody. Call. 911. It's an *emergency*."

A manager deployed her cell phone to call 911. The covey of janitors, servers, and customers gathered as Martin and Sweeney headed for the exit. Sweeney barked into his cell phone, "I can't get a *signal* on this cursed thing."

As they hustled out the door, no one heeded them. They trotted across the parking lot, scrambled into their unmarked car, and zoomed onto the turnpike.

Martin and Sweeney regarded the outing as a complete failure. But their commanding officer was pleased they'd at last learned how the drug dealers were protecting their operations. He told them, "Your investigation was a success. We learned what we needed to learn."

What also happened was the partners had learned about one another. Martin saw that Sweeny was intrepid and kept his wits under fire, and if he was in a real jam, his audacity could be heroic. Sweeney saw that if he were in a tight spot, Martin would come to his aid.

In 2000, their partnership grew strong in the nursery bed of mutual respect. By 2013, Sweeney and Martin were regarded as one of the best detective duos in the state. Not the best interracial partnership, but one of the best detective teams, period.

During their time together, Martin saw he could rely on Ronald's acuity when studying local, state, or regional crime statistics. He read case studies and national accounts about the clear downward trend in the crime reports from the fifty states and the District of Columbia.

"That's what the numbers tell us," Sweeney would say. "Crime is down in all categories. It's been going down since the late 1970s. More than thirty-five years. No one knows why.

"But they don't air that on the evening news. If there's only one murder to report, talking heads will broadcast different stories about it four nights in a row. So citizens get a steady diet of mayhem and believe crime is rising, even when it's been declining for decades. It's pointless to argue with the news hucksters. They are selling fear on TV, and the public is buying it."

FIFTEEN

JULY 23-27

On July 23, Armando Beluga convened the alternative seminary in an assembly room at UniPhil on Fairmount Avenue near Broad Street.

"In the twentieth century in Latin America," he said, "renewed support for a so-called preferential option for the poor came from advocates of a movement known as liberation theology. What's the basis for the preferential option? Is it connected to the idea of liberation theology?"

Three raised their hands. Armando scanned the class of fifteen. "Can we hear from someone who hasn't spoken in a while?"

Most other participants stared at the floor.

Armando persisted. "Anyone? How about our newest member? Can you help us out here, Henry? Is there any known basis for this ministry?"

Henry said, "Yes. Two familiar bases are Matthew 25:40 and Luke 4:18. After Vatican II, it was included in the revision of the *Code of Canon Law.*"

"Code of what?" asked Armando.

"In catechism we learned the *Code of Canon Law* is all the laws of the Church not concerned with our worship — about two thousand rules. They're called canons, and they're arranged in seven books. Book two gives the rights and obligations of all the Christian faithful. One obligation is 'to promote social justice and, mindful of the precept of the Lord, to assist the poor from their own resources.' It's a bridge between the Gospel and us."

"Who could be against that?" Armando asked.

One student said, "Our government saw communists, not Christians, whenever anyone was helping the poor. And while Reagan was asleep, Oliver North was helping the hooligans in the Salvadoran army."

"Sounds good, Patricia. Thank you. Do you have any evidence to support that statement?"

The woman who'd made the comment said nothing.

After a time, it was clear no one was going to respond to Armando.

Henry said, "In 1989, Senate Foreign Relations Committee members criticized the Salvadoran army's death squads, who'd murdered tens of thousands of civilians. Many victims were Catholics who opposed the government's brutality. In the mid-1980s, the president said the army was our ally in the fight against the communists in Latin America. But the committee didn't agree."

Armando said, "You claim to know a lot about this senate committee."

Henry said, "I worked on Capitol Hill from 2007 until 2010. As far back as the late 1980s, many in Congress were skeptical of the old anticommunist song. When the murders of the Jesuits came to light, there was a lot of criticism in the media."

"That's the US Senate?" Armando asked. "So you're telling me the US government was behind the subversion of liberation theology?"

A tense silence descended on the alternative seminary classroom.

Henry said, "There's disagreement about that. But most agree there's a big divide between the wealthy and the poor in Latin America and that we were not helping the poor. Liberation theology holds that freedom for all oppressed people is a fulfillment of the Kingdom of God. That's in the writings of Gustavo Gutiérrez, a Dominican priest from Peru."

"So, Henry, you're familiar with the writings of obscure Peruvian —"

Henry interrupted Armando to say, "He's not obscure. He's at Notre Dame."

Armando said, "And he plays free safety —"

Laughter erupted in the class, burying the rest of Armando's aside.

Henry spoke after the laughter subsided. "His football-playing days are behind him. He's in his eighties. But he reminds us the Gospel is explicit about bringing a sword to the fight to help the poor."

"Ah, and your citation?"

"Matthew 10:34. Luke 22. Isaiah 61. And here in Philadelphia, UniPhil has done this work since 1981."

"We know, Henry. They're our hosts tonight."

Henry nodded.

"Did you want to add a comment?"

"Yes. I'd say not just radical priests but the Vatican also calls us to our Christian duty. Pope John Paul II asked us, 'In the spirit of the Church, which is the spirit of Christ, and supported by its teaching, let us get back to work in this field.'"

"When was that, Henry?"

"In 1979 or 1980. He asked us to 'speak in the idiom of Vatican II, Paul VI, and John XXIII. Speak to the experience, suffering, and the hope of contemporary humanity.'"

"What does that mean for us today?" Armando asked.

Silence returned to the classroom until Armando recognized a swarthy-faced man wearing a brown wool herringbone tweed suit. "Go ahead, Rodrigo."

"It means Jesus and his followers of the early church advocated peace, feeding the poor, welcoming the stranger, and caring for the sick. Then, Roman emperor Constantine hijacked the church in the fourth century to protect the interests of the ruling classes, the rich, and the propertied. John XXIII and John Paul II say we need to return to our roots. The Church needs to live a life in keeping with the Gospel . But it is not going to happen."

Armando asked him, "Why not?"

Rodrigo said, "Because the Catholic doctrine favoring human dignity always loses to the rich who oppress the poor. It's been going on for seventeen hundred years. And it's getting worse. Since 1980, the distribution of wealth has worsened. The gap is wider between rich and poor, and the middle class has shrunk.

"And everybody is in on it. The call for a recommitment to early Christian principles is called liberation theology. Pope Benedict XVI opposed it and called it Marxism."

He paused.

A man wearing dirty trousers and a stained long-sleeved shirt asked Armando, "Can I give another reason why the rich get preference over us?"

"Who's us, Jerome?" Armando asked.

"The poor. It's not just Pope Benedict who's against the poor. Jesus is too, in the parable of the talents."

The comment hushed the room.

"Those are strong words, Jerome," Armando said.

Jerome challenged him. "You sayin' strong or wrong?"

Armando scanned the classroom. "Does anyone have a reply for Jerome?" The room was quiet. "How about you, Alicia?"

An attractive, well-dressed Latino woman stared at Armando and did not speak.

When Henry spoke into the silence, he first looked at Jerome. "I think you're right, Jerome. That parable has always troubled me." Then, turning to face Armando, he said, "In catechism classes, I was told to make good use of my talents. But no one explained why we needed slaves to teach the lesson. Or why it was all right for the master to reap when he hadn't sown. Or if the parable was used to defend capitalism for the rich and ruling classes."

Armando raised his eyebrows in surprise at Henry's forceful comments. He said, "Anyone else have a response for Jerome?"

A woman raised her hand.

"Yes, Shaundra. Did you have a comment?"

"It's cool how the press buys into the agenda of the ruling class."

Armando asked, "How does that happen? Do you have any evidence to support that statement?"

"Sure," Shaundra said. "In 2009 there were parades celebrating the twentieth anniversary of the fall of the Berlin Wall. We also remembered the twentieth anniversary of the murder of six Jesuit priests in El Salvador by the Salvadoran army. The priests supported liberation theology. But using US government talking points, *New York Times* hack Clifford Krause reported in 1991 that the murdered priests had been 'leftist intellectuals.'"

Shaundra paused before saying, "So? Does that count as one piece of evidence?"

Armando noticed the other students were attentive to Shaundra's remarks. He said, "Maybe. Not sure we can determine who's a hack."

The students laughed. Armando continued. "But it's evidence if it can be corroborated. Do you have any other evidence the press is in on it, as you say?"

"Well, yes. In 1991, Archbishop Quinn of San Francisco criticized the Krause story as an example of how the establishment discredits anyone opposing the government story. They use critical-sounding names. Leftist. Intellectual. Quinn quoted Brazilian archbishop Hélder Câmara, who made the same point. 'When I give food to the poor, they call me a saint. When I ask why they are poor, they call me a communist.'"

Armando said, "Yes, Archbishop Câmara has been criticized for his activities."

Rodrigo said, "So you admit —"

Armando interrupted him. "I am trying to keep calm here while discussing a controversial subject. And this isn't a debate. It's a learning experience in the Socratic tradition."

Rodrigo said, "OK. But do we agree on the point? There are instances when the mainstream press is little more than rewriting CIA and White House press releases?"

Armando said, "We grant it may be one instance. Subject to corroboration."

Rodrigo said, "And why do we have to fight so hard to get you to —"

"I'm not fighting with you," Armando cut in. "If you don't have your facts in order, you are little more than a clanging brass. Your facts must be clear and organized and well presented, or you can't be an effective advocate for the poor in this city or anywhere else."

Rodrigo and Shaundra nodded their assent.

Henry found the exchange edifying, and he raised his hand.

"Yes. Henry," Armando said.

"Are we also in accord that the Church has abdicated its radical Christian roots for the past seventeen centuries? Except for a few pronunciamentos and encyclicals from Rome?"

Armando said, "Good question, Henry. Does anyone want to address it?"

No one spoke. Armando let his question hang in the air for a moment and then said, "It's getting late. Maybe it's time for us to sit in silence for a bit before wrapping up for tonight."

Everyone sat for a time of quiet. After two minutes, Armando said, "Next time we'll continue with our discussion of liberation theology and the preferential option for the poor."

Students gathered up their notebooks. Henry and Rodrigo put the folding chairs on a storage caddy and retrieved their coats. As they started to leave, Armando said, "Henry? Can I see you for a moment, please?"

Henry stood in front of Armando, who said, "Heard you had a little run-in with some thugs last time we met. At Family Church on Eighteenth."

"Where'd you hear that?" Henry asked. The words were out of his mouth before he thought about them.

Armando's countenance reddened. He looked up at the ceiling and then stared down at the floor, as mortified as his timid students who had avoided him an hour earlier.

Henry did not want to worsen Armando's embarrassment, so he said, "Yes, that's right. I got a little whuppin' last time. But —"

Armando interrupted him. "Henry, I saw what happened to you. At first, it was just noise, but then —"

Henry tried to interrupt him. "That's right. And it was scary, but —"

Armando tried to speak over him, but before Henry could let him continue, Armando began to cry. He curled his hands into tiny gnarled fists and thrust them at his sides to punctuate the heavy sobs that drained him of breath. He said, "I heard...and then..."

Henry put his hand on Armando's bony shoulder and let it rest there. At five feet seven inches, Armando stood several inches shorter than Henry, and his bowed gray head emphasized his frail presence.

At first unsure how to respond, Henry embraced the old man. Armando was no longer the commanding and enlightened class-room presence. He was an old man convulsing with tears of shame.

"I was *afraid*," Armando said, in a voice approaching a howl. Then he pushed Henry away, and in a whisper laced with his spittle, he added in a manic burst, "I was afraid. I was too afraid to move, Henry, and —"

Henry interrupted him, pulling him back into a gentle embrace. "It's all right, Armando. It was the right thing to do to stay out of it."

Armando, his head buried in Henry's shirt, shook his head and said, "Oh, I was afraid...I was afraid..."

Henry was at sea. Thinking he had no more reassurances to give Armando Beluga, he just held the man, taking care not to squeeze his delicate bones.

After a moment, Henry said, "OK. You were afraid. But it happened so fast you couldn't have stopped them. Staying in the alley kept you out of the ER. That was the smart thing to do."

Armando pulled away from Henry and cursed. Then he spoke without pausing. "Oh, gawd, look what I've done to your shirt...oh, gawd, I'm sorry."

Henry said, "Those streaks of salt tears and mucus'll come right out, Armando. My shirt cleaner gets all the stains out. Chocolate gelato, roasted beets, sautéed zucchini —"

Armando laughed, interrupting Henry's list of stains. Then he said, "You are a forgiving man, Henry. Forgiving and understanding."

Henry released the old man from their embrace. Cupping Armando's bony jaw in his right hand, he gave him a playful tap on the side of his head and said, "So we're all right here?"

Armando nodded. "Henry, that was a loving gesture. I've been worried about making this confession to you, and now you have delivered absolution."

"OK. So we're all right, eh?"

Armando nodded. They departed.

Henry's brisk mile-and-a-half walk home took him down Sixteenth Street in twenty-five uneventful minutes.

His exchange with Armando affected his tattoo's examination of conscience. He reflected. The *Code of Canon Law* obliged the Christian faithful to promote social justice and, mindful of the precept of the Lord, to assist the poor from their own resources. *Am I fulfilling this obligation? Tithing isn't enough to fulfill it.*

He thought, too, of Martin. *In exercising my rights, have I taken into account the common good of the Church, the rights of others, and my own duties toward others? Or have I been stubborn and self-centered in my behavior?*

On July 27, 2013, Gwynneth and Henry went to dinner at Carmen Stanhope and Mike DelVecchio's home on Kater Street near South Twelfth. Many guests praised its authentic restoration, exposed brick walls, and gas fireplaces. Henry was enthralled by the 360-degree views from the tiled deck on the rooftop. He said, "This oasis up here is eerie, Mike. Is it always this quiet?"

Mike, a general contractor, said, "Yes, since the jackhammering stopped."

"Construction?" Henry asked.

Mike nodded. "It took two years to rebuild it. But now we live in a four-bedroom house where all three kids walk to school and Carmen walks to work. She sits up here most days."

At dinner, Stanhope seated Gwynneth next to Rudy De León, Mike's uncle and a senior manager in a pharmaceutical company located across the Delaware River in Cherry Hill, New Jersey.

De León asked Gwynneth pointed questions about how she viewed the rewards and perils of scientific research in a corporate setting. Gwynneth spoke from broader experience than as a scientist who taught at a university and worked in a lab. She said, "Colleagues have moved to drug companies from academia, in New York and here. They claim they're living up to their scientific principles *and* supporting a business model. 'You can do both' is what they tell me."

"Principles?" he asked.

Not wanting to be rude, she hesitated and then said, "Are you more comfortable with 'technical requirements for registering pharmaceuticals for human use' or 'good clinical —'"

De León cut in. "I see. Those principles."

She smiled and let it go by repeating, "Yes. Both. Principles and business." Gwynneth suspected he did not see, but it was not apt to challenge him in Henry's boss's home. And this was her host's uncle. It was enough to remember that De León's corporate brethren could express displeasure by firing scientists and their managers when the results of clinical trials did not support outcomes they sought — to remember it and be quiet about it at this dinner table.

De León may have suspected Gwynneth had more to say and wasn't saying it. That, too, impressed him. As espresso and Patxaran were served, De León asked her, "Would you be interested in talking to pharmaceutical company executives who might be looking for someone with a strong scientific background? Who also thinks research can thrive in a corporate structure? Someone such as you?"

Gwynneth responded with a nonverbal *maybe* by nodding and canting her head. "Not all my former colleagues have been happy in the pharmaceutical industry," she added.

But later, as they left the Stanhope and DelVecchio home, De León said, "If you want, I can call Anita Stromberg. She's at Merck, in R&D. She works one or two days a week at their offices in One Liberty Place. They're not hiring now, but she could give you a view of the corporate landscape. If you're interested."

Having had a chance to consider the proposal, Gwynneth now gave a more direct answer to his question. "That would be generous and welcome."

Her brief and candid reply started a five-month chain of events that moved her from a bench scientist and teacher in academe to a management post in a Fortune 50 corporation.

At first, three weeks rolled by, and Gwynneth turned her attention to the fall semester at Drexel, working with Hildegard Zimmer, teaching biochemistry, and starting up her lab. She forgot about De León.

SIXTEEN

AUGUST 21–24

At eight on Wednesday morning, August 21, Gwynneth left her home and walked four blocks to the Penn Medical Center at 800 Walnut Street. At the fourteenth-floor OB/GYN clinic, her obstetrician, Dr. Barbara Quinn, confirmed her pregnancy and estimated Gwynneth would deliver in the second week of April 2014.

On Saturday, August 24, Henry and Gwynneth met for an urban hike to explore the Fabric Workshop and Museum, at Twelfth and Arch Street, and the African American Museum, at Seventh and Arch.

If there was time after their visits and they weren't in a stupor of museum fatigue, Henry also wanted to show her Tiffany's mural of Maxfield Parrish's *The Dream Garden*, a 100,000-piece mosaic installed in the lobby of the Curtis Publishing Company, at Sixth and Walnut.

Starting out at noon, they walked up Eleventh Street and turned left onto Walnut. As they did, Henry recognized Martin Perez sharing a small round marble table at the Caribou Café with a dark-skinned African American woman. They were chatting over their al fresco repast on a warm summer Saturday.

Gwynneth saw quite a different sight. She saw Henry's landlord having lunch with her obstetrician, Dr. Barbara Quinn. She may not have seen them first, but she commented first.

"The woman he's with is my obstetrician," Gwynneth said. "Dr. Barbara Quinn from Penn Medical. You'll see her again in the coming months."

Henry nodded.

"What's he doing at a bistro? I thought you told me he cooks his meals at home. Isn't that why he shops at Acme?"

"He cooks every day, as far as I know. Maybe he asked her out to lunch. Maybe it's a date."

It was a coincidence to see his friend Martin and Gwynneth's physician together. But he didn't want to talk about Martin or Barbara Quinn.

His mind was on being with Gwynneth in the city and walking to the museums they'd planned to see that Saturday afternoon. He'd missed seeing her in June and was glad they were both in Philadelphia, not 150 miles apart. He was happy she was pregnant. He was pleased to be with her in what he considered a real city. And he was enjoying a few hours of respite from his Chinese language studies and group projects for his Lauder program.

Gwynneth followed up. "Does he have a girlfriend? Or are they —"

Henry cut in. "We haven't interrogated him, but he says he's solo. That's his word. Solo."

He paused before going on. "The night I got mugged, before he left my apartment, he called someone. I heard some of what he said. He answered some medical questions. When he rang off, he thanked her, in a special tone —"

Gwynneth interrupted him. "Special?"

Henry hesitated before answering. "What happened that night is still a bit foggy, but he spoke with tenderness, in the intimate voice of a man who was thanking a sister or close friend."

They continued walking along Walnut Street. As they reached Twelfth Street, Gwynneth asked, "How old is Martin? Do you know?"

Henry shrugged. "He's lived in Philadelphia 'all fifty-six years.' That's what he told me the first time we met. My guess would be —"

Gwynneth broke in. "Fifty-six?"

"It works out. He was twenty or twenty-one years in the marines, including five years on a cryptology gig at Fort Meade, in Maryland. He started with the state police about sixteen years ago."

Gwynneth wasn't keen to hear about Martin's work history. She wanted to chat about her obstetrician. "Dr. Quinn is a little older than that, if we can trust her bio on the Penn website."

Henry put his arm around her shoulders and pulled her to him. He asked, "Can you show me your bio sometime? I'd enjoy reading it. Just to see —"

She pushed him away with a playful shove as they made their way north on Twelfth Street. "I wanted to tell you. The first time you suggested the Fabric Workshop, I didn't understand what you were saying. It's an unusual name."

He frowned. "The Fabric Workshop and Museum?"

"Whatever," she said. "The word *workshop* doesn't fit."

Henry said, "In the seventies, artists here were invited to create work from unconventional materials. Fabric was one. Ceramics was another. There's a video and walk-through-audio exhibit of the Arecibo Observatory, the one in the rain forest in —"

She broke in to say, "I know about the observatory, Henry. It's in Puerto Rico." She didn't intend the remark to be patronizing. Her mother was from Puerto Rico. Gwynneth had visited her mother's family there a dozen times.

"Ever been to the observatory?" he asked.

"No. It's a two-hundred-kilometer round trip from Condado, where we stay when we visit."

She paused and then said, "Thanks for the background about the Fabric Workshop. At first I thought it might be a used-clothing stall."

To tell her he reckoned they were in accord about their destinations, as they turned off Twelfth onto Arch Street, he took her hand. She was glad to let him hold it.

SEVENTEEN
AUGUST 30–31

Philadelphia's Labor Day weekend celebration was as big a production as the one for the Fourth of July. Concert artists on the Ben Franklin Parkway included Beyoncé and her husband, Jay-Z, two of Gwynneth's favorites. They'd be sure to draw tens of thousands of fans even at $100-plus for admission. But when Henry asked Gwynneth if she wanted to go, she declined, unsure whether she could endure two hours on her feet in the crowds. Nor did she want to return to Penn's Landing for another round of fireworks.

Henry suggested they investigate Fishtown together. "Good idea. It was becoming gentrified in 2009 and '10 when I was at Penn. Never got over there. You've been?"

"Went twice after work with Michael Larsen. First time we ate at Loco Pez."

"You went to Fishtown to get crazy fish?"

"We tried three or four different tacos. Not bad."

"That what you got in mind for us? Tacos?"

"Once we ate at Pizza Brain. It's right on Frankford, near Little Baby's Ice Cream."

Gwynneth smiled and frowned at him and said, "Bizarre names in Fishtown."

He laughed at her quip. "It's hip. Many galleries. Good restaurants."

"Good," she said. "Did I tell you May is coming for a visit this weekend?"

"You said she might."

"She's taking the Megabus Saturday morning. Going back on Monday."

Henry nodded.

"So Friday is gonna work for us in Fishtown," Gwynneth said.

Henry asked, "And brunch Saturday morning at Reading Terminal?"

"Yes. May's bus isn't due here until two in the afternoon."

After work the Friday of Labor Day weekend, both Henry and Gwynneth went home to change out of work clothes into dungarees and shirts then met at her place. Later they took the Market-Frankford Line train to the Berks station and walked a few blocks in the twilight to Loco Pez. Gwynneth was enchanted with the place.

"Oh, man, no credit cards and tacos for less than three dollars? Great choice, Henry. This was worth the subway ride."

They sipped *aguas frescas de watermelon*. Gwynneth ordered a taco salad with chicken and Henry a mushroom, a chorizo and potato, and a fish taco. It was crowded and dark and loud, so they suspended verbal conversation, confining their remarks to thumbs up.

When they came out of the restaurant onto Norris Avenue, Henry steered them south through Fishtown. Between stops in three of the small art galleries, they saw fireworks shooting into the night sky at Penn's Landing, a dozen blocks to the south. At ten o'clock, they boarded the Market-Frankford Line train at Girard, alighted at Fifteenth Street, and spent the night at Henry's place.

Saturday morning, they walked in the rain to Reading Terminal Market for brunch.

"Don't we avoid the crowds on Saturdays?" she asked.

"It'll be OK," he said.

While Henry stood in line for a double scoop of mocha chip ice cream from the Bassett's concession, Gwynneth bought a whole roasted chicken, six rotisserie wings, and a pint of roasted carrots at the Dienner's Bar-B-Q Chicken stand.

They met as she was paying for her chicken. After a search, they found a table for six located deep in the market, joining a family of four — to the dismay of the father and the curiosity of the two children. The wife's focus was on her mobile telephone. She tapped its screen, careful not to smear it with the residue from her Olympia gyro or to damage her manicured and painted index fingernail.

As Henry and Gwynneth began to talk, the children gaped at them. The girl looked at the boy and tilted her head in their direction. "Look at that," she seemed to say. "Two adults eating and talking to one another in a public place. And neither one holding a phone."

Henry said, "You've become a big fan of Dienner's."

"Sunday night Hildegard and a few others are coming for paella. And Maria and Bennie," Gwynneth said. Most of this will go into the pot." She pointed to the plate of wings and the wrapped bird. "Bought it now 'cause they're closed Sunday and Monday."

She stabbed a roasted carrot with her plastic fork and then nibbled at her first chicken wing. She offered one to Henry.

He shook his head. "No, thanks," he said, glancing at his ice cream cone. "Gotta finish this before it melts."

After a moment, he said, "You're eating healthy. Is that because you're nourishing one and nine-fortieths of you?"

"Trying not to be too fussy about food. Gab told me, 'When you're hungry, just eat what you want.' Her ideas on food are working OK. She's also mentioned other issues…."

"What does Dr. Quinn say about your diet?"

Gwynneth raised her eyebrows and said, "She's cautious. Got a list of things she wants me to avoid. Mocha chip ice cream is on her list of no-nos."

Henry let his mouth drop open in mock disbelief. "Anything else?"

She smiled and said, "Right. No pulled pork tacos. No margaritas. 'Go with leafy green veggies,' she says. 'Collards. Spinach. Bok choy.'"

"Not keeping you to raw scallions and steamed kale?"

"She's my obstetrician, Henry. She's not torturing me. She wants me to stay healthy."

When the man at the table smiled at Gwynneth's crack, the woman across from him looked up from her appliance and scowled at him, as if she'd caught him committing a misdemeanor. Henry and the man made eye contact and exchanged expressions of "Oops." Then they both aimed their eyes down at the table before they were exposed for ridiculing the woman as a harridan.

To keep himself from laughing, Henry snatched a paper napkin from a receptacle on the table and used it to wipe away a nonexistent bead of melted ice cream. The woman sighed and returned her attention to her screen.

Gwynneth stared at Henry. "Your life is simpler if you follow the Gospel. You don't worry about what goes into your mouth, just what comes out of it. Right?"

In a soft tone he said, "Right. Good point. But were you going to say something else about what Gab told you?"

"Yes," she said, but she looked off balance and did not continue.

Henry conveyed his patience and support with a subdued "Mm-hmm."

She looked at the tabletop for a moment, then said, "Henry, you may want to know this…" She let her voice drop and then stopped talking altogether.

The man and woman at the shared table froze in their places, hoping their absence of movement might be rewarded with hearing Gwynneth continue with a juicy tidbit of personal information.

Henry waited. He repeated his silent prayer. *Peace. Be still.*

Gwynneth said, "We haven't talked about it much, but Gab told me to expect complications. Not trouble — complications. That's the word she used."

Again, he waited. He could see Gwynneth had been affected by something Gab had said to her.

"It's about what the demographers call the birth rate for un-married women. That's the phrase they use to describe me and my situation. Not *our* situation. *My* situation. The phrase doesn't include the whereabouts of the father. The father doesn't exist for that demographic statistic."

She paused again then said, "And there will be complications."

"Right. Complications."

"Complications. The details we can manage if we have accord on The Six."

"Right. We talked about it —"

"Yes, Henry. We got it together in the car when you drove us here from Washington. Ten weeks ago?"

Henry studied her. She seemed pensive but not annoyed.

Gwynneth went on. "Gab says, 'Those details are complicated' and they're coming our way."

Henry watched her solemn expression as he continued listening to her.

"One problem detail we haven't thought about is that you can't see me in the hospital except as a guest. You won't be entitled to talk to Dr. Quinn or any other doctors. Nurses won't be able to tell you if my temperature is abnormal. Candy stripers won't have to tell you what cursed *room* I'm in. And that's if all goes well and there are no problems with delivery or me or the baby. It's just *one aspect* of what's coming."

Gwynneth was exasperated at the legal and social conventions attached to having a baby.

Henry reached across the table for her hand. She let him take it. In her frustration, Gwynneth appreciated this gesture and his silence.

The man and woman at the shared table looked at one another and decided this might be a good time to end their meal. The woman pointed to her e-map and said to the man, "We go out where

113

we came in." The children picked up their rain gear but not their food wrappers or plates or plastic ware and followed the man toward the exit. The woman stayed behind to clear the table and put the paper and plastic dreck in a nearby trash container.

Gwynneth resumed after they were gone. "Gab said we'll be dealing with a hundred other people. It's what happens when you're pregnant. You're not invaded by them. They just seep into your life. Doctors. Nurses. Medical lab techs. Radiologists. My employer. Insurance people. And it'll be more complicated because I'm in the demographers' category of *unmarried women*. Which is where I put myself. And I'm not even counting our families and friends. Their questions are based on their assumptions, not our reality. It's happening already."

Henry waited a moment but spoke when it was clear Gwynneth had reached a stopping point. He leaned toward her and said, "An observation?"

Gwynneth's mild rant had relieved for the moment the pressure she felt about complications. Her face was relaxed. She exhaled and nodded, then whispered to him, "Yes. An observation."

He said, "Gab is helping us. There are complications for *every*one who's having a baby. It's an earthquake for *every*body. It's better to know about them ahead of time. And we can handle them."

He waited, making sure Gwynneth wasn't upset about what he'd said. After a moment, he continued. "Last year, I overheard my mother tell my aunt Katrina that forty years ago, fathers weren't allowed on the same hospital *floor* as their wives who were delivering babies. They had to wait in the fathers' waiting area until after the babies were born to see their wives and their own children."

Gwynneth knew those had also been the standards at Columbia Presbyterian Hospital, where she and her siblings and cousins had been born, just as it had been true in Mineola on Long Island, where Henry and the other children in his family had all been born.

He finished his point. "And now, we'll survive too, doing it our way."

Gwynneth yanked a paper napkin from its dispenser, folded it, and dabbed her moist eyes. She was not weeping, but her moist eyes left two crescent-shaped arcs on the napkin. Henry reckoned Gwynneth was vexed over how the world responded to pregnant women.

He added, "Do you believe we're strong?"

She nodded, grateful for his caring words.

"But if you're tired of being strong or you don't *want* to deal with the complications, we can get married. It's no disgrace to abide by tradition. We could do it this afternoon. I'll kidnap a Quaker on Arch Street who'll marry us right over there."

He pointed behind her for emphasis.

"There, between the fruit stand and the Thai takeout."

She coughed and laughed at the same time at his jest. The Quaker reference was an exaggeration, but his sentiment was clear, and it was true that a justice of the peace could marry them if they had a marriage license. And his offer was a blessing. She believed him. She felt such deep respect for his reassurance that it intensified the reddening of her café-au-lait cheeks. She felt less troubled when she recalled the annoyances she'd discussed on the phone with Gab. The complications.

After a few moments, she said, "Oh, you are a gallant, Henry. You are a real man."

Henry, trusting her comment was a compliment, was still.

She took another napkin and said, "All right. And thanks for not telling me I'm an emotional wreck and that this hysteria over nothing is common among women in their first pregnancy."

After a pause, he said, "I want to follow up on me and Martin."

She frowned and asked, "To say more than you told me last week?"

"Yes. We really haven't had a chance to talk about it while we're sitting down. I've given you the substance, but —"

She cut in. "It's fine. Go ahead."

"OK. Martin is unhappy because he doesn't have a signed report —"

"A statement with your signature."

Henry blinked. Gwynneth seemed to know all about it. Yet he wanted to tell her in his own words. "Martin needs a signed report from me to request a warrant. If the police don't witness a crime, they need a warrant to make an arrest."

She frowned again. "Didn't you tell me this?"

"No. When you asked me whether Martin was investigating the mugging, I said no. That was a little too cute. The reason Martin isn't investigating it is because he needs —"

She interrupted again. "He needs your signed report to get a warrant if he wants to make an arrest. And your idea is to turn the other cheek. Pretty sure we covered this, Henry." She was perplexed but not impatient with him.

"Maybe you're right," he said. "I felt I hadn't told you the whole story, but —"

"OK, look. Are you trying to tell me something else? You need a place to stay because he's getting ready to throw you out?"

"No. And that's significant. Our disagreement about the report sounds fierce when we're discussing it. But it hasn't developed into a feud or kept us from walking to Mass together. He's becoming a lot more than a landlord."

"Despite the wrangle about the report? That's impressive, Henry. Quite a man who's renting you a place."

"He told me police in the South don't investigate —"

Gwynneth interrupted. "Ah. So it's not the mugging, and it's not your report. To him, he's a police officer trying to do the right thing. His job. And you? You're a Christian trying to do the right thing. To live according to the Gospel by not sending another cursed fool to prison."

They sat for a moment, both admiring Gwynneth's summary.

"So that's it?" she asked.

"Yes. Yes, that's it. Glad we got to clear it up."

After a moment, she sighed, as if to punctuate her intention to change the subject. "What's on your schedule for the rest of the day?"

"Depends."

"On what?"

"On if you want to do something together in this rain," he said.

"Well, it's a relief we're not going to stand in it to hear Beyoncé this evening. I'd go anywhere she's performing, but maybe not today."

"Do you have something you want to do?"

"May wants to see Maria and Bennie's shop," Gwynneth said. "We might do that this afternoon. Or just sit and visit. Catch up. What would you do then?"

"Go to late Mass at Saint John. Study Chinese. Draft my chapter for our group project."

"All right. Maybe we'll get together tomorrow?" Gwynneth proposed. "I'll plan to be with May this afternoon."

"Good," he said. "I'll call you tomorrow. Around nine?"

Gwynneth tilted her head, considering. "Make it ten."

She gathered her trash and stowed the food she was taking home in a shopping bag before rising from her chair and standing still, looking pensive but relaxed.

He got up from his chair, walked around the table, and stood behind her. He put both hands on her shoulders and rested the side of his head against her ear. "Can I walk you home?"

"Yeah, Henry. It'll help me to have a few more minutes with you today."

They trekked through the gentle summer rain down Market Street to Eleventh and then south past Smokin' Betty's barbecue and comfort food emporium.

"Henry?" she said as they walked.

To show he was listening, he draped his arm across her shoulders.

She went on. "Fourth of July weekend was the first time we talked about your drawing. But drawing isn't what goes on, is it?"

"No," he said. "It's not a conventional exercise of putting onto paper what I see in the streets or parks. It's asking what's going on at the end of the pencil. And I haven't figured out…" He shrugged, his voice trailing off. "I should've waited to tell you. It's vague —"

"I'm glad you mentioned it, Henry. You, the buttoned-down consultant, is in the vanguard of —"

Henry stopped her. "I'm not in a vanguard of anything. I'm only going out there to see how the pencil views the world."

"Can you say anything about how your pencil views the world?"

"The pencil can connect poverty to anger, hatred, and negativity."

Excited to hear such words coming from him, she said, "I'm glad you told me, Henry."

When they reached her home, they kissed one another goodbye.

Having seen her off, Henry walked south on Eleventh, cut through the tiny oasis of Louis Kahn Park, and then made his way to 1589 Pine Street in the now heavier rain. At home, he resumed reading *Every Day Is for the Thief.* Later, he went to the Saturday afternoon Mass at Saint John. That night, he studied Chinese and drafted a chapter for a report on Asian business and social trends. During his tattoo, he pondered whether his full and rich life was guided by the Gospel. He sensed that as he was engaged in forming a new family and expanding his professional life, a part of him was being reborn.

EIGHTEEN
AUGUST 23–SEPTEMBER 3

I n August of 2013, Andre and Carmichael admitted they'd neglected a thorny personnel issue when James Wainwright, head of their Washington office, wrote a defamatory evaluation for Henry Knudsen. He'd also violated ACI's employment procedures when he hired Knudsen without verifying his previous jobs or checking all his references. The catalyst for Andre's remorse was Henry's stellar performance in the ten weeks since he'd moved from Washington to the Philadelphia office in June.

Carmichael, who'd had misgivings about defending Wainwright's behavior and retaining him, was also disquieted. The spark for his contrition was a conversation with his wife, Toni.

On Fridays, they reviewed the firm's pipeline of active contract proposals. At their meeting on August 23, Carmichael said, "That's it for proposals?" He sounded tentative, as if he had something else to say. Andre nodded.

"Toni brought up the Wainwright mess. She's known about it for months."

Andre said, "Yeah. It's still a mess."

"Last night, Toni mentioned that I've been edgy. She wanted to know if it was about Wainwright, about how I've ignored his deceit, thinking only of the business he generates for this company. Maybe I forgot deceit is bad for business, she said." He paused. "And she's right. It's been bothering me."

Andre waited.

"She said, 'You're no different from elitists who think rules don't apply to them.' I said nothing. So she asked, 'Maybe you think you're different? Can you say *how*?'" He looked at Andre and said, "When she's onto something, she repeats her questions. Twice was enough. I thanked her and went for a walk." Carmichael sighed.

Andre had known Antoinette Carmichael for seven years. Toni had a keen willingness to confront unscrupulous behavior. At five feet ten inches tall, darker skinned than her husband, Toni was also a commanding physical presence. After bearing and raising three children, she'd kept the same athletic profile she'd had when she played basketball at Marquette. If she raised her voice one notch in a group conversation, others stopped to listen. She did not curse. Even at low volume, her powerful voice had more impact than a common rant.

Andre returned to the business at hand. "Wainwright's been good for us."

"He's earned our esteem. Sold a lot of business. Developed key staff."

"But we didn't respond to negative signals our all-star was sending out to —"

Carmichael interrupted him. "Halo effect."

"Yes," Andre said. "Right. Halo effect. We wouldn't — or couldn't — see the serious defects."

"We're swapping generalities here," Carmichael said. "Halo effect. Denying the negative signals. His behavior was wrong. My behavior was wrong, no matter what buzzwords we use. I should've listened to you, but that's behind us. Let's think. What do we do now?"

They agreed to let the matter rest for a week.

The following Friday, August 30, Carmichael reopened the conversation. "We need to tell Wainwright his hiring and most recent evaluation of Henry Knudsen were both false and unethical."

Action was long overdue. They were not deterred that Wainwright had changed Henry's evaluation to a positive one early in 2013.

"How would *you* tell him?"

Carmichael said, "I'd say we're still disturbed about his 2012 evaluation of Knudsen, that it looks worse every time we recall it, and that we're asking whether there's still a place for him at ACI. Ask him what he thinks."

"He'll be here next week for the executive staff meeting. Can it wait?"

"No. I want to give him some advance notice. You think that's a mistake?"

Andre shrugged. "It's giving him notice we don't give others."

Carmichael reached for the telephone. "I know. But as you say, he's been good for us. It seems mean to ambush him."

"Good point."

Carmichael put the telephone back in its cradle and said, "If he quits in a pout? Do we have anyone who can sit in that seat for a few months?"

"Not sure. Welles could manage it for a few months as an interim guy."

"What about Knudsen?" Carmichael asked.

"No."

"No?"

"No. As we know, he's studying at the Lauder on our scholarship. And it hasn't come up in a direct way, but Stanhope says he's looking in the city for a house to buy. Asked about the Kater Street area."

Carmichael frowned. "South Philly?"

Andre nodded. "Yes. And Antique Row…and Yorktown and Mount Airy."

Carmichael was annoyed at the distraction and swung the conversation back toward the issue of an interim director in the Washington office. "What do we know about Welles?"

"Strong performer. Enrolled in the MBA program at George Washington University now. Smart guy. Phi Beta Kappa at Vanderbilt."

"Family?"

"Long-term male partner. Don't know if they're married. No kids that we know about. Keeps his private life private."

Now it was Carmichael who nodded. "And you think we could ask him to stand in for Wainwright if there was a sudden need?"

"Yes. Manages one or two major proposals every year. He was one of Wainwright's first hires, seven years ago. He'd step up if we said we were in a jam."

"OK." Carmichael tapped buttons on the telephone console to speed-dial Wainwright in ACI's Washington office and put the call on speaker.

Wainwright answered. Carmichael said, "James, Andre's joining us on this call."

Wainwright greeted them.

"We want to give you a heads-up. We need to meet, the three of us, before the executive staff meeting." Carmichael paused. Wainwright said nothing.

After a moment, Carmichael resumed. "We're still disturbed about your 2012 evaluation of Knudsen. It looks worse every time we recall it. We're asking whether there's still a place for you at ACI. We want to hear your thoughts. Take the weekend to think about it."

Carmichael paused again.

"Appreciate the heads-up," said Wainwright. "Yes, there's a place for me at ACI, and I'm happy to talk about it. See you next week."

"Good," said Carmichael. "Next week." He ended the call.

As Wainwright's departure moved from remote possibility to a potential occurrence, Andre stopped in to see Henry. He posed an abstract problem in succession planning, asking for Henry's thoughts about candidates to run ACI's Washington or Boston office.

Henry blinked at the query and asked, "You mean to replace Wainwright or Gallagher?"

Andre said nothing but kept up his calm eye contact with Henry. He was being disingenuous, but he felt a need to hear from Henry the information he'd heard from Stanhope.

Henry was puzzled by the question. He said, "Are you asking for names?"

Andre again replied with a wordless nod.

"In Boston, not sure. In Washington? Bob Welles. He's the best guy...if he'd take it."

"Why wouldn't he?" Andre asked.

Henry said, "He's happy in his role there."

Again Andre nodded.

"If he agreed, he'd be strong. We didn't interact much, even in that small office, but staff there hold him in high esteem."

Another nod.

Henry felt good about being asked for his opinion on something as important as the head of ACI's offices in Boston and Washington, even though Andre's mien was casual. Were Andre and Carmichael planning management changes?

Neither spoke for a few moments. Then, without feeling pressed to say anything about himself, Henry added, "Don't know if this is relevant, but I would *not* be interested in returning to DC."

Andre asked, "Can you say why not?"

"No," said Henry.

They both laughed at the sharp negative reply.

Then Henry said, "In confidence?"

Andre nodded yet again, waiting for Henry to tell him what Stanhope had already related about his looking for real estate. Henry did not oblige, but gave Andre information he'd given to no one else. "My beloved Gwynneth is happy in Philadelphia. Carmen Stanhope has introduced her to some executives in the pharmaceutical business."

Andre let his eyebrows express his surprise at Henry's statement.

"You don't have to tell me more. You're talking about important personal —"

Henry interrupted. "I followed Gwynneth here, and it looks as if she'll be staying, either teaching or moving into the corporate world."

Andre nodded.

"Gwynneth and I are having a baby. It's gonna happen next spring, and it's gonna happen in Philadelphia."

Andre's memories of Catherine's four pregnancies flashed upon his inward eye. He allowed himself a smile. "Exciting to think about," he said.

"It's not a secret, but we're waiting until the second trimester to tell people."

Andre said, "I appreciate it, Henry. Both the news and your trusting me with it."

"I'm glad to be studying at Penn, we're enjoying Philadelphia and looking at houses." Henry paused and then asked, "And about Bob Welles? In confidence?"

Andre exhaled. "Go ahead."

Henry said, "Welles was the guy who kept in touch with Moskowitz and Capriella."

Dana Moskowitz and Mary Capriella were two all-stars who left ACI's Washington office in 2011 to set up their own firm, M&C. Wainwright had trained them and regarded their departure as a betrayal. Carmichael and Andre had disagreed and told Wainwright to stay in touch with them and treat them with the same care as any future business partner.

"Welles collaborated with them by stealth."

Andre said, "Because Wainwright wouldn't deal with them. ACI worked with them, but it was Welles, not Wainwright? And Welles got the job done and kept quiet about it?"

Henry nodded, relieved Andre hadn't asked him to say it. "You knew this last year, though. Right?"

"No. This is the first I've heard of it."

Henry nodded, gratified by Andre's candor.

After a brief silence, Henry said, "You can share all this with Dave Carmichael if it feels right to you."

"Thanks, Henry. I'll let you know if I do."

Andre recalled conferring with Welles on a project in 2011. M&C and Welles had partnered on a planning contract for a consortium of insurers who wanted a strategic paper on insuring driverless cars. Auto insurers and IT firms did not want to devote sizable resources for a promising but still niche market yet wanted to monitor its development.

In their initial research, the consulting team examined premiums charged for auto insurance in a dozen states. They found clear patterns of significant price differentials by zip code. Premiums charged to customers were as much as fifty percent higher in zip codes where people of color and lower-income citizens lived. The pattern of higher premiums was at least forty years old, could not be related to risk or claims experience, and had been verified by a university's thorough research study.

The insurers' premium-setting patterns created a dilemma for Welles, Moskowitz, and Capriella. Their contract required them to recommend premium-setting metrics for driverless cars. Could they fulfill their contract without mentioning the current scheme? And could they do it without raising questions about industry behavior that was racist? Their answer was no, but since it wasn't their decision, they conferred with Andre about it.

In their conversations, Andre learned that Welles disagreed with Wainwright's view that the customer is always right. Welles said, "Isn't it our business to point out errors and propose effective corrections? Isn't that what we do?"

Andre concurred. "The customer is not always right. We don't manage ACI by slogan. If clients whine about our employees or our findings, we investigate, and then we do what's right."

But the larger issue of mentioning the clients' racist pricing policies affected ACI, so Andre included Carmichael in the deliberations. They told Welles to present their methodology, findings, and recommendations in objective terms and leave all value judgments to the client.

So, in addition to their descriptions of three pricing scenarios with premiums at higher, the same, or lower levels, they appended two summaries without comment. The first was the university study. Its summary pointed out the racism inherent in premium-setting practices of insurers. The second was an insurance industry analysis showing dollar values of fraudulent collision claims tended to be filed by policyholders who lived in zip codes where income was higher but where premiums were still kept at lower levels than in zip codes with lower income.

Clients were unhappy to see data from the second document presented to them on the letterhead of their own industry association. The consortium decided to accept the report from ACI and M&C, but they suspended further contract work.

Both ACI and M&C lamented the loss of the auto insurers as clients but were not desolate about it. There was plenty of work in the consulting market.

ACI's executive staff was scheduled to convene at nine o'clock on Tuesday, September 2, the morning after Labor Day. At eight, Wainwright joined Andre around a small coffee table in Carmichael's office. Carmichael did not recount their displeasure with his unprofessional behavior when hiring and later managing and evaluating Henry Knudsen. His demeanor showed that he was waiting for Wainwright to speak.

"I made some mistakes about Knudsen," Wainwright said. "It was wrong to misrepresent his performance —"

Carmichael interrupted him but spoke in a soft tone. "You were not forthright with us about him, beginning with your hiring him. Let's keep events in sequence."

"Sure," said Wainwright. "If you want to revisit all the details."

Andre said, "We need to be clear. When you say 'some mistakes,' let's say what they were and keep them in chronological order."

Wainwright took a breath. He was speaking to ACI's cofounders. They were in accord about his mistakes and sounded unhappy about them. He said, "Knudsen had an impressive résumé. I was in a hurry to bring him aboard, and —"

Carmichael interrupted again. "That's perplexing. You abrogated our protocols for hiring?"

Wainwright sighed and looked away but said nothing.

"ACI protocols you'd followed for six cursed *years* until Knudsen showed up? And you stopped because you were in a cursed *hurry?*" Carmichael frowned, looking puzzled but not angry. He hadn't raised his voice. He sounded as if he wanted answers to his questions.

Wainwright's gestures demonstrated he had no answers to make. He held out his hands as if expecting someone to pass him a basketball. No words came from his mouth as he shook his head. He looked away from Carmichael's and Andre's unwavering gazes but didn't slump in his chair. He sat erect, showing a determination to avoid defeat.

Carmichael said, "Your mistakes in hiring Knudsen are troubling. We uncovered them by accident. Were there others we don't know about?"

Wainwright's diffident reply was expressed in wordless headshaking.

"You are saying no? Am I right?" said Andre.

Wainwright said, "I believed the work history on his résumé was true. Is that a crime?"

"It's not how we do business," said Carmichael. "You could've hired a temp to verify his work history." And when you didn't, you put our firm's reputation at risk."

Wainwright shrugged at the mild rebuke.

Carmichael said, "We called you last week to tell you we'd be having this conversation. Let's put our questions aside. Have you given this any thought? Do you have anything to say for yourself?"

Wainwright nodded, but when he paused before responding, Andre spoke.

"You've been good for ACI for seven years. You opened the DC office. You hired and trained the staff. You grew the business and were ACI's best ambassador. Then you decide ACI's rules don't apply to you? You understand your behavior is confusing to us?"

Wainwright nodded. "It was harmless. I cut a corner. It's common in executive circles."

Carmichael said, "We saw how executives cut corners before we started this firm." He let it go at that, trusting Wainwright would understand that ACI sought to govern its employees by one set of rules.

Wainwright heard the statement as a scolding but continued. "And as a senior officer, it's condign for me to punish a junior's insolence."

Carmichael said, "You jeopardized ACI's credibility by not checking all his references. You cut a corner, and because he worked out, you got away with it. But even after training him, you threatened his career with a bogus and libelous evaluation. And you did it behind his back. Is that how we behave?"

Wainwright looked at Carmichael and said, "I told Andre I thought Knudsen was ridiculing me. It was disrespectful behavior. I admitted I was wrong about that, too. It was someone else."

Carmichael, his tone still calm and controlled, said, "So what do we do at ACI when we make a mistake? Do we talk to our colleagues or employees face to face, verify our facts, and come clean? Or do we just smear their repute?"

Wainwright sighed and again shook his head.

"You vilified him. You acted as if you were an aristocrat with privilege, not a corporate officer in this firm. Maybe you think doing what's right is for chumps. So you just attacked the junior associate with a false report to us and didn't even let him see it."

Wainwright did not respond. Violating ACI's protocols when hiring Knudsen wasn't being regarded as harmless. It was deemed a serious offense. His hubris had compounded it. And since he hadn't told Knudsen about the false evaluation, Carmichael had added a charge of personal cowardice.

Andre said, "Firms differ in how they treat such misconduct. But ACI's personnel policies are explicit."

Wainwright flinched. ACI's hiring practices and nondiscrimination policies were stated in clear terms in all employees' offer letters. The penalty was termination.

Carmichael said, "If I tell you your behavior has disqualified you from remaining at ACI, how would you respond? Can you help us out here?"

Wainwright nodded and hesitated. As a calculated gambit, he reached inside his coat to retrieve an unsealed business envelope and set it on the low table. Andre picked it up. He removed, unfolded, and read Wainwright's letter of resignation. Then he set it on the table in front of Carmichael, who let it sit there.

"OK. OK." Carmichael paused to look at Andre, who shrugged. "Here's our response. We accept your resignation effective now."

Wainwright stiffened. ACI's cofounders had trumped his ruse.

Carmichael went on. "You may collect your personal belongings tomorrow at our DC office. Leave your keys, building pass, and credit card on the table here." He pointed to the envelope in front of them and added, "You go forth with our benediction and a sadness I have no words for. You are a brilliant and enterprising man, James. I'm sure you'll find a company where you'll fit in."

Carmichael and Andre stood, as if it were prearranged. Wainwright did too, shook hands with both, and departed.

"Call Welles. Ask him if he'll stand in for Wainwright until the end of the year. If he agrees, add those personnel changes to the executive staff meeting agenda."

Before either of them moved, Carmichael sighed, as if to add another agenda item, and then stared at Andre. "You think this untangles the disorder we created?"

"Maybe," Andre said. "Except for telling Knudsen."

They stared at one another and said nothing. Andre broke the silence. "Stanhope told me Knudsen thought it was right to talk to Wainwright. That was in May."

"When he knew he was transferring here. About what?" Carmichael asked.

Andre said, "About Wainwright's change from a supportive mentor to a sullen overseer."

"And?"

"Stanhope said she told him to go ahead. This is all secondhand information."

Carmichael said, "I understand that."

"So Knudsen did, and he gave her an account of their conversation. Whatever Wainwright said to him, Knudsen didn't believe it. He told Stanhope he just thanked Wainwright and left."

"This Knudsen." Carmichael said. "He's a stronger kid than I thought."

Andre nodded. "Stanhope said she told Knudsen if he said what he had to say, his initiative was ethical. She suggested he move on."

"So what does that mean for us? We forget it? Don't tell Knudsen about Wainwright's assassination attempt?"

Andre shook his head. "Not now. Maybe later. There's no value in it. Stanhope says he trusts us to judge him on his performance."

Carmichael said, "Which has been superior."

"Better than any of us expected."

"All right. Now we turn to executive staff. That meeting starts in forty minutes. I need to refocus here. You'll call Welles?"

Andre nodded his concurrence and left Carmichael to prepare for their meeting.

Minutes later, Andre reached Bob Welles. Then, as Henry entered ACI's offices, Andre hailed him and told him to write a two-line message to all hands, announcing Wainwright's resignation and Bob Welles's promotion to interim director of the DC office, both as of that morning. "Run it by Stanhope before you send it but get it out before nine. It'll be the first agenda item at the executive staff meeting."

At 8:40 a.m., his message complete, Henry marched into the room where executive staff were gathering and handed his draft to Andre. "Stanhope had to take her youngest son to the ER this morning," he said, explaining his presence. Andre nodded and initialed the two-line draft. Henry sent it at 8:45 a.m.

NINETEEN

OCTOBER 11–28

On Friday, October 11, May Kim sent Gwynneth a text message. "Hi. Back to Phila next Thurs. Job interview. Can we meet?"

Gwynneth replied, "Yes. Stay w/me if you want."

As planned, May called after her job interview on October 17. They met at Gwynneth's place, and Henry joined them. They walked up to Eleventh and Sansom Streets for comfort food at Smokin' Betty's and returned to 1110 Clinton for after-dinner drinks. They sat. They talked. May was circumspect about her interview.

"How'd they find you?" Gwynneth asked her.

"Long story," said May.

"We've got time. If you want to tell us," Gwynneth said. Henry nodded.

"Larry Berzinski was my classmate at Cal Tech. We worked on an IT project and copresented in a statistics seminar. We —"

Gwynneth interrupted her. "Didn't you study math there?"

"It was a multidisciplinary doctorate. Math, computer science, IT, and statistics."

Gwynneth's widened eyes and nod showed her admiration of May's stunning academic pedigree. When they'd lived together in Washington, DC, May had dismissed her own work as data analysis at the World Bank and never mentioned her PhD.

When Gwynneth didn't ask a follow-up question, May continued. "Larry and I worked on projects together in the early days of the cloud. We did well. We learned to trust one another and then got tight but weren't lovers. That rare genesis begat a strong friendship.

"Six or seven years ago, he moved to a bank here. I went to Sun and the World Bank. He knows the hiring officials at Consolidated and their need for help in moving into markets in Africa. He told them to talk to me."

May shrugged and then added, "And please...don't repeat any of this?"

Gwynneth and Henry nodded to seal the covenant.

"This thing with Consolidated isn't going anywhere. I asked Larry why he hooked me up with these jokers who didn't understand even the basic computing terms I was using. He said I needed to get back into the IT vanguard. Maybe he's right."

Henry and Gwynneth sat there, dumbfounded by what May was telling them about the executive leadership of a Fortune 100 company.

"But these white men at Consolidated know one thing. They know they're megastupid."

Gwynneth asked, "Not rookies?"

May was firm in her answer. "No. Stupid. If they were technical rookies, they might acknowledge they have a lot to learn."

Henry listened with care. It was true May was expressing contempt for the men she'd spoken with, but her voice was free of rancor.

May went on. "They were stunned when I described our work at Sun. When they weren't staring at the table or fiddling with their cell phones, I could see on their faces they were full of fear, afraid I'd ask them a question about their own systems that none of them could answer. And they're *running* the place."

May took a breath and continued. "It's pathetic. They still don't know a computing platform from a loading platform, and —"

Henry frowned and interrupted her. "We're looking for someone."

May and Gwynneth turned to him, waiting for him to explain what he meant.

He asked May, "You're going back to DC when?"

Looking at Gwynneth, May said, "Tomorrow. Maybe Saturday?"

Gwynneth said, "You can stay here over the weekend if that helps."

Friday morning, Henry, May's résumé in hand, spoke to Carmen Stanhope about May's availability and how she might fill their staffing needs for the risk management work in Philadelphia and the economic development work assignment in Africa. Stanhope showed May's impressive résumé to Andre.

"Strong," he said. "Can we afford her?"

"I think so. Even including the income tax breaks employees get at the World Bank, she took a big pay cut to move from Sun. And we can do better than the bank."

Andre said, "Right. We can. But is this a good move for us *and* for Dr. Kim?"

"It looks good for us. We can use her skills and her experience for the risk management work. And she has contacts in the business community in Botswana and South Africa for the larger work assignment."

"And can you tell me how *we* found her?"

"Through Henry's friend Gwynneth, where she's staying. Consolidated interviewed her yesterday. She was disappointed there. Henry told her we might be hiring."

Andre shook his head. "This seems too good to be true. Will she talk to us?"

Stanhope said, "Henry says she will. And she's still in town. You want to wait a few weeks?"

"No," Andre said. "Her credentials are impeccable." He looked at his calendar.

"Henry read two papers she cited on her résumé and spoke with a former colleague at Sun Microsystems before he approached me."

Andre nodded. "Can you join me if she can come here at eleven this morning?"

"Yes."

The three met at eleven in Andre's office.

Carmen Stanhope began. "Dr. Kim, we —"

May interrupted her. "I'm May Kim. Please call me May."

"All right, May," Stanhope agreed. "Do you know about our new work assignments in risk management and banking in Africa?"

"Yes. Henry told me about their scope, in a general way. Are there other —"

Stanhope interrupted her. "No. Just these two right now. You have experience in these areas?"

May nodded. "Yes."

Andre asked, "May, how would you approach the risk management work?"

It took May a minute to draw a colloquial verbal sketch about banking industry metrics and how she'd assess Broad Street's risk management systems. Comparing them would identify gaps in their systems and how banking industry best practices could address them.

Andre nodded and asked, "And the banking effort?"

May countered with a question. "What resources do *you* bring to this work?"

Stanhope said, "We have partnered with an MNO —"

May interrupted her. "Does your mobile network operator have experience in sub-Sahara Africa?"

Andre answered, "Yes. They've worked with an informal consortium of internet cafés, cell phone airtime resellers, and an established bank. Here, our staff and Broad Street —"

May cut in again. "Which bank...if it's not a secret?"

Stanhope looked at Andre, who nodded. She said, "Bank of Gabarone."

"And the level of effort for your MNO?"

Stanhope said, "The MNO is in the budget in the low seven figures."

May smiled.

As their discussion extended well past a half hour, Andre said, "We're at a decision point on starting our hiring protocol. Before we do, we'd want to know if you're interested in moving ahead with it."

May said, "My initial answer is yes, depending on what I find out about you and your client."

Andre asked, "What drew you from Menlo Park to Washington, DC?"

"When Oracle bought Sun in 2010, my team was disbanded. We were a cohesive bunch of high achievers. We all wound up wet-nursing project directors who knew less than we did. That happens in mergers. It isn't something you can fight. I asked a trusted colleague for ideas. He put me in touch with officers at the World Bank."

She paused. Andre waited. Then May said, "My mother's a Motswana. Through her, I have dual citizenship in Botswana and in the US. That helped. Officers boasted of hiring me, an African woman. It was proof they'd shed their colonialist ways."

Her reply was drifting beyond Andre's question. But he listened.

"I'm talking to you because in my view, your firm's banking contract could do more to benefit Batswana and other African people than the Bank has done in recent years."

Andre asked, "Are you saying *Batswana?*"

"Yes," May said. "Botswana with an *o* is the country. Its inhabitants are Batswana, with an *a*, but there's also a singular form. One person from there is a Motswana. Those are the demonyms."

It was a new word for Andre. "Demonyms. Thanks for the definition."

May said, "It *sounds* complicated, but it's as simple as the demonym for people from the Netherlands. We call them —"

"Right. We call people from the Netherlands the Dutch and think nothing of it. Thanks."

Andre regarded himself as informed and sensitive to such matters as names people had for their entire populations. He appreciated

May's informative answer, which had been delivered in an even tone, free of any criticism or complaining.

The interview ended.

Later, when writing to his daughter, a sociologist who taught at Carnegie Mellon, Andre mentioned the exchange with May Kim. His word processing software highlighted *demonym*, alerting him it was considered a misspelling.

While completing the hiring process, Sharon Beyerly, ACI's comptroller, who managed all finances as well as dealings with federal and state governments, told Andre, "We're required by law to verify citizenship. Did you know Dr. May Kim is a citizen of both the US and Botswana?"

Andre said, "Yes. But thanks for keeping us alert and out of trouble."

After interviewing May's former employers, verifying her publications, and reviewing Ms. Beyerly's homework, ACI sent May an offer letter to work on the risk management and the economic development work assignments as a senior associate for up to one year.

May accepted and came to Philadelphia to work for ACI. She was to start Monday, October 28, 2013. Carmen Stanhope would be her supervisor.

Gwynneth checked with her aunt Maria to see if they could offer May housing in a spare bedroom for a few months.

"She can stay longer than that if she wants," Maria said.

Gwynneth was explicit when she extended the invitation to May. "Maria says you can stay with us as long as you want."

May accepted the invitation. On October 27, she moved onto the third floor with Gwynneth at 1110 Clinton Street, where she shared a bedroom with four large antique armoires.

TWENTY

NOVEMBER 26–30

In her first full semester of Drexel's 2013–2014 academic year, Gwynneth's successes in the lab and outstanding work in the classroom were overshadowed by a colleague's major advances.

Then, two days before Thanksgiving 2013, Gwynneth retrieved a draft report from the group printer. Under her report was a one-page letter addressed to her brilliant colleague, and under that was an attachment, a three-page array of data. The letter, written on a major pharmaceutical company's letterhead, made clear reference to the three-page attachment.

Not cursing, Gwynneth reflected, "I can outshine Hans Gunther but not Hans Gunther and a team of ghostwriters."

She went to see her mentor and supervisor, Hildegard Zimmer. "Dr. Zimmer," she began. "I have a dilemma. Can we talk?"

"Yes. Sit down for a bit. Let me finish this report to the dean. All this *paper*work. It's a miracle we get any scientific research done here."

Gwynneth eased her pregnant self into a chair and waited. Ten clicks later, Hildegard spun away from her computer. "All right, then. A dilemma, eh?"

"Dr. Gunther is cheating. His data is ghostwritten. It's not from his lab work; it's coming from a pharmaceutical company. A note they sent him was in the group printer. The note is on company letterhead. Data is attached to the letter. Any ideas what to do about it?"

Hildegard reached a broad hand across the desk, her wordless Teutonic request for the pages. Gwynneth gave them to her and said, "I've copied these and sent them to remote storage."

"*Merde*," said Hildegard, scanning the four pages and shaking her head. Her French accent was terrible. "Fraud, not major advances in my own lab, under my own stupid nose. And it *is* a dilemma."

The word *dilemma* sat in midair between them, a wayward drone hovering over the desk. Hildegard added, "I'm going to need a few minutes to process this."

Gwynneth sat up straight in the wooden chair, waiting.

"Can you just let me ruminate on this overnight? And can you be still about it?"

"Yes," said Gwynneth

"Thank you."

After a solemn moment, she offered a ride home. Gwynneth accepted.

As they rode an elevator to the parking garage, Hildegard asked, "Twenty weeks to go? Is my arithmetic correct?"

"Yes, though Mother Nature has her own metrics."

"Mother Nature needed help with our second child. They called it inducing labor."

Gwynneth nodded. "Right. They supplied the Pitocin, and you supplied the labor."

The next day, the cheater was terminated. Gwynneth honored Hildegard's request to be still about it, though she told Henry on Saturday, during their return drive from celebrating Thanksgiving with her family in the Bronx.

In the front seat of their rented car, she gave him a brief summary of her role and the university's prompt response to what she called the Gunther ordeal.

"Thoughts?" she asked him.

"Good to have a plan in place for unexpected devel —"

"Let me put it this way, Henry. What would *you* have done?"

He paused. *Peace. Be still,* he prayed. Then he asked, "No one caught a trace of shenanigans when one triumphant paper followed another in short order?"

She made a vigorous reply to his question. "You mean was anyone keeping the whole cursed department under surveillance? Is that a tenet in your Gospel?"

Henry took a breath while shaking his head. "No. That's not what I mean."

She waited for him to respond to her jab about his Gospel.

He said, "The facts are always friendly, right? We're supposed to know the facts. Maybe it's easier with time sheets. But someone's responsible, and someone signs them."

"You?" Gwynneth's question had a sharp tone, but she was not angry.

"Yes. I sign some of them, for some projects."

Gwynneth asked, "And on a related topic, what about pressure to perform?"

"We're a team. ACI executives know I've brought in work this year. But we all know it was because Stanhope plowed the field for two years. It wasn't me thriving under pressure."

"Right. No one works alone. Anything else?" she asked.

He nodded and said, "Sure. What did you think about his papers?"

"Dr. Gunther worked hard and avoided mistakes. Kept to himself. We knew little about him. Then his output shot up. Three papers in five months. I was suspicious but had no proof he was cheating."

She paused. "Scientists aren't ballplayers. They don't use steroids or cocaine to jack their performance. They may use something else."

Henry canted his head to one side as if to ask, "What else?"

Gwynneth shrugged. "They can usurp others' work or devise faux data. Or both. But in our lab, we had no evidence of that. The papers were excellent work. Criticizing someone who was helping the team more than me would've been whining."

After a moment, she added, "So that's why I kept quiet."

Henry waited, but she said no more about it on the drive home. They arrived at Gwynneth's place early Saturday evening.

He accepted her invitation to come in for a drink. Inside, she sat in a large stuffed chair, looking tired after the two-hour drive. He made them a pot of tea and brought hers to her in a large mug. She held the mug with both hands as he sat on an arm of her stuffed chair.

After a pause, he asked, "On another matter?" He set his mug down, slid beside her into her chair, and asked, "May I join you?"

She sighed and nodded to welcome the snug fit.

"Are you both getting the help you need from me in this trimester?" He pulled one of her shoulders into his chest and wrapped both arms around her.

"Yes. Don't change a thing, Henry. You've been fine to me through all the cravings and emotional swings."

"Good," he said.

"Gab called," she said. "She and Laura are coming next weekend. Taking in the New Barnes and the Rodin. Gab said they'd be at the Warwick."

Henry nodded. He looked forward to seeing his sister and his fourteen-year-old niece.

"I told her they could stay with me."

Gwynneth occupied the entire third floor of her aunt Maria and uncle Bennie's home near Antique Row. She shared its twenty-five hundred square feet of space with May and a dozen large pieces of fine eighteenth-century furniture.

Three bedrooms and a den in the rear of the place were semi-furnished with tall armoires and enormous wooden chests with elaborate inlays. Toward the front were two and a half baths, a full kitchen, a dining area, and a cavernous living room. One wall of the living room was adorned with two distinct and rare English walnut cupboards.

There was plenty of room for Gab and her daughter. Henry's studio apartment south of Rittenhouse Square could accommodate only emergency short-term guests.

He leaned forward, nuzzled, and then kissed her on the helix of her tawny ear. "You are an amazing woman, and I am glad to be here with you tonight."

Gwynneth took a deep breath and exhaled slowly. "Some days you make it easy to be an amazing woman."

"Good," he said, turning her face toward him to kiss her and slipping his other hand under her slacks onto her bare belly.

"Oh, yeah, that *is* good," she said, responding to his touch. "But it'll be better in bed."

After their lovemaking, he let her sleep while he returned the rental car. Later, he wakened her and as she stirred, he asked, "Got everything you need?"

She smiled, glad to be spent, and said, "I got a man who knows what I need."

"I'm going to get myself home now."

"No," she said, pulling him beside her. "Please. Stay the night."

TWENTY-ONE
AUTUMN 2013 (1)

It took many weeks to set up Gwynneth's first meeting with Dr. Anita Stromberg, who introduced her over lunch to two senior executives from AmeRxOne. The executives were seeking candidates for a new associate director for monitoring with strong experience in planning, conducting, and reporting research findings. They didn't need an expert in immunology, but they needed a clear-thinking scientist who was comfortable managing effective, legal, and ethical operations that included teams of scientific researchers.

Gwynneth knew AmeRxOne, as did most Americans. The firm had cultivated and earned a good reputation for combining ethical practices with a century-long record of strong profits.

But earlier in the summer, AmeRxOne had experienced a setback when it was caught promoting and selling billions of dollars' worth of drugs to hospitals, doctors, and patients for unapproved purposes. The offense, called off-label marketing, sounded less weighty than evading entrance fees to a national park. But it was a serious federal crime that had endangered thousands of lives.

In August 2013, to put the criminal misconduct behind them, lawyers at AmeRxOne had proposed to US Justice Department prosecutors a settlement of a few hundred million dollars. The sum was pocket change for the company, but the grave damage to AmeRxOne's public reputation needed more urgent and substantial repair.

Mark Palumbo, AmeRxOne's director for pharmaceuticals, and Brigitte Gerhardt, general counsel, told Gwynneth at initial meetings that they'd been tasked by the board and corporate leadership to find a new associate director for monitoring. In October, AmeRxOne retained a human resources consultant to evaluate Gwynneth's suitability for the post. He reported to Mark Palumbo, "Her papers are first rate. Nine years of top-tier work. Respected in the lab."

Palumbo had shot back, "So why haven't we heard anything about her?"

The savvy consultant answered with a barbed question. "She's not into self-promotion?" He let the question sink in and then added, "If it were my company, I'd hire her."

And when they reviewed her background and conferred with other officers in AmeRxOne, Palumbo and Gerhardt agreed the associate director for monitoring position might be a good fit for both Gwynneth and the company.

Gwynneth conferred with Stanhope about the slow pace of discussions with AmeRxOne. During a call on the Friday before Halloween, Stanhope told her, "This is how long it takes for companies to make a hiring decision. They make no-go decisions faster."

"No-go decisions?"

Stanhope said, "With a go or no-go question, it's easier to say no, to eliminate an unsuitable candidate. If you weren't being considered, they'd've told you months ago. For all their dilatory ways, they are still interested in you. Why not wait and see what they have to say?" She added, "Does Hildegard Zimmer know you're talking to them?"

"Yes," Gwynneth said. "And we're both intrigued by their apparent interest. But we're also having a good fall semester here at Drexel."

On November 4, Palumbo and Gerhardt called to invite Gwynneth to meet with them again in Anita Stromberg's office.

When they sat down on Friday, November 8, they told her the position of associate director for monitoring was still open. It sounded as if they were about to offer her the job, but their focus was on the incumbent deputy associate director.

Brigitte Gerhardt said, "We think the incumbent can be a good deputy."

"Are you posing a riddle or declaring a condition?" asked Gwynneth.

Mark Palumbo said, "We want to offer you this job. But first we'd like to know how you'd feel about Ms. Gerhardt's proposal. Keeping the current deputy to maintain continuity."

Gwynneth said she wanted to think about it over the weekend. They agreed to resume their discussion on Monday.

Henry offered a succession-planning case study. Gwynneth read it and spoke with Stanhope, who told her, "Follow your instincts."

"I'm asking for *counsel*," Gwynneth said. "I don't have enough experience with this sort of thing to have any useful instincts."

Stanhope said, "Be skeptical. It's possible keeping an incumbent deputy might be a good idea for supporting a new boss, but I've seldom seen it work."

"Why don't they put someone else in the deputy's slot?" Gwynneth asked.

"To avoid a lawsuit if they fire him, or maybe the guy *is* an all-star. Depends on who's sitting in the seat."

At their meeting on Monday, Gwynneth seized the initiative. It looked as if she wanted to change the subject from the deputy to herself. "An associate director for monitoring is an important figure in your company," she said. "My experience is scientific in an academic setting. You're planning to sell me as the new AD, to announce in your press releases that I'm one of the sweeping changes you'll be making? To demonstrate your ethical rectification?"

Uncomfortable as they were about her summation and questions, Mark Palumbo and Brigitte Gerhardt did not contradict her.

Gwynneth paused and then said, "Director is singular. One guy in charge."

They nodded.

"OK. So who'd be the boss?"

Mark Palumbo said, "You'd be the boss, the associate director. The current deputy would be *your* deputy. Part of his job would be to orient you about the corporate structure and culture and to smooth communications with the general counsel."

"And you're proposing here that I'd be the one who makes sure he does that job?"

Mark Palumbo and Brigitte Gerhardt were disquieted by the power of Gwynneth's insight. They had not anticipated her poise and confidence.

Before Mark or Brigitte could respond, Gwynneth said, "You're talking about a guy who hasn't been promoted into the job for which he's the deputy. What does that mean?"

They looked at each other but did not reply.

Gwynneth did not press. In a spirit of comity she asked, "Was he so oblivious he didn't know about the off-label marketing? Or is he bright and qualified and *did* know about it and is disappointed about not being promoted and ready to sabotage a new AD?"

"We can't comment on his history," said Palumbo. "But he knows we'll be watching him."

Gwynneth said, "And you want to put me, a rookie, into a key job that's critical to your new-drugs pipeline and your profitability? With an incumbent deputy? And it'll be OK because you're going to watch him?"

Her challenging rhetorical questions prodded Brigitte Gerhardt to ask, "What's your proposal?"

Gwynneth sought clarification first, "OK. So in this AD job, I'll get you into compliance with all the new requirements that are part of your settlement with the government for your fraudulent practices. And run the associate directorate for monitoring with a deputy you're afraid to promote into the AD slot. Is that where we are?"

Again, neither Mark nor Brigitte said anything. They spoke their assent by avoiding eye contact with her. And while they did not enjoy her assessment, they did not refute it.

After a pause, Brigitte said, "We're sure an innovative approach is in order here. The old ways and the old teams couldn't get it done. No one disputes it."

Gwynneth replied as if she were talking to graduate assistants in her lab who didn't understand a basic point. She said, "Your deputy is satisfied with his standing as a noble retainer who's compensated —"

"I'm sorry," Palumbo interrupted. "Noble retainer?"

She answered without sarcasm. "A serf with some heroic qualities. In the Middle Ages someone the lord of the fief could trust. You're not talking about a well-compensated executive. You're paralyzed by a loyal servant who can't cut it."

The two sat in silence, as if to acknowledge they'd been defeated in the exchange by an academic scientist who'd studied just one undergraduate course in medieval history.

Gwynneth went on. "I apologize for the feudal cliché *noble retainer,* but it doesn't seem to be suffering from overuse in your company." She let her tone project a small measure of condescension but not contempt for the unread executives sitting across from her.

She continued. "Isn't it irregular to keep him? He's been passed over. You're saying you couldn't find another soul in the firm who could function as my deputy or chief of staff?"

"There are other factors complicating the situation," said the general counsel.

Gwynneth's riposte sounded as if she had experience with such dilemmas. "Then simplify it. Send him off with a year's severance. Pay his tuition to get an MBA he can show a future employer. That's one proposal."

Brigitte agreed. "Yes. Separating him as you suggest could be simpler."

Gwynneth added, "You'd also send a valentine to your sinecures. 'We've eliminated a deputy associate director who was not adding value to this firm.' They'll get the message they could be next."

Brigitte Gerhardt looked down into her lap. Such a stratagem had not been put forward by the HR consultant. She said, "You've raised some good points. I'm glad we're all operating here within the shelter of a nondisclosure agreement."

"I'm glad, too. So where does this leave us?"

Palumbo said, "We'll confer with our CEO and a few board members."

"And?" Gwynneth was careful to sound neither smug nor dismissive. "And you'll get back to me?"

They ended the meeting.

Gwynneth thought at some point Brigitte might have mentioned her swelling belly. But although she had mentioned her grown daughter and son, and, Gwynneth presumed, at least two pregnancies, she hadn't made any outward connection between them as two women.

In Gwynneth's experience in work settings, women introduced discussions with other women by complimenting them. *You look impressive in that jacket* or *Your manicure is a new look*. It was something women did to create common ground. Brigitte had made no such comments. Gwynneth thought Brigitte's detachment seemed pathological. Merry Godmother opined, *That's a bit harsh, dear. Maybe Brigitte is an introvert.*

Gwynneth had shared with Henry accounts of her meetings with Mark Palumbo and Brigitte Gerhardt. That Monday evening, she told him about AmeRxOne's questions, comments, and what she felt was an imminent job offer.

"What do you really want to do?" Henry asked.

"Excellent question, Henry. I want the job. I can do the job. I know others who've made the successful transition from academe to the corporate world. We're in touch from time to time. But there's no battalion of supporters waiting for me at AmeRxOne. And I do not want to be waylaid when I step in there."

She paused and shifted the subject. "I can handle myself in any fight. These overpaid bozos think they're tough political infighters, but they win only because they write the rules. We all saw how stupid and puny they acted when the government nailed them last summer. But here, I'll be playing by their rules, on their home field."

Henry said, "And what about Hildegard Zimmer?"

"I've told her everything, and she's been supportive. She got me admitted into a special business consulting program at Drexel. I think she's proud of me. She's been the successful mentor watching a protégé fly away. She says I should do what's best for all."

"Interesting developments," he said. "How'd the program come up?"

"A friend of hers called, looking for a scientist for a business consulting team. She wanted to know if Hildegard knew of a candidate. She knows I've been talking with a search committee for a pharmaceutical firm and thought it might be a good opportunity for me. Drexel faculty and staff collaborate with corporate execs on three- or four-month projects, online and in classes, on the second and fourth Wednesday nights. It starts January 8. So I'm in a formal business program without a single moment of anxiety over my schedule or my budget."

"Or the baby," Henry added.

"Right. And it's humbling. My brightest colleagues lament they have no time to do what you have to do to get admitted to a tier-one business school. And if they have the time to apply and get admitted, they wouldn't have time to study for the classes or write papers to present at seminars and feed the husband and pick up the kids after day care and every other cursed thing. Yet here, in November 2013, after my nine years of graduate study, scientific research, and teaching biochemistry, admission to a grad school business program has fallen out of the sky into my lap."

After a pause, she added, "My colleagues' requiems for graduate study that could help career advancement had one common trait. They were all women."

Henry nodded.

Later that evening, Gwynneth conferred again with her spiritual guide, Merry Godmother, about how she might respond to a job offer from the pharmaceutical company.

Well, dear, you remember Caroline and May's idea? That worked out well for you. Write down these questions: What do I want in my professional life now and in the near future? If I take the job, could I live with the current deputy? Give these some thought, and see what comes up.

So for a few evenings Gwynneth engaged in a discernment process, posing those two queries. The fourth night, she had her answers. She might take the job...but not the deputy.

The Monday after Thanksgiving, December 2, 2013, Gwynneth met Mark Palumbo and Brigitte Gerhardt for lunch at R2L, on the fiftieth floor of Two Liberty Place. Brigitte proposed installing her own deputy as an interim deputy assistant for monitoring.

They reiterated that Gwynneth would be one of thirteen associate directors, managing a dozen middle managers responsible for monitoring research activity, clinical practices, and compliance with state, federal, and international legal requirements, including the stringent requirements imposed by the government as a part of the off-label settlement.

On a separate but parallel track, after weeks of intensive negotiations, Scriptaphage bought AmeRxOne. The deal was reported in the press early in December and would be final January 1, 2014.

Negotiations with Gwynneth were concluded when AmeRxOne agreed to pay the costs for her Drexel seminar, approved telework up to six days a month, and added a fourth week of vacation.

On her starting date, December 16, 2013, her compensation package more than quadrupled, from $48,500 to $195,000.

At 1110 Clinton Street with Henry on the Friday before Christmas, Gwynneth reflected. "It's been quite a week at AmeRxOne. I'm not in a lab doing research and not in seminar rooms teaching biochemistry. I've started as the megachecker at big pharma, managing a cohort of *their* checkers."

"Getting into compliance with government regulations and terms of a settlement," Henry said.

"Yes. It's strange walking the hallways with checkers who've shown they can't be trusted to obey the law, meet their ethical standards, or behave with human decency. They disrespected their customers. They committed crimes. No one is showing any remorse. When the AmeRxOne name is be gone in ten days, that'll help obliterate the public relations mess. We'll be marching under the banner of Scriptaphage. And I'll be in the vanguard because I understand clinical trial data." She hesitated and then added, "And because I'm clean."

Henry said, "Other changes are ahead of us. You'll see them in your first paycheck. I'm seeing them already."

"How so?" Gwynneth asked.

"Selling millions in new bank business has been lucrative. Our bonuses will be six figures."

She shook her head. "How can that be? Your *salary* just got raised to six figures."

He explained that though the revenues at his firm were small compared to the billions at AmeRxOne and Wall Street banks, ACI would earn profits of one per cent and a fee of three per cent on a multi-million-dollar work assignment Henry had sold. ACI's profit and fees could amount to several hundred thousand dollars.

"Andre told Stanhope and me ACI will keep some, but he told us we can expect bonuses in the low six figures."

Gwynneth nodded. She understood the arithmetic, but, stunned by the implications of Henry's remarks, asked, "So, what will you do with that kind of money?"

"You and I will have a less abstract discussion of what stewardship means to us."

"And what does it mean to you?"

Henry did not answer. He didn't want each of them to fashion a statement about what stewardship meant, then somehow combine them. He wanted to discuss what stewardship meant to the two of them as a couple. But since they weren't a couple and he'd never had such a discussion he was at sea about how to proceed.

She interrupted his contemplative moment. "Do you not want to say what stewardship means to you?"

He shook his head. "I'm fine with discussing it together but not clear about how to do it."

"And the problem is what?"

He said, "As I say, I'm not clear about how to proceed but now it's different."

"Different," she said.

"Here's one big difference. We're not sure if we're a couple. That makes it hard to discuss our stewardship goals. Another is the scale of our income is majorly different. After a year on the Hill and two years at ACI, I drew up a financial plan for myself. My view of the future was as a consultant, in a lower middle-class income band. My goal was to save and invest so I could live comfortably and not be a burden to anyone. Now I'm in an upper middle-class income band and those old goals will be met in one or two years."

She said, "I'm in a similar position."

He said, "So when the goals are met, what then?"

There was a lull in the conversation, as they pondered his question. Then Gwynneth shrugged and said, "You'll consult the Gospel to set new stewardship goals?"

He shook his head. "No. Some Gospel guidance is for those who want to be perfect. That's not me. Other counsel, the parable of the talents, isn't helpful.

"This is a luxury issue, and we need to discuss it or we'll wind up in a dreary mansion in Chestnut Hill asking how we got there. And it sounds as if we're a couple. Agreed?"

Gwynneth nodded her accord, then turned to him, straddled his lap with her knees, squeezed his hips, and began to unbutton his shirt. "Yes, let's discuss it."

"Yeah," he sighed, fondling her. "Some other time."

They took themselves into the bedroom.

TWENTY-TWO
AUTUMN 2013 (2)

While Gwynneth negotiated her position at AmeRxOne, Henry, May, and Michael Larson were preparing for their risk management project. In early December, two of ACI's senior staff, Ernestine Tewksberry and John Carlucci, oriented them in four daily sessions on banking principles and the vocabulary of risk management.

To get acquainted with the project staff, Susan Hazari twice joined the sessions then both times went to lunch with May, Henry and Michael. At their second lunch, Susan asked Michael where he'd gone to school. Michael knew ACI had appended his résumé to its proposal to the bank. Susan could've read about his two-year AmeriCorps gig and his college. Bemused at her query, he looked at Henry, who tilted his head, suggesting that Michael answer her pronto.

"Georgia Tech, 2012, mathematics," he said.

"And how did you find ACI?"

"Wainwright found me at a job fair, at the Washington Convention Center."

Susan nodded with a look of mild dissatisfaction that told Michael she really wanted to ask more about him. But instead Susan asked May to compare Philadelphia to Washington. May smiled and, said, "Not enough data points yet."

In mid-December, May, Henry, and Michael produced a summary of banking-industry-relevant best practices and identified six vulnerabilities in the bank's systems. As they proceeded, Henry asked Ernestine, "How can you not require two signatures for all six-figure transactions?"

"Banks do," she said. "But opening new lines of business, or reorganizing, or merging two firms are complex deals. Here, a merger left a few gaps that put the bank at risk. They were accidental, not deliberate. Finding and eliminating these risks is regarded as unglamorous. Bank hotshots think it's work for the auditors. But they also know rogue traders have destroyed hundred-year-old banks, so they'll acknowledge the risks."

Carlucci added, "Our challenge is to convince bank officers the risks are serious and to eliminate them. We make our findings clear, but also make them understand that implementation plans are their business. One of our jobs is to convince them to take prompt action."

Ernestine said, "And if they do what we recommend, they'll likely have a positive view of ACI, and may want to do more work with us. This isn't just project management. It's marketing too."

Henry stared at her. Stanhope and Wainwright had also made these points.

Later in December, Henry made one of his weekly calls to Susan Hazari. "We'll be early with our recommendations on risk management."

"My mentor told me you might be early," Susan said.

Henry plowed in. "Who's your mentor?"

"Janet Davies. She's a VP in commercial real estate but started in corporate and investment banking. The bank's C-level executives were impressed when she told them about ACI's work. They're anticipating doing more business with you guys."

"Mm-hmm," Henry answered.

As they finished the risk management work, Stanhope told Andre and Carmichael she'd met with Janet Davies. Janet reiterated that Henry, May, and Michael had dazzled the bank officers, who were sure they'd made the right decision to use ACI to manage their $10 million business development initiative in Africa.

TWENTY-THREE

JANUARY 3–13, 2014

By January 3, 2014, Gwynneth had navigated with panache her first three weeks at Scriptaphage, née AmeRxOne. She'd been gifted a world-class assistant when Brigitte Gerhardt, the general counsel in both the old and new corporation, assigned her own deputy, Maxine Palapye, to plan and manage the pace of Gwynneth's orientation to the firm.

At five foot one inch, Max was shorter than Gwynneth and darker skinned. She favored pinstripe slacks and wore complementary red or black jackets over white blouses. Disdaining high heels, she wore flats for comfort and let others decide whether her petite stature was a problem. Her confidence arose from her high-level competence in the firm's legal affairs and her strong personal network. Max knew most of the important executives in the old company, AmeRxOne, and leading players in the new one, Scriptaphage. She also kept in touch with colleagues in other firms and was active in community affairs.

"You can call me Max," she told Gwynneth when they met. "Palapye is assonant with *lullaby*, if anyone asks for pronunciation help. And you're Trevor?"

"Yes, that's right," said Gwynneth.

Maxine looked as if she expected a few more details. Gwynneth supplied them.

"It's Welsh. My mother is from Puerto Rico. We grew up in New York. In the Bronx."

"Ah," said Max.

"And you?" Gwynneth asked.

Acknowledging she was the one who'd asked about the Trevor name, Max sighed and looked with suspicion at Gwynneth. In her experience, Americans who asked about her background struggled to hear and repeat the unusual-sounding city and family names when Max answered their queries. But she answered, "In Molepolole. It's —"

Gwynneth interrupted her. "Outside of Gabarone."

Max finished her sentence. "In Botswana." She stared at Gwynneth, impressed she'd heard of her hometown.

"Not many people know about it," Max said. "The ones who know about it can't pronounce it. The ones who can pronounce it have never been there."

Gwynneth laughed. "Oh, man, if my friend May Kim heard that, she'd howl."

"Friend?"

"May's American, born in Los Angeles. Her father's Korean, and her mother's a Batswana. We lived in a friend's house in Washington for a couple of years. Now we're both here."

"In Philadelphia? Both of you?"

"Yes, but she's not going to be here for long. May's working with Henry's —"

"Henry?" Max asked.

"Henry Knudsen. My man," said Gwynneth. "May will be working in Gabarone on a banking project. She and Henry work together for a small consulting firm here. ACI."

Max smiled at Gwynneth and said, with raised eyebrows, "Small world."

Gwynneth was scheduled to attend her first executives' meeting on January 13 at the start of her fourth week at Scriptaphage.

To prepare for the meeting, Max and Gwynneth sat side by side on the sofa in Gwynneth's office at seven in the morning, reviewing on their tablets bios of executives on AmeRxOne's old website and Scriptaphage's new one. Max spoke at length about associate directors who were responsible for scientific research, monitoring, and legal and financial matters. There'd be nineteen executives at the meeting, including Gwynneth.

The twelfth bio they reviewed was the associate director for scientific affairs. When it appeared on their tablet screens, Gwynneth emitted an involuntary curse.

"Problem?" Max asked.

Gwynneth said, "No. A surprise."

"George Cramer?" Max asked, looking at her own pad.

Gwynneth said, "We were colleagues at Columbia in 2007. I'd lost track of him."

"He was here before he went to Columbia, and he came back in 2008. It was a strange sort of move, a reverse sabbatical. We thought he might stay there." Max tapped her touchscreen, and a full bio appeared.

Gwynneth tapped her screen to pull up the same bio. "He hasn't done much here in the past couple of years. Can you say something about him?"

Max shrugged. "We don't have much to do with the scientists and the research they do."

Gwynneth was emboldened to challenge Max's statement. Max had just given her details about the research activities of other associate directors. And Gwynneth knew George Cramer. In 2007 they'd been engaged to be married, but it hadn't worked out. Now she wanted an update.

So Gwynneth said, "Well, that's bizarre. For the past half hour, you've told me in some detail about many others' scientific and legal —"

Max reddened as she interrupted Gwynneth. "I don't want to gossip about him."

"You gave many details about other ADs. And then you decide you're gonna send me into my first execs' meeting —"

Max interrupted again. "His misbehavior has only come to the attention of Tim Shekel, the CFO."

Gwynneth waited. When Max didn't continue, she said, "OK. Well, if Tim knows about it, *I* want to know about it. What kind of misbehavior?"

Reluctant to answer, Max said, "I haven't heard him myself —"

Gwynneth cut in. "What misbehavior has Tim —"

Max stopped her. "All right. George has a reputation for saying untrue things about women who work here. And he's supposed to stay current on research his directorate supports, but the word is he —"

"He isn't?" Gwynneth asked.

"It's a little worse than that. He doesn't make site visits or —"

"He doesn't confer with investigators who are working on his own cursed research agenda?"

Max nodded but said no more.

"OK. I wouldn't call that gossip, Max. I'd say it was giving me good information ahead of time so I don't waltz into a meeting unprepared. Or cursed *clueless*."

Max nodded and said, "Sorry. We can talk more about him later if you want. But that'll get you through your first execs' meeting."

At eight o'clock, Tim Shekel brought to order five other financial officers and thirteen associate directors, including Gwynneth. The gender mix was three women and sixteen men. As usual, each exec gave a five-minute recap of developments since the previous meeting. Most addressed the impact of the merger of AmeRxOne with Scriptaphage. The meeting ended at ten.

As participants left the room or fell into small caucuses, one man lobbed a taunt into the conference room. "Women. They should all be back in the kitchen."

No one responded to the sneer.

After a moment, in a calm voice loud enough for all to hear, Gwynneth asked, "Are you mocking me or mocking yourself, George?"

Others stood by their chairs, toying with their electronic pads, not watching either George or Gwynneth.

George said in a low voice, "Women are getting promotions *handed* to them —"

Gwynneth interrupted him. "George? How many papers have you published in the past year?" She knew the answer to her question. She'd read it in his bio on the new Scriptaphage website.

It was a sharp challenge. George was quiet, as if in synch with the silence that had stilled the conference room. He was unsure whether it was smart to answer the woman's question in front of his colleagues.

Unconstrained by any such reluctance, Gwynneth spoke into the silent gathering. "One. One paper. Right George?"

He was incredulous that the woman had launched a counterattack. And he'd miscalculated both her tactical firepower and her willingness to use it in front of others.

She went on. "You show up as the seventh coauthor. Was that just a courtesy gift from your friends who knew you hadn't written a single paper in a year? You don't even meet with your own clinical investigators."

She paused as George glared at her. Then she said, "But that's a risk of your sinecure, George. You wind up attacking people who are getting things done and publishing their findings in scientific journals."

George said, "It's pretty clear you're getting hysterical here." He started to leave the conference room.

Tim Shekel, the CFO, said, "George, she's not hysterical, and the comment addresses and debunks your notion that women are getting promotions handed to them here."

George scowled at Shekel. No one else said a word.

"Did you mean Dr. Trevor had a promotion handed to her because she's a woman?"

"You're getting a little hysterical yourself, Tim," said George.

Tim paused, measuring his response. "She published five papers last year, George. She was the lead author on three of them. You're the one who's hysterical. Your hectoring her is unprofessional. It's disappointing to hear it in this room."

George looked down at his papers, waiting for a word of support from one of his colleagues. All he heard was an uneasy silence. There were feelings of loyalty for George Cramer but no hint of succor for him or his remarks.

Shekel said, "There was a time when a woman had to outperform all the competition to get an executive post here. We're past that time. And we're not doing it to be nice, George. We have to hire the best and trim the rest if we're going to stay competitive in today's markets."

When Shekel paused, George neither rebutted his comments nor ridiculed what he called in private the firm's latest moronic jingle, "We hire the best and trim the rest."

Shekel continued. "Five papers, George. That's the reality. One in a Spanish medical journal. She's doing a management seminar at Drexel, George. No one has handed her anything.

"And as CFO, I see it as an outrageous waste to pay anyone six hundred thousand dollars because someone told her she 'should be back in the kitchen.' We're interested in paying that money for recruiting, George, not to a plaintiff suing us for witless and offensive talk in a boardroom."

In a well-publicized development, a rival pharmaceutical company had paid that memorable sum two months earlier to settle a lawsuit for an instance of sexual harassment.

George braced himself and said, "So my forty papers and presentations at three international conferences —"

"George, your past performance was extraordinary and good for the firm's bottom line and reputation. You're one of our best chemists. We all acknowledge your loyal service. But in the last year? Maybe one paper. And your attitude and juvenile talk mystify all of us. Why are you behaving this way?"

George Cramer did not answer.

After a pause, Shekel said, "I'm going to wrap this up, George. I hope we can agree your remarks are not helpful. Your claims of others' hysteria are feeble. Given the legal risk you're asking us to take with your loose talk, your remarks have been pretty cursed stupid, too."

Shekel gathered his tablet and slid his chair toward the conference table. Then he walked out of the room.

Gwynneth waited for a few seconds, then also left the room.

"So am I taking the fall here for what everyone says in the dining room?" George asked, addressing those remaining.

In a sympathetic tone, Bob Peterson said, "George, you're the only one in the dining room who attacks women. For years, you've ignored our hints to stop. Don't you see we're not laughing at your lame and sexist jokes?"

"*Years*, Bob? You can't be serious," George said.

"Yes, George. My hints started when our daughter was nine and outscoring all the boys in fourth-grade math. Kids taunted her on the playground for being a show-off. She started making deliberate mistakes on her math tests. When we figured out what was going on, we met with her teacher and principal. They said we were overreacting. It was just kids being kids. Amanda is fourteen now, George, so yes, it's been five years."

Unimpressed, George sighed aloud and looked at the conference room ceiling in faux exasperation.

"Is that when *you* started taunting women and getting away with it, George? Fourth grade?"

George glared at him. Bob Peterson had made his point but responded to George's defiant look with a brassy riposte. "You're a brilliant chemist, George. But sometimes you sound as if emotionally you're still stuck there. Stuck in the fourth grade."

Another man said, "George, I told you last year your crude ways could lead to trouble, and you told me —"

George interrupted him. "I remember attacking you, Marvin. And in defense of the tradition of patriarchy and my commitment to it, I called you names I should not have called you."

Marvin Felderman knew from years of experience this was the closest George could come to making an apology. He said, "On the drive home that night, I played my favorite Gloria Gaynor cut, George: 'I Will Survive.' If you keep up with this talk, it looks as if you may not."

"That's right," said George. "When my friends told me the world had changed, I decided they were all wimps. What *happened* to all you guys?"

Marvin looked at Bob Peterson and shrugged. George would not be persuaded that it was smart to treat girls and women with the same respect he extended to boys and men. He thought that was idiotic. As for Title IX, he believed the law of the land had been hijacked and was no longer worthy of his esteem.

George might admit he had a few outdated notions about women and how they should be treated and managed in big organizations. His colleagues and superiors viewed his beliefs and behavior as offensive misogynistic burdens they no longer wished to carry. Those sharp differences had endured for many years and continued because of a powerful inertia. They would not be resolved without an extraordinary intercession.

TWENTY-FOUR

MARCH 3

Early on Monday March 3, Max knocked on Gwynneth's door, then swung it open. Gwynneth as usual had been at work since six that morning.

Max said, "Hi. Good weekend?"

Gwynnneth tilted her head and said, "You could say that. Henry and I got married. And we put a contract on a house in Antique Row."

Max said, "Whoa. Quite a weekend."

"We've considered ourselves committed to each another for months."

"Sometimes there's a ceremony," Max said.

"After the baby comes, we'll tend to that. Meantime, our relations with people and institutions will be easier for us. And living together will simplify our intimacy and our householding. That'll happen soon."

Max nodded and said nothing, surprised to hear Gwynneth had married. Six-figure down payments were standard for homes in Antique Row. Buying a house there was another significant commitment. She deferred asking whether the marriage and home-buy were public information.

Later that Monday, Gwynneth, Max, and Stanhope met for lunch in a quiet restaurant that made conversation easy. To introduce

Max to Stanhope, Gwynneth said, "When I got to AmeRxOne and since the merger with Scriptaphage, Max has been a mentor and guide, not just our—"

Max cut in. "So you're not upset when I haven't repeated rumors—"

Gwynneth looked at Stanhope. "We're working on Max's understanding that passing along buzz she hears doesn't make her a gossip."

Stanhope nodded.

Returning her gaze to Max, Gwynneth said, "And a comforter. You've protected me. And I've appreciated it."

Stanhope waited, and when she saw that Max understood and Gwynneth had finished, she swung the conversation around to the topic of Gwynneth's pregnancy.

"Almost eight months in?" she asked. "How are you guys doing?"

Gwynneth smiled and said to Stanhope, "We're excited. Henry's sister, Gabriella, has known about it from the start. She has three kids. Same as you. And she's been an angel. Same as you."

Max listened to their intimate exchange, sensing that Stanhope knew about the weekend marriage.

Stanhope said, "Glad to help. Glad to see Henry's doing all right, too."

"Yeah," said Gwynneth. "He's about recovered from his setback."

Max asked, "Setback?"

"Four skinheads beat him up pretty bad after his Tuesday-night Bible study last June. He's mostly over it now, but it took time."

Stanhope nodded. "He's moving around a lot better than he was last year."

Max tried to smile, but she lowered her head and stared at the tabletop.

Their lunch came. They ate. The check came. They paid it.

That afternoon, Max called Antoinette Carmichael, her best friend and counselor, about her dilemma. Toni was a deacon at the African Episcopal Church of Saint Thomas on Lancaster Avenue in Mount Airy, where Max and her family were also parishioners.

Max had met Toni and Dave Carmichael in 1995 when she was at Penn Law and working part-time at the university's children's center. Toni worked mornings at the Penn library when Dave was in the MBA program at Wharton, and their three children were enrolled in the children's center.

Toni had often invited Max to stay with them during Max's vacations from law school when she could not get home to Botswana. Over the past seventeen years, Toni had watched Max's legal career evolve from an associate in a small telecoms law practice to a position of counsel at a pharmaceutical company on Market Street.

But Toni was troubled by the difficulty Max presented to her.

During the call, Max said, "I'm working with a new associate director, Gwynneth Trevor. Last June, her husband, Henry Knudsen, was mugged outside a Bible study class. It took him months to recover."

Toni did not ask Max how she knew Gwynneth and Henry were married. Her understanding was no one at ACI seemed to know or care about it.

Max went on. "The state police investigated and tried to interview my boss's son. The investigation is still open because the assault case was never solved. I think Brigitte's son, Heinrich, was involved, and I don't know what —"

Toni cut her off. "All right, Max. Settle down here. You're upset. Take a breath."

Max was indeed upset, but she was nowhere near as off balance as Toni. Henry worked for her husband. They'd both learned of the mugging in July of 2013, a month after it occurred. She also knew that both her husband and the firm's cofounder, Andre Morneau, had been perplexed when Henry asked them why the police wouldn't let him ask an assailant why he was beating strangers on Philadelphia streets. When Dave and Andre explained that police kept perps and witnesses apart, Henry stopped talking to them about it.

This complicated backstory flashed through Toni's mind while she was trying to calm down her young friend Maxine. She said, "Let's just think about what we know for sure, Max. It is a coincidence that your boss's son might be involved in a mugging, but a few of those happen every day in this city. Henry is all right. And it doesn't —"

Max interrupted. "No. The state police *know*. Brigitte told me the detectives who came to the house asked Heinrich if he'd been on Eighteenth Street the night Henry was attacked. It's the same street —"

But here, young Max began to raise her voice and was at risk of sending herself into a crisis.

"OK, Max. Let's step back here and see what's what."

Max quieted. Toni thought her friend may have been soothed by what she'd said, but on the telephone it was hard to tell.

So Toni said, "OK, you're probably right, Max. And it's a difficult situation. Do you want to meet for a cup tomorrow? Chat about it face to face?"

Max had managed to compose herself enough to say, "Yes. Thanks, Toni. Maybe it's just what I need…to get out of this office and talk to you."

"Tomorrow morning at ten? Dunkin' Donuts, Market and Fifteenth?"

"That's fine, Toni."

Toni sat on a stool at the island in her country kitchen, overlooking the intersection of Sedgwick and Greene Streets. As she recalled Max's distress, her right hand and fingers crept across the granite countertop, feeling for a pack of Newports and her silver Ronson lighter. She caught herself. *That'll never go away*, she thought. *I haven't smoked in ten years, but when I'm stressed, my fingers still tell me I want a cigarette.* She looked up at the skylight and then out the French patio doors, down toward Henry Elementary School. She took a breath and then said aloud, "What a mess. Henry Elementary. An ironic mess."

"Mama?" her twenty-one-year-old daughter asked as she walked into the kitchen. "What mess you talkin' about now?"

"Just talking to myself, darlin'. No mess in here."

But, Toni thought, *there could be a mess of something out there.*

TWENTY-FIVE

MARCH 10

C hapter was the word Gwynneth and Max used to refer to their early-morning meetings to review the day's agenda. It was a tradition in many churches, including Max's. Brigitte Gerhardt stopped in at their chapter meetings two or three times a week.

Although it was clear Gwynneth was going to have a baby, it wasn't until mid-March, late in Gwynneth's pregnancy, before Brigitte mentioned anything about it. Even then, her question was not about Gwynneth but about someone else.

"Who's your obstetrician?" she asked.

Gwynneth said, "It's a team at Penn Medicine headed by Dr. Barbara Quinn."

"She practices at the university? Has admitting privileges there?"

"Yes. The whole OB/GYN team is located near the hospital where I'll be delivering."

"And your husband is excited about being a father?"

Without mentioning their recent marriage, Gwynneth said, "Yes, we're both excited."

Brigitte at last asked a question about Gwynneth herself. "Is it your first?"

"Oh, yes," Gwynneth said. She wanted to change the subject but could not think of words to shift the topic away from her pregnancy and back toward Scriptaphage work.

Brigitte's mobile phone chirped. She examined its screen and said, "I have to answer this one. Talk to you tomorrow morning."

"Tomorrow," Gwynneth said. "Before you go, will you be able to get back to me this morning about whether you're OK with Vance Barker's notes of our meeting with Norman Hughes?"

On her way out the door, Brigitte said, "Yes. Make sure he knows our timetable."

Gwynneth asked Merry Godmother. *So? How'd we do?*

Merry Godmother was reassuring. *You did fine, dear.*

Gwynneth mused, *Many are interested in the pregnancy. It happens for most pregnancies. So it isn't happening to me. It's just happening. And it's OK.*

Max rapped on the door to Gwynneth's office and asked, "Brigitte just passed me outside."

Gwynneth said, "Before she had to leave, she asked about my pregnancy. Mothers seem to ask each other the same questions year after year."

Max shrugged and said, "You'd *think* they'd be the same questions. Trajectories of most uneventful pregnancies are the same."

After a pause, Gwynneth smiled and said, "I've heard the questions women ask one another. Heard them for ages. Just never had them directed at me."

"When Americans see you're pregnant, they think they can ask you anything. Or walk up to you and put their hands on you while they ask, 'Oh, can I feel the baby?' You might want to have a good reply for that. And not, 'Hey, creep, get your cursed hands off me.' Something *nice*."

Gwynneth laughed at her scoffing. "Thanks for the alert, Max. It hasn't been a problem, but I'll come up with something."

Max paused for a moment. Then, although they were the only two in Gwynneth's office, she lowered her voice to say, "Brigitte could be conflicted about the baby making."

Gwynneth frowned and looked at her.

"Trouble with the son. She's shared some of it with me in the two years we've worked together. Not minor stuff. Not shoplifting or smoking reefer. Megatrouble."

"Sorry to hear that."

It was clear Max was not going to elaborate about Brigitte's son. So, after another pause, Gwynneth said, "Time for chapter? Today's schedule?"

Max said, "Yes. At least one tough one today, but not as troublesome as Heinrich Gerhardt."

Gwynneth frowned again.

"That's Brigitte's son's name. Heinrich."

"Ah."

Max awakened her tablet and opened her electronic calendar. "You have a follow-up with Norman Hughes at ten this morning."

"Any other meetings today?"

"You have another lunch with Carmen Stanhope."

"We have reservations at the tea room at two."

"That's what you told me," said Max. "The Mary Cassatt Tea Room."

Gwynneth said, "We keep in touch."

Eager to leave the weekend behind them, Gwynneth resumed their discussion of the day's plan. "And later today?"

"Right. Later you have three calls scheduled, at four, five, and six. The six o'clock is with the general counsel's staff in the Seattle office."

"Thanks, Max. Let's review the agenda for the meeting with Norman Hughes."

"This will be our second meeting with him."

"He denies any deficiencies or wrongdoing."

Max nodded and swiped a finger across her tablet. "It's not criminal, but it's not a pretty record. His turnover is three times higher than it is in other divisions. All four of his branch directors are men. Three white, one Asian. Overall, of the sixty-one in his division, four of color."

Gwynneth said, "And you can verify we've had no correspondence with him since our meeting with him January thirtieth?"

"Yes. No word. His last two annual evaluations mention his high turnover, but there's no written reply from him and no record of any involvement from HR."

Gwynneth closed her eyes as if to concentrate on the reality of such a poor record. "Human Resources hasn't been involved? What about general counsel?"

"No. He says he's meeting all his performance and financial goals and that ought to be enough for anyone."

"Right," said Gwynneth. "All true in sales and revenue, but his labor costs are sky high compared to other divisions. And they seem to be getting worse."

Max asked, "On diversity? Does it count that their one Hispanic guy doesn't speak Spanish?"

Gwynneth glared at her and said, "Not funny, Max."

"TFB, but true."

"TFB?"

"Too. Bad."

Gwynneth rolled her eyes but suppressed a smile. She said, "Yeah. Too bad."

She picked up a green file folder from her desk and said, "Two other divisions also monitor clinical studies and state, federal, and international legal requirements, as well as competitors' best practices. His monthly reports say nothing about tracking any competitors' best practices."

Max said, "Could be an interesting meeting if those come up today."

"They're coming up. We told him they would when we met in January. Didn't they come up before I got here?"

"We knew about them, but they were never mentioned."

"Why was that?" Gwynneth asked.

"Lack of fortitude. Norman Hughes can be loud and intimidating. No one has wanted to deal with him. That's been the scuttle."

Gwynneth frowned. "Who's coming from general counsel?"

"Vance Barker, same notetaker as before." She failed to suppress her sarcasm.

Gwynneth said, "OK, look, this is business."

"Sorry. But he didn't say a word last time we met Norman Hughes. Just took his notes."

"Right. That's why he's here."

Max looked at her cell phone. "Ten of ten. Need a few minutes to get yourself ready?"

"Yes," said Gwynneth.

Max left her alone. Gwynneth put her file folders on one of the chairs around the table in her office and draped her coat on the other. This left two seats open for the meeting, both on a sofa with a lower height than the chairs.

Barker walked into Gwynneth's office five minutes later. A tall and lean African American, Barker clasped a laptop computer in his long fingers, carrying it easily, as if it were an empty file folder. He wore a dark suit, button-down pink shirt, paisley tie, and black wingtip shoes. Gwynneth removed her coat from the chair and gestured to it with an open hand. Accepting the invitation, Barker sat erect in it, opening his laptop and positioning it on his thighs. Gwynneth wanted Norman Hughes on the sofa, opposite her, in a less dominant position.

She asked Barker about his children and his thoughts about Hughes's HR record.

"Haven't formed an opinion," he said, ignoring her inquiry about his kids.

"Good," said Gwynneth. "We need to be open minded about this from the start."

A few minutes later, Norman Hughes walked into the office. A big man whose physique had begun to sag, he wore a dark-navy suit, black loafers, and a white shirt with a formal tall spread collar. His red-and-black striped cravat was tied with a Windsor knot. Gwynneth and Vance Barker welcomed him with handshakes.

"Why don't you take a seat there wherever you want," said Gwynneth, indicating the sofa. It was the maneuver of a parent who asks her children in a casual way whether they want to order spaghetti or mac and cheese at a restaurant. Hughes seemed indifferent to where he sat. Maxine joined them a moment later and sat next to him. Gwynneth and Vance Barker sat in chairs that were two inches higher than the sofa.

Gwynneth let Hughes sit for several seconds before turning in her chair to face him. "Good morning, Dr. Hughes. We have some important business to discuss with you today."

The wording of Gwynneth's opening sally made it sound as if Norman Hughes was entering a meeting that might prove adversarial. And her use of the word *we* made it sound as if they were beginning the meeting with three pro on her side and one contra on his.

Gwynneth took another few deliberate seconds to reach to the tabletop for her files. The message in body language said, *We are in no hurry and are going to do this right.*

"As you know, I've been meeting with division directors to review position descriptions and performance."

"Good," Hughes boomed. "Looking forward to reviewing our division." He looked at her and made strong eye contact. "Glad to discuss my numbers with anyone who needs to be brought up to speed."

Gwynneth let the comment pass. "Then this will proceed apace," she said.

"Right," said Hughes. "We don't want to get bogged down discussing soft issues."

"There are no soft issues on my agenda for today. Did you have one in mind?"

He hadn't expected the quick response. In reply, he posed his own query. "Shall we start with the issues you *do* have?"

"Yes. Good idea," said Gwynneth. Again, she paused before saying, "We rely on you and your large staff to assure compliance with research protocols as well as to manage our relations with regulatory bodies."

"State, federal, and international," Hughes said.

Gwynneth did not respond to the comment. She said, "Holding aside those regulatory and research responsibilities, in this directorate, two other divisions also monitor and report on our competitors' best practices. Yet their annual labor costs are much lower than yours. Is that because they're better managers than you?"

The meeting was just three minutes in, and Norman Hughes had been confronted with a serious challenge. A small bead of sweat formed on his chalky upper lip. He did not reply.

Gwynneth glanced at Barker, whose light-skinned, thin, and muscular fingers lay still on his laptop's wrist rest. As she started to speak, Barker resumed his typing, keeping pace with her and Hughes's comments.

Hughes extended and lifted his right hand almost to his ear, as if to show that Gwynneth's question was akin to an erratic buzzing mosquito. He said, "I thought we were going to review financial performance metrics this morning."

"We are reviewing a number of performance metrics. One is monitoring best practices in the pharmaceutical industry. You are not getting it done. We raised it in our first meeting. In January."

"Oh, I remember that one," Hughes said. The tone of his remark had an edge that was dismissive and scornful, but he kept his body language calm and inoffensive.

"And we asked you whether you're responsible for knowing about best practices in this business. The other pharmaceutical divisions in this directorate *do* know about those best practices." She watched as Norman Hughes sat back in the sofa. Barker continued to record the proceedings on his laptop.

She added, "I mean for monitoring clinical trials and conducting effective relations with state and —"

"I know what my position is," Hughes snapped. His calm evaporated when he raised his voice.

To emphasize her composure, Gwynneth dropped her voice a notch but kept her tone firm. She said, "Well, that's good. So we agree. We agreed in January, too. That you'd be back to us about your remedial action. Is that right?"

Hughes was reluctant to reply, but he did, with a curt nod.

"Thanks," Gwynneth said, adding — in Barker's direction but not to Hughes — "We're recording your nod as a yes."

Vance Barker's rapid and audible typing continued, heeding Gwynneth's prompt and keeping pace with the exchange.

"So we agree it's part of your job to know about competitors' best practices, to keep us current if not in the vanguard on —"

Hughes retorted with a loud firmness some might have found intimidating. "I *know* what my —"

Gwynneth interrupted him, but with patience. "You said that already, Dr. Hughes. But you also said that on January thirtieth. And we haven't heard from you about how you plan to raise your performance levels up to those of the other divisions in this directorate. That's a disappointment."

Hughes glared at her with contempt laced with bitterness, but he said nothing. His blank countenance suggested he was displeased at her outspoken calm and steady eye contact.

Gwynneth continued. "We haven't heard from you. It's March tenth. We're asking again. Can you just answer my questions? Are you and your division responsible for knowing about best practices in clinical research? And for keeping us current or perhaps in a leadership role in managing relations with government regulators?"

Hughes did not reply. He removed a white linen handkerchief from the inside pocket of his light-gray flannel suit and dabbed his upper lip. But because the handkerchief had been starched and ironed, its fibers were pressed flat. The sweat on his upper lip was repositioned, but only a small fraction of it was absorbed.

Gwynneth said, "We can come back to that if you prefer."

She waited for Barker to finish typing. Norman Hughes said nothing.

Maxine bent down to straighten her trouser leg. The move was designed only to let the others know she was still in the room and awake.

Gwynneth consulted her notes. "You said you wanted to discuss the issues I do have. The second is your responsibility for HR management. I'm sure —"

Hughes interrupted her with a patronizing tone. "HR manages human resources. If you look at my job description —"

Gwynneth interrupted him with a steadiness that matched his but again without raising her voice. "I *am* looking at your position description, Dr. Hughes. It's written there, and it is explicit about your responsibility for overall management that has impact on the business results of this directorate."

She slid a four-page document from beneath her notebook, unfolded its vertical crease, and pointed to a highlighted paragraph. "Do you need to see this? It's your PD. It calls for you to recruit and manage your staff and monitor their compensation levels. You are not fulfilling those provisions. As a result, your performance is not satisfactory."

Her statement and the presence on the table of Hughes's position description shifted the balance of power in the room to Gwynneth's clear advantage. Norman Hughes had been put on the defensive by her flurry of statements, supported by written evidence.

And by leaving the highlighted position description on the table in full view, she was inviting him either to contradict its terms or to fabricate a claim that he was in compliance with it.

He felt the sting of her sharp attack. In his defense, he bellowed in a rhythmic cant, "You. Have. No. Right. Even to *suggest* my perfor —"

She interrupted him with a coolheaded gambit. "I'm not suggesting anything, Dr. Hughes. I am *telling* you." Gwynneth allowed herself to mimic him by emphasizing *telling*, again without raising her voice. She continued. "I've already reminded you that I'm new here, but this is a serious performance deficiency. It's been a serious performance deficiency for some time. We discussed it in January, and now it's March."

Gwynneth stopped for a moment, not just to let Vance Barker finish recording the exchange with Hughes but also to rein in her pace. She paused and took a breath.

When she heard Barker had stopped typing, she said, "And because of your deficiency, this directorate for monitoring is carrying you. We have established there are at least two shortfalls that cause us to carry you. One shortfall we can measure is your high staff turnover. It is high, and it is bad, Dr. Hughes. It's bad because it's expensive. It's costing us millions in fat salaries paid to people you train who then walk out the door in six months."

Again, she waited for Barker. "It leads us to your second and related deficiency. Your talent-management skills are lacking. Your division is overstaffed yet still isn't monitoring our competitors' best practices. These failings highlight your poor performance."

Hughes responded with a taunt. "You mean I'm not making the minority quotas put out by HR."

Gwynneth said, "No. I haven't mentioned anything about racial or gender quotas because they're not used in this firm. And they're irrelevant to this discussion."

Norman Hughes was not enjoying listening to Gwynneth's points. His assessment was that she was too poised and well prepared to be intimidated. He was for the moment stumped about how to reply.

To keep her deliberate rhythm, she extended her next pause by picking up and glancing at her notes. "Moreover," she continued, "leaving aside your ignorance about our competitors' best practices, your behavior here is unprofessional. You know there are no personnel quotas at Scriptaphage, yet you trotted them out in January and again just now. There are consequences for unprofessional behavior in this directorate, especially for those drawing executive salaries."

Hughes frowned. He was unsure what Gwynneth meant by *consequences*.

"On one aspect of the business at hand, your turnover is higher than any other division in the monitoring directorate. Can you address your turnover problem?"

"None of these college kids wants to do any work. *That's* the problem, and —"

"No," she said, interrupting him. "No. That is not the problem." She took a light-blue sheet from her file folder and glanced at it. "This directorate's other divisions are hiring from the same labor pool as you and in the same metro area as you. Philadelphia."

"I do not need to be told where we are, thank you," said Hughes.

Gwynneth ignored the remark but looked again at the sheet of light-blue stationery. She said, "Their annual turnover levels are seventeen to eighteen percent, in line with the rest of our industry in the northeastern United States. Yours is about fifty percent."

She waited to be sure Hughes had heard her figures and that Barker had recorded them.

"And so your labor costs are higher than in other comparable divisions here. This came up in our meeting in January, and you rebuked me for suggesting that HR could help you improve your performance by lowering your labor charges.

"But the numbers tell us your recruiting, hiring, and training expenses are three times higher than others in this directorate. And you haven't taken a single action to curtail your excessive spending for these items."

She paused and in a softer but supportive tone asked, "Have you talked to HR about adjusting your hiring approach to cut your turnover costs? Can you say anything about this?"

Hughes growled his reply. It was another question. "What do *you* have to say about it?"

"Two things. First, I'd hoped you might describe the steps you've taken to lower your high turnover. Or tell us which managers you've talked to in the other divisions here, for example, who are doing well in the areas where you are underperforming. Or with HR. To hear their thoughts for improving —"

He interrupted her with another nasty blast. "I don't need any help from anyone."

Gwynneth nodded and continued. "And second, if you didn't want to seek help from HR or your colleagues, then perhaps consultants you might have brought in could've assessed why your staff expenses are astronomic —"

Hughes stood up from the sofa and towered over Gwynneth. "I do not have to listen to this from you. You are out of control." He cursed her and continued to stand over them.

She and Max watched his performance as if he were an untethered balloon exhaling its frantic way to the floor. Gwynneth sent a clear message with her composure that his loud histrionics did not scare or upset her. And while Max and Vance Barker blanched, they sat at ease, following Gwynneth's calm and unruffled example.

Gwynneth said, "General counsel is here to record our discussion."

Hughes heaved a noisy sigh. He took a few steps and stood behind the two-seat sofa, regarding the three others as if they were insidious microbes he needed to keep at a distance. "Sure. General counsel," he sneered. Another drop of moisture formed on his pale upper lip.

Gwynneth said, "Here is an important package for you, Dr. Hughes." She held out a sealed manila envelope. He did not reach for it. She put it down on the table near where he'd been sitting.

"This package includes a letter approved by the general counsel suspending you without pay for unsatisfactory performance, beginning now. The package contains a copy of AmeRxOne's and Scriptaphage's appeals procedures for your suspension. You may use either. And you may return to this building's security desk this evening after six o'clock for your personal belongings."

Norman Hughes attempted to regain his composure. "No," he said. "No. You can't just —"

"Yes. Yes, I can. I have. It's done, Dr. Hughes. You can take this package with you or —"

"*No.*" He jeered his reply.

They did not respond to his one-word outburst.

"Regardless of your choice, you'll need some help, starting now."

Gwynneth picked up her cell phone, awakened it, and sent a prepared text message to Jasmine Lugo, her administrative assistant, who was sitting at her desk just outside Gwynneth's office.

Seconds later, three security staff entered the office. The two men were each taller and heftier than Hughes. The woman was more sinewy but just as tall as her colleagues. All three wore white shirts, navy blazers, tan slacks, and black patent leather shoes.

"Thank you for being here," Gwynneth said to them. "We'll know in a moment how this suspension will proceed."

The security detail stood still, waiting.

Hughes shook his head and sighed. He walked around the sofa, picked up his package, and started to leave the office.

Gwynneth said, "Mr. Williamson will accompany you, Dr. Hughes. You will need his access card to use the elevator and to get into or leave the garage. Yours is inactive."

Hughes nodded. He took a step toward the door and then stopped, staring at Gwynneth. After a moment, he said, "If this is about my not meeting my racial and gender quotas, there is going to be trouble here."

Gwynneth said, "This is about overruns in labor costs due to turn-over and failures to keep current on best practices in our industry."

With a tilt of his head, Mr. Williamson stepped to the side of the table, where they all now stood. By a subtle turn of his shoulder and without touching Norman Hughes, Mr. Williamson encouraged him to continue on his way out of Gwynneth's office. The other two security officers followed behind them. Barker typed a few words into his laptop.

Gwynneth said to him, "Please let me know when you can send us a draft of your notes."

Barker stood. "By noon if I can get approval. Maybe later if I can't."

"You can text Ms. Gerhardt now and ask her where you can reach her later this morning. I assure you she's looking forward to reading your draft minutes and letting me see them before noon today."

After he left, Maxine said, "Please excuse my snarky comments earlier. This went well because it was managed as if it were another piece of important business."

They sat in silence for a few moments. Then Gwynneth said, "We all have lapses. The idea is to recover and do what's right."

"Where did you learn your choreography for this one?"

"I read case studies. I have allies in HR as well as mentors and friends. They've been generous with their time in the past few months. I'm having tea with Stanhope to review what's happened here today."

"What are you going to do about the mess in Hughes's division?"

"We're gonna get a wizard in there who can do the job."

"This morning?"

Gwynneth smiled and said, "No, but today we'll name an interim replacement for Hughes. Brigitte has to approve Barker's notes first."

Max nodded. "Can I ask something personal?"

Gwynneth looked at Max but said nothing.

"I've seen him destroy people who called him on his rudeness. Political incorrectness."

"Political correctness is a poor net for catching anything," Gwynneth said. "We keep to the business issues at hand. Do our homework. Take our mentors' counsel. Look for the win-win resolutions. And remember this isn't a sandbox in a playground. Our goal isn't to get everyone to play fair. It's business. And this was a team effort. Jasmine did most of the research in-house. She's studying computer science at night at La Salle. Did you know that about her?"

"Your admin guy?"

"Yes," said Gwynneth.

"No. Didn't know anything about her, but I just got here myself."

After a pause, Max asked, "Where'd you get the comps about staffing in other companies?"

Gwynneth twisted her lips into a smile that carried the message she wasn't going to divulge her sources. She said, "I have a couple of contacts. They're helping me with other stuff, too."

"What other stuff?"

"Pay comparability is one area. Best practices. And diversity is another. Not for fairness but for aligning us with our customers and other firms in the industry. And models for risk management in clinical trials. But I just got here, too. Finding my way."

"Yeah, well, I'm impressed. Everybody knew this had to be done, but no one ever did a single effective thing about Norman Hughes. Until this morning."

"No, not this morning. We were prepared before today. Jasmine Lugo compiled and arrayed most of the data. General counsel's suggestions were key to wrapping it up tight. And the tactics had to be tight. We needed to give Norman Hughes at least one other chance to tell us his plan for remedying his business shortfalls. These things take time and concentration and patience."

Max nodded. "All true," she said. "But we've had people in here who said they had all that, and they got nowhere. Because you also need the backbone to do it. And keep in mind, those spineless wonders are still here."

"OK, thanks. But I have a call to make before lunch, and I have to get at it."

Max said, "See you this afternoon."

TWENTY-SIX

MARCH 11

Next morning, Gwynneth was in her office early, preparing for chapter with Max, when Brigitte Gerhardt knocked on her open door.

"May I come in?"

"Of course. Good to see you," said Gwynneth, standing up to complete the formal welcome.

When Brigitte walked into the office, they greeted one another with firm handshakes. Brigitte wore a tailored blue suit whose cut veiled her stockiness. The pewter buckles on her shoes were clean and brushed but not shiny. Her stacked heels raised her height to five feet three inches, still two inches shorter than Gwynneth, who was wearing flats.

Gwynneth tilted her head to one side and gestured to a chair. Brigitte sat in it and said, "It's only seven thirty, and I've already had a bad day." She looked away, but Gwynneth could see she was upset.

Brigitte said, "I have enjoyed working here for many —"

Gwynneth interrupted. "You're not leaving?"

"No." Brigitte smiled and shook her head. "No. This could be an exciting time here."

"Exciting?"

"You know I read and approved Vance Barker's notes about your meeting with Norman Hughes yesterday. I told him to send you a copy."

189

"Yes. He sent the draft notes yesterday at noon, along with a note that you'd seen and approved them."

"Good." Brigitte stared at the table in front of her. "No one did squat to expose Norman Hughes's incompetence…" Her voice trailed off. Then she began again. "I need to restart that sentence. I did nothing to expose his incompetence and rudeness and unprincipled ways. That's how he lasted so long. We were bumblers, and we were afraid to do what we needed to do to hold him accountable."

Gwynneth said, "It was his supervisor's job to do that. Not yours."

Brigitte sighed and shook her head. "Well, his supervisor wasn't doing anything, and we were afraid to talk to his supervisor. Your predecessor, who —"

Gwynneth broke in, "It was his supervisor's job and the board's ethical —"

"Please don't interrupt. Please. I'm here to thank you for doing in less than three months what we couldn't or wouldn't do in four years. Maybe longer. We are in your debt. That's why I'm here this morning. To thank you."

Gwynneth paused for a moment. When it was clear Brigitte had finished her point, she said, "Well, Brigitte, I appreciate your taking the time to come here and say it. We're glad you can join us for chapter a few days a week. But you're the only one who's dropped by or even mentioned it."

Brigitte cursed and said, "I hope that's not right. I hope what you say is wrong." As her voice rose, she pronounced *what* with a soft Teutonic *v.* She took a breath and, lowering her voice, added, "I hope I'm just the first of many."

"We'll see about that. But from my viewpoint here, Norman Hughes was the first of many."

Brigitte raised her eyebrows.

"We have a few in this directorate who are bad for business. We've carried them for too long. We need data to address them and challenge them, just as we needed data to confront Norman

Hughes. And help from you to make sure it's done right. If we get our job done, we'll be a much stronger company later this year."

Brigitte sighed again and said, "I haven't said a word today about your pregnancy. You look fabulous, so I presume you're doing well?"

"Yes, so far," Gwynneth said. She swiped at her tablet and saw the time was nearing eight o'clock. "You started to say something else? About how you loved it here?"

"Yes. I still love it. My career has brought us a home in Chestnut Hill and great schools for our kids. My daughter is studying mathematics at Michigan. She's doing well. But now my son is in real trouble."

"Trouble?"

"Heinrich has done something. He won't say what. But the police have been to the house. It's real trouble, and I can't tell anyone what it is. Because…" Brigitte started to cry without sobbing. "Because I don't know what it *is*. How can you help someone in trouble if they won't tell you what's going *on*?"

Gwynneth nodded and kept still.

"I asked him again this morning, and he walked away. That's why today has started so…" Brigitte's voice trailed away as she fought back tears.

In a moment, she'd recovered some of her composure. "We didn't smother him. He did well in school. He was a tutor at the AME church in Mount Airy. He gets along with his father. But now he's fallen in with some unsavory men." She shook her head in confusion over her son's prospects and then retrieved a facial tissue from her jacket pocket. She dabbed her eyes.

Brigitte returned the tissue to her pocket. "Our therapist says it's his life and that he's responsible for what he does. And if he's not in school, we ought to ease him out of the house. He needs to be on his own."

Gwynneth was glad there was a sensible-sounding therapist helping with a difficult family situation. She felt no need to add a comment.

Brigitte sighed again and flicked away a few paper filaments her tissue had shed onto a pant leg. "And by the way…Vance Barker?"

Gwynneth nodded.

"I asked him to help with the Hughes meetings. He's stronger than he looks. He's an introvert. I've overheard some wisenheimers call him the secretary. But he's first rate. I think he's a fine emissary for the University of Tulsa."

Gwynneth continued listening with care. She was glad to hear a bit of praise for the general counsel's man Max had called a notetaker.

"Will he be acting as your deputy while Max is over here helping us?"

Brigitte was not prepared for a question and seemed distracted for a moment. "I'm sorry. You asked about Vance?"

"Will he be acting as your deputy?"

"Yes. No. He's not sitting in Max's office. He's not getting a promotion. But he's occupying her slot for a while. We'll see if he can handle it. Then maybe he'll move up."

They heard the sound of the outer office door opening. "Max is here," said Gwynneth.

"Good timing," said Brigitte. "If I'm not a mess?"

Gwynneth shook her head. "You look fine."

Max entered the office. "May I?"

"Yes," said Gwynneth. "Come on in. We're wrapping up."

"I came here to thank your boss for her work on the Hughes suspension."

Max smiled and nodded. "Yeah, well, she isn't into high fives. She's on to the next."

"Thanks again, Dr. Trevor. Well done." Brigitte made her exit.

Gwynneth said, "Chapter?"

Max and Gwynneth sat.

"Not much on the calendar today," Max said. "Did John Knowlton accept your offer to serve as interim for Hughes?"

TWENTY-SEVEN

MARCH 12–13

H enry's tattoo on Wednesday night brought him yet another unexpected message. After listening to the recording of tattoo and reciting his three compline psalms, he began his examination of conscience.

On January 1, 2014, he'd resolved to add to it an informal but deliberate review of twenty-three sections in book II, part I, title I of the *Code of Canon Law*, on the obligations and rights of all Christian faithful. Its canon 217 reaffirmed he was "to lead a life in keeping with the teaching of the Gospel." He devoted three weeks during his tattoo to pondering the question, *Am I leading a life in keeping with the* Gospel's *teaching?*

In the next portion, title II, he reflected on the obligations and rights of the lay Christian faithful. In early March, he examined the item requiring him "to imbue and perfect the order of temporal affairs with the spirit of the Gospel...especially in carrying out these same affairs and in exercising secular functions."

That particular item prompted thoughts about its meaning to him and Martin. He was puzzled during his March 12 tattoo to see law enforcement as a temporal affair in the spirit of the code and to realize his ego was open to considering anew Martin's request for a report of his mugging the previous June. During his examination of conscience, it became clear to him that Martin was right. It was a simple obligation of the lay Christian faithful to cooperate with him.

He took prompt action. At seven thirty on Thursday morning, March 13, he sent a text to Martin. "I'm ready to give you a report about June 18. Let me know a convenient place and time."

At seven thirty on Thursday morning, March 13, Martin and Ronald Sweeney were analyzing data compiled about physical evidence processed by the medical examiner's office. Martin glanced at his phone when it announced an incoming text. He was baffled as he read it.

"Trouble?" asked Sweeney.

"Henry says he's ready to give a report about his mugging last June. So no, it's not trouble."

Sweeney said, "Nine cursed months."

"So you're saying you had nothing to do with this?"

Sweeney projected his most innocent expression. "How could you suspect —"

"Answer," Martin snarled.

"No. Haven't spoken to the man. It's a shock. And it'll be an enjoyable shock if the perp is still around."

Martin said, "When will we finish here this morning?"

"Eleven thirty if we don't get —"

"Let's make sure we're done by then." Martin dictated his reply to Henry. "Foyer at 1589 Pine Street at noon?" He tapped Done to end his recording and then sent it.

Henry answered right away. "Noon at 1589."

It was a two-mile drive from the ME's office to Martin's place, a shorter commute for both the state police detectives and for Henry than the six miles plus to the Troop K barracks on Belmont Avenue. As he drove across the Schuylkill River on the South Street Bridge, Sweeney said, "This community on the right is the Devil's Pocket. Used to be a rough Irish working-class area."

Martin said, "The row-house owners are dying off. Now it's filling up with people who want to walk to work in Center City."

Sweeney nodded. He parked the car. When they entered 1589 Pine Street at 11:50 a.m., Henry was waiting for them. "My place or yours?" he asked.

Martin said, "Mine."

Sweeney and Henry followed Martin into his apartment. They sat down at his large, bare dining-room table while he powered up his laptop. "Coffee? Coke? Anything?" No one spoke in reply.

In a few moments, Martin asked Henry to look at a document on the computer screen. It was dated June 22, 2013. Martin had drafted it on a Saturday.

Henry read it and asked, "Is this what you're asking me to sign?"

Martin said, "The date'll be March 13, 2014, and yes, I'm asking you to sign it. But it has to be right. Everything. The Koosh ball, keys, knife, skull, all have to be right."

"There was a witness. Armando Beluga."

Sweeney stared at Martin, who explained, "He led the Bible study that night at the church on Eighteenth Street. I'll amend the report."

Henry gave him Armando's telephone number. Martin added Armando's name and telephone number to the report.

Then Martin took the laptop into another room. After a few seconds, they heard a laser printer lowing. Sweeney and Henry were still sitting at the table when Martin returned with two copies of the modified one-page report. He put them in front of Henry, who took out a pen and signed both. Then he asked, "That it?"

Martin nodded. Henry left.

After Martin scanned and made copies of the signed report, he and Sweeney went back to work.

TWENTY-EIGHT
MARCH 14

O n Fridays, Andre and Carmichael met to discuss ACI's business prospects. After their chat on March 14, Carmichael said, "On a separate matter, something's come up about Henry."

Andre blanched. "*Henry*? Has he sold a hundred million dollars in new —"

Carmichael interrupted, shaking his head. "No. Henry's stuck at twelve million dollars this fiscal year."

"Still, we hadn't expected —"

Carmichael cut in, "Agreed. His twelve million dollars in business with the bank has impressed everybody. Up from zero in sales last year. What's come up about Henry came in over the transom at home."

Andre sat back in his chair.

Carmichael said, "Gwynneth Trevor is tearing 'em up at Scriptaphage. She's got a small team of all-stars working for her. One is Maxine Palapye, the deputy under General Counsel Brigitte Gerhardt, who's assigned her to be Trevor's assistant. Trevor was troubled by an underperforming senior exec. Max, as she's known, told her boss, Gerhardt, about Trevor's plans to separate the guy."

Andre nodded.

"You're nodding. You've heard all this?"

"Not this level of detail," Andre said.

"All right. Gerhardt, the general counsel, talked to Trevor. She was pleased with Trevor's case. It was data based and well organized.

Its focus was on the business. Gerhardt suggested doing it in two stages several weeks apart and having one of her attorneys in on it."

"And?"

Carmichael canted his head. "Trevor checked with her mentor and then said OK."

"Do we know who her mentor —"

"Yeah, we do. It's Carmen Stanhope."

"That fits," Andre said. "Stanhope introduced Trevor to pharma world last summer."

"Right. Stanhope told me Trevor calls her twice a week. Stanhope's asked me not to say —"

Andre cut in. "Full disclosure? Stanhope talks to me too and asked *me* to keep it quiet."

Carmichael smiled and nodded.

Andre said, "This crowd came through your transom?"

"No. But it turns out that when Henry got mugged last year..."

Andre winced. It had taken Henry months to recover from a June 2013 beating. He said, "When he asked us about not reporting it to the police, we suggested he reconsider."

"Right, and when we did, he didn't mention it to us again."

Andre shrugged.

Carmichael said, "On a parallel track, Brigitte told Max all last year that she's worried about her son. She doesn't know who he's hanging with or what he's doing, and it's driving the parents nuts. Then this year, Trevor introduced Max to Stanhope over lunch. When Max heard them say Henry was recovering from last June's beating, her suspicion was that Heinrich Gerhardt might be involved. Max knew from Gerhardt that the police had been to the house. But you can't take suspicions to —"

Andre cut in. "So she went —"

"To a trusted friend. Antoinette Carmichael."

Andre shook his head. "Intriguing narrative."

Carmichael continued. "Max has been a virtual member of our family for about twenty years. She and Toni are fellow parishioners at Saint Thomas Episcopal Church on Lancaster Ave and she called Toni.

"Maxine was in a lather. Toni got her calmed down. They met last week."

"And?"

"And Toni told me that Trevor and Henry and two Gerhardts and Max could be connected somehow."

Andre said, "Right, 'could be.' But there are thousands of Gerhardts all over Philadelphia."

Carmichael shook his head. "Max told Toni the police came to Brigitte Gerhardt's place and told the kid they knew he was in on the mugging."

"But they needed Henry's signed statement to arrest him," said Andre. "So they had to wait."

"Right. That's what Toni's doing. We can, too. Maybe this'll get resolved without anyone's brilliant maneuvering."

Andre nodded and said, "Agreed. We wait."

"Another development. Henry and Gwynneth Trevor are now married."

Andre blinked.

Carmichael said, "Sharon Beyerly encouraged Henry to tell us he opted out of our health plan because he's getting health insurance through his spouse. He upped his retirement account contributions."

Andre said, "Our Comptroller is an all-star and protects employee confidentialty. When did Henry talk to you?"

"This morning. A JP married them March 1."

"Did he say anything more?"

Carmichael smiled and nodded. "They put a contract on a house off Antique Row, near Gwynneth's aunt and uncle's home."

"An intrepid couple makes some bold moves."

Carmichael said, "They've been talking to Stanhope and her husband about real estate. And Henry said, 'We're committed to each other. We're a family. The marriage was a formality that eliminates lots of complications.'"

"Complications," Andre repeated. "Who needs them?"

TWENTY-NINE

MARCH 15

At seven on Saturday morning, Sweeney and Martin met at the state police barracks on Belmont Avenue. Sweeney drove them to the Gerhardt residence on Crefeld Street. In the sunrise quiet, they approached the mansion and three-bay garage via its driveway, Sweeney in a dark-gray suit, French-blue shirt, and a yellow-and-black striped tie that highlighted his pale countenance. Martin wore a black suit and a light-gray tie that contrasted with his dark-skinned complexion. They both wore heavy black walking shoes.

Martin pressed the doorbell, activating as it had at their visit nine months earlier the first movement of Bach's Third Brandenburg Concerto. The recording stopped when Brigitte Gerhardt opened the door. She was wearing a pink fleece jacket, black sweatpants, and black Converse low tops.

Martin presented his identification and said, "Detectives Martin Perez and Ronald Sweeney, Pennsylvania State Police. Are you Mrs. Gerhardt?"

Brigitte nodded but did not examine their credentials.

"We have a warrant for Heinrich Gerhardt's arrest. Is he at home?"

Brigitte said, "I don't know." Then she added, "Come in. I'll see if he's in his room."

Martin and Sweeney crossed the threshold and stood at the edge of the large reception hall as they had on June 19, 2013. Two minutes later, Brigitte returned solo. She said, "He might be in the garage." She stood in front of them, unsure what to do.

Sweeney was the first to hear the hum of an electronic garage door opener. He opened the front door and scooted toward the driveway. Before following Sweeney, Martin asked Brigitte, "Is he armed?"

"I don't know. Maybe," she said, resting her face in her hands.

Martin tapped the holster on his right hip to feel the heft of his Glock and stepped outside. He told Sweeney, "His mother doesn't know if he's armed. She says maybe. Careful here."

Sweeney said, "Yeah. Careful." His sidearm was a Taurus Raging Bull with a two-and-a-quarter-inch barrel. Its .454 Casull cartridges had more stopping power than Martin's Glock Gen4, and the weapon was a match for any perp's sidearm. Sweeney touched it to verify the safety was engaged.

Heinrich emerged from the shadows of the leftmost garage bay into the early-morning light. He was wearing a camo hoodie, and his hands were in its pockets. His facial expression showed surprise but neither fear nor evasion.

They moved apart, Martin sidestepping toward the driveway and Sweeney toward the front corner of the mansion. In three seconds, they were ten yards apart. Heinrich, now positioned between them, the trio forming a triangle, seemed impressed by the ploy, as if it were a clever move in a game. He turned his head from Sweeney to Martin and then back to Sweeney.

Sweeney said, "We have a warrant for your arrest, Heinrich. Let us see your hands."

Sweeney's comments seemed to amuse Heinrich. He smiled for a moment and then slipped his empty hands out of his pockets and let them fall to his side. As he did, he said, "I'm not talking to you."

To reassure Heinrich, Sweeney said, "You don't have to talk to us or anyone else."

Heinrich seemed relieved to hear Sweeney's response. He told the detectives, "I hafta close the garage door. Then I'll come with you."

Sweeney hesitated, but before he spoke, he glanced at Martin, who said, "No. I'll close it."

Heinrich, his demeanor tranquil and agreeable, said, "OK. Switches are on the left side. Use the top one, and mind the electric eye."

Martin hustled toward the open garage. He spotted the switches, reached in, pressed the top one, and then removed his arm, keeping it close to the door rails so as not to activate the safety beam. They listened to the garage door's motor and chain hum and rattle. A few seconds later, the door closed with a soft thud.

In a casual, unemotional tone that suggested they might be taking a trip to New York, Heinrich said, "OK. Let's go."

They marched him toward the street, Sweeney holding Heinrich's left upper arm. Martin, vexed that Sweeney hadn't frisked or handcuffed him, walked close behind them. Using his right hand, Heinrich took his cell phone from his shirt pocket and showed it to Sweeney. "Can I call my mother? Tell her where we're going?"

Sweeney nodded and told him their destination. Heinrich spoke into his cell phone. "They're taking me to their barracks, 2201 Belmont Avenue."

Martin frisked and cuffed Heinrich before securing him behind the steel cage of their patrol unit. They drove to the barracks, where they booked him for assault and assault with a deadly weapon. A young woman, perhaps on call from the Gerhardt family law firm, waited for them as they photographed and fingerprinted him. The lawyer posted bond and drove Heinrich home.

As they were finishing the paperwork, Sweeney said, "Mighta been a mistake not to cuff him or stop him when he grabbed his cell phone. Mighta done that because he's rich and white."

Surprised at Sweeney's clumsy apology, Martin nodded to acknowledge it and then said, "I'm not gonna report you. Glad he wasn't shot and killed when he came out of the garage."

"You mean if he was black, I would've shot him? Don't you ever let up?"

"I mean I'm glad we got him arrested and booked without any drama."

Later on Saturday, they called Armando Beluga, then went to see him. With Sweeney sitting on an adjacent folding chair in the living room of Armando's group house, Martin took the lead on speaking with the old man about the events of June 18, 2013.

Martin asked, "Can you tell us what you saw that night?"

Armando shook his head. "It was dark. Three or four men attacked Henry. But I didn't know that until later."

"Could you identify any of the assailants?"

"No," said Armando. "They were twenty or thirty yards away, and it was dark."

"Did you call anyone? Someone in the church or 911?"

Armando shook his head. "No. I was scared. And my phone was in my briefcase. By the time I put my cane down and unlatched the briefcase, the fight was over, and the hoodlums were gone."

Sweeney asked, "Could you recognize anyone's voice? Was anyone wearing an unusual coat or hat? Or carrying a weapon?"

Armando said, "I'm sorry, but I can't. It was so far away and so dark and —"

Martin said, "It's all right, sir. Hard to see much in the dark. Do you have any questions for us?"

"No. It's sad, but I don't have any answers or questions, either. But I'm glad to talk to you, to meet the police who arrested Henry's attacker."

Martin and Sweeney ended the interview.

THIRTY

APRIL 9–10

Early Wednesday morning, April 9, Gwynneth was in her office, editing her portion of a presentation her team was scheduled to deliver that evening. Her Drexel colleagues were finishing a four-month collaboration with a health care firm on growth strategies in global markets. Her segment examined research findings about how diversity improved sales teams' performance and profitability and ways C-level execs might support it.

After a morning of meetings with division directors in Scriptaphage's monitoring directorate, she caught the Market Street bus to Eighth Street, to the Penn Medical Center. At the OB-GYN clinic, she took the elevator to the fourteenth floor. The nurses regarded her protruding belly. One greeted her in Spanish with a smile and respectful nod: "*Senora.*" Gwynneth returned the smile.

In the examination room, Dr. Barbara Quinn told her, "Everything looks fine. Both your heartbeats are strong. And you're dilated a few centimeters. You can make an appointment to see me here, but the next time we meet it'll probably be in the delivery room."

Gwynneth was glad to hear the doctor's assessment and excited that the baby's birth was imminent. But she did feel overwhelmed by negative thoughts that streamed into her mind without ceasing. *You didn't check to see if those sleepers are fireproof. You don't know a single thing about taking care of a baby.*

Back in her office, she asked her Merry Godmother for a little assistance to stanch the river of bitter criticism her imagination pumped through her. *We've covered this*, said Merry Godmother. *Julian tells us, "All is well, and all will be well." Your mind is not your friend. Just do a good job on your presentation tonight.*

The reassurance brought her only temporary relief. Unable to think her way out of a bad mood, she called Henry and told him Dr. Quinn's good news. He said, "Glad to hear that others agree you've done a fabulous job caring for yourself and the baby." Then he added, "Can I get something for you this afternoon? Need anything at all?"

She challenged him to help her. "Got any non-Gospel, non-preaching ideas for shutting down streams of negative thoughts?"

Henry smiled but did not laugh into the phone. He said, "Yes. I invite the voice in and —"

"In where?" Gwynneth spat.

"It's all imagined. May I finish?"

"Sorry. Go ahead."

"I say, 'Tell me more,' whether it's negative ideas about a client, my future, or whatever. I show I'm listening by putting my arm around its imaginary shoulder, as if I'm comforting a nephew, and ask, 'Can you say more about that?' It takes five seconds and almost always stills the voice. When the voice returns, I just repeat the lines."

Gwynneth was quiet on the phone. Then she said, "Thanks, Henry. I'll let you know how it works."

"All right, then. Hit a home run tonight for your team."

Gwynneth stopped at home, where she resisted an insane urge to scrub the kitchen floor. She said to the lunatic voice, "Tell me more about the floor." When the voice withdrew, she smiled, cursed at the line's success, and took a nap.

That evening, Gwynneth and her team responded as Drexel classmates and faculty peppered them with questions on their assumptions, data, and conclusions about diversity. It seemed to her the questions were more adversarial than they needed to be. And although she kept her composure, she did push back at one corporate exec by asking, "What's your experience in sales? Have you sold anything in any foreign market?"

The pestering exec was still.

She softened her tone and said, "Let's remember we're supposed to be collaborating on this issue and improving your prospects in foreign markets. Do you think it's a good business strategy to take a sales team made only of white men into *any* international market? Or even a local, regional, or domestic market? The research says no."

Her question had been proffered in a quiet voice and with a nod, showing everyone her question was a sincere one. The corporate exec blushed and confessed he hadn't served on any sales team anywhere. And again, Gwynneth let a cordial nod be her only reply. The facilitator thanked the team for its good work.

Although she'd had a long and active day, Gwynneth felt energized and hoped she'd be able to sleep. While in the cab that sped her homeward via South Street at eight o'clock, she called Henry to tell him her presentation had gone well.

He again offered to do anything he could for her, and again she turned him down. "I need to get to bed," she said. "That's something I can do by myself. But here's an update. Today I asked a lunatic voice to tell me more about it, and the voice went away. So...thanks. I'll talk to you tomorrow."

At six the next morning, April 10, Gwynneth imagined herself in shallow water, swimming to the hospital to have a baby. She was disoriented as she gauged whether she was asleep and dreaming or awake and in distress. She decided she was awake. She wasn't in distress, but her amniotic sac had ruptured, and she'd released some of its fluid.

Lying in the wetness, Gwynneth reached for her cell phone and called Henry. "Hi. Sac burst. We need to get to the hospital pronto. Can you come in a cab?"

Henry, awake and alert, said, "Yes. On my way. Call you soon."

Within three minutes, he'd dressed, hustled down to Pine Street, and hailed a cab. As the driver neared Gwynneth's, he called to tell her he was a minute away. She said she'd stay in her bedroom.

When the cab arrived at 1110 Clinton, Henry asked the driver to wait for them. That the cabbie was willing to do it was a stroke of good fortune.

Henry used his key to unlock the front door and raced up the stairs. She was standing next to the bed, holding her long woolen winter coat.

She said, "The fluid soaked my clothes and wet the sheets. Maybe the mattress pad."

He helped her into her coat. She put her phone into the outside pocket of a small bag she'd packed for a quick, unexpected getaway. As they eased down two flights of stairs, he said, "We're close to the hospital, and a cab is waiting. We take our time on these stairs."

A minute later, they were in the warm taxi. Henry asked about her insurance card.

"Same pocket as the phone," she said with a gasp. Then, splayed out in the back seat of the cab, Gwynneth announced with loud groans her first labor pain.

She called and left a message at Dr. Quinn's office.

"Hi. Gwynneth Trevor. Six fifteen a.m., Thursday, April 10. Water broke this morning. In a cab on my way to the hospital." She ended the call and wedged the cell phone back into its pocket. Henry patted her hand to show he admired her clear message and control in delivering it.

The cab driver knew it was just a short hop down Clinton to the Pennsylvania Hospital campus. But the hospital occupied an entire city block, and their destination was the ER entrance on Spruce between Eighth and Ninth Streets. The neighborhood's one-way streets extended their trip to seven blocks.

When he stopped the cab at the ER entrance, the driver looked into his rearview mirror and caught Henry's eye. "It's thirteen fifty including waiting time." Henry gave him a twenty-dollar bill and thanked him.

He helped Gwynneth out of the cab. Then, with no one in sight, he commandeered an idle wheelchair, put her in it, and rolled her into the ER. A triage nurse sitting on a tall stool at the edge of a reception desk took in Gwynneth's pregnant belly. She picked up her electronic tablet and asked, "Doctor?"

"Dr. Barbara Quinn. She knows I'm —"

"Insurance card?"

Gwynneth handed it to her.

The triage nurse's questions sounded curt, but her expression was pleasant. Her short blond hair was brushed back at the temples, and her ruddy complexion suggested she ran or played tennis outdoors to keep herself trim. She wore no makeup or jewelry other than an analog watch with a sweep second hand and an ancient leather band. She was dressed in green scrubs and silver New Balance walking shoes with blue trim and laces. When she rested her right foot on a rung of her stool, the *N* on the outer surface of her shoe looked like a *Z*.

As her well-tended but unpolished nails skipped over her tablet, recording Gwynneth's information, she asked, "You feeling well enough to take a little ride to obstetrics? It'll be about five minutes."

Gwynneth nodded.

"Good. Looks as if you're in for an exciting day." As she spoke to Gwynneth, the nurse printed out Gwynneth's information onto a stiff white cardboard strip, folded it in half, and slipped it into the window of a red plastic ID bracelet. She used a clamp to lock it onto Gwynneth's wrist and then asked, "Your first?"

Gwynneth nodded again.

The nurse spoke in an serious but soft tone. "You're in the best place in the world you can be. The best. We've been delivering babies for two hundred and sixty-three years, and we're gonna take good care of you today." Then, to get Gwynneth off to obstetrics, she called to a man standing nearby. "Conrad?"

A thin black man almost a foot shorter and thirty years older than Henry approached them. He wore maroon hospital fatigues and white running shoes. His two-by-four-inch Lucite photo ID frame hung from a stout black fabric lanyard. Two access cards were attached to the lanyard with thin, red carabiner-style clips. Below his photograph, a dark-brown plastic nameplate displayed the hospital logo next to CONRAD imprinted in white capital letters. His fatigue top was draped with earbuds and a thin white wire that dangled near a cell phone clipped to his belt. He might have been the best-equipped hospital orderly in the place.

"You can just leave her in that stolen vehicle, Conrad," the triage nurse said with a smile. Then, holding her smile, she said to Henry, "Conrad will take over the navigation from here, Mr. Trevor. He knows the way to get your wife into safe and capable hands."

Henry, not inclined to correct her about his name, said, "Good. Thanks."

In the next few minutes, Henry followed Conrad as he pushed Gwynneth down a maze of corridors. He used one access card to unlock doors to an adjoining wing in the hospital and a different card to open the doors to an elevator. As they rode it to obstetrics admitting, Henry stood next to Gwynneth, his hand resting on her shoulder. He let his hand fall away when the elevator doors glided open. Conrad wheeled her into the hallway toward an open area in front of them, where two nurses were at work.

One nurse saw them coming. She got up from her chair and motioned to Conrad to follow her into an examination room. Henry watched them pass behind opaque curtains of light-blue nylon hanging from stainless steel rods to within a foot of the floor.

In a few seconds, Conrad returned to the nurse's station with his empty wheelchair. The two men stood in the quiet and unoccupied hallway, relieved Gwynneth was no longer in their custody but under the care of the obstetric staff. After a moment, Conrad took a breath. He lifted the front wheels of the vacant wheelchair with his hand and right foot, spun it 180 degrees and, on his way back to the elevator, said to Henry, "Have a nice day."

After Conrad's departure, Henry approached the other nurse, who was typing at a keyboard. When she looked up at him, he said, "I have Gwynneth Trevor's cell phone and purse. May I leave all this with you, or do I hang on to them...or what?"

The nurse pulled a large clear plastic bag from a dispenser underneath the counter and told him to put whatever he wanted to leave for her in the bag. She returned to her typing, sending him a message that his presence was not critical to her getting her job done just then.

Henry hesitated. The nurse said, with a hint of compassion, "That's how we handle it. It's safe to leave it with us, and she'll need the phone to contact you and —"

A series of sharp, loud bursts from a wall-mounted horn exploded into the corridor, accompanied by a voice broadcasting an announcement Henry couldn't understand. The nurse brought her short narrative to an abrupt end. She pushed herself away from her computer keyboard and marched down the hallway. Without breaking stride in the fluorescent gloom, she veered toward a wall-mounted dispenser to anoint and massage her palms with hand sanitizer before disappearing into an adjacent corridor.

Henry put Gwynneth's stuff into the bag she'd offered him and then sat in a plain, brown, hard-bottomed folding chair a few feet away. The cold seat chilled his butt and thighs. The light fixtures buzzed from time to time. The combination of the chair and the bright lights reminded him of the first time his father had taken him to Shea Stadium, when they'd sat in the bleachers in the wind and cold on opening day to see the Mets play the visiting Phillies. In the fourth inning of a tie game, it had begun to snow.

He retrieved his cell phone and pulled up the line score of Wednesday night's Mets game: Atlanta 4-NYM 3. He shrugged and pocketed the phone.

Ten minutes later, the first nurse returned and slipped a card into an envelope of the heavy-duty plastic bag holding Gwynneth's cell phone and purse. She added Gwynneth's clothing and shoes.

She picked up the cradle to her telephone and spoke into it. Her remarks were not audible. Two minutes later, a woman in scrubs came out of the elevator, walking at a rapid pace toward the nurse's station.

As the woman in scrubs reached them, the nurse at the desk said to Henry, "Your wife is OK. She's just started labor, so she's gonna be here awhile. Right now we're tending to an emergency with another patient."

Henry was grateful to know Gwynneth wasn't the subject of this particular emergency.

"Dr. Quinn has your telephone number," she said.

That's good to know, Henry thought. *If it's true.*

The nurse and the woman in scrubs hustled down the corridor.

Henry recalled from his sister and brother-in-law's experiences at the Virginia Hospital Center that as the father, he might not draw any attention or get any information from anyone in the Obstetrics Department for several hours. He took the elevator down to Spruce Street and walked toward 1110 Clinton.

On the way, he called Maria Irizarry to tell her Gwynneth was in labor. Maria was thrilled to hear her niece was at the hospital.

Then Henry asked, "Can we wash the bed linens in the second-floor washer?"

Maria told him no, that she'd take care of it.

Henry said, "I'm leaving the hospital now and can be at your place in five minutes. Maybe we could both —"

"Yes, Henry, thank you," she said.

When he arrived at 1110 Clinton, they stripped the bed and carried the soiled linens down to the first floor, where Maria loaded them into a commercial-size washer and said, "I'll put these back on the bed before lunch."

While the washer filled with water, Henry recorded a text and sent it to Gabriella, his sister; Sonia, Gwynneth's mother; and May Kim, their friend. "Gwynneth in Pennsylvania Hospital obstetrics in early labor and in good hands."

He walked home, showered, changed into work clothes, and then went to his office. Michael Larson was at the office waiting for him. After a cursory early-morning greeting he asked Henry, "Ever been obsessed with a woman?"

Henry, surprised by the blunt query, stopped and made full eye contact before answering. "Sure. It was a big distraction." He noted but said nothing about the energetic presence of the handsome young black man.

Michael shook his head. "It's not just a distraction. It's a tsunami. It overwhelms whatever I'm doing."

Henry waited. Michael's facial expression and erect stance sent a message that he was eager to say more. Henry waited for him to continue.

"I've been attracted to women before, but this is crazy different."

Henry nodded.

"Thinking about or wanting to be with someone who's *ordinary*." Michael seemed exasperated that he was describing the object of his interest as ordinary. Henry frowned at the word.

Michael replied to the frown without sarcasm. "Ordinary. Ordinary means not a movie star or a celebrity or majorly rich. Another female working in the city, not a perfect body or giant intellect."

"Can you say who this is?"

"Susan Hazari."

Henry smiled. "Yeah. Susan Hazari."

"Anything in your Gospel about whether I need an MBA to ask her to dinner?"

"No. It's nowhere else either. Is it a problem for you?"

Michael glared at him as if it was an insulting question.

"All right then. If it's not a problem, ask her. Or we can invite both of you to dinner if you want to meet her at a small gathering. I'll talk to Gwynneth. She's mentioned others she wants to invite."

"That's a righteous offer, Henry. You guys must be wicked-busy with jobs and the baby coming. I appreciate your listening to me."

Later, from seven thirty until noon, Henry finished a draft report for the Broad Street Bank. He updated Stanhope about Gwynneth and handed her the draft.

After a pause, she said, "Listen, Henry. This is your time to be with Gwynneth and the baby. Trust me, they want you there with them. It's your most important business now. Come back to work after Easter."

The first workday after Easter was Monday, April 21, eleven days away. Henry thanked her for her counsel.

When he returned to 1110 Clinton, it was after one o'clock. Maria had remade Gwynneth's bed. Henry vacuumed the bedroom floor and emptied the wastebasket. Then he walked back to the hospital.

THIRTY-ONE
APRIL 10, 6:00 P.M.

G abriella Knudsen Mendoza, Henry's sister, arrived in Philadelphia at six o'clock on Thursday evening. From the stretch of Market Street west of Thirtieth Street Station where her Megabus disgorged its passengers, she took a cab to Gwynneth's place on Clinton Street. After greeting Maria and Bennie, she dropped her small overnight bag in a vacant bedroom on the third floor and walked the four blocks to the hospital.

During her walk, Gab called Henry. Her call went to voice mail. She left a message, telling him she was in town and on her way to visit Gwynneth.

Gwynneth's room was obscured by the door the nurses had left ajar to keep her out of view of passersby in the hallway. Gab knocked on the doorjamb.

"*Hola, mi hermana,*" she said, greeting her sister-in-law Gwynneth in Spanish. "*Soy yo, Gabriella Knudsen Mendoza, aquí para visitarlo a usted y a su bebé.*"

From inside the room, Henry said, "Come in."

Gab pushed the door open. When she saw no bed in the room, she gasped.

Henry was seated upright in a large faux-leather recliner. It also folds out into a single-size sleeping contraption, suitable for a visitor staying overnight with a hospital patient. Sitting up and holding his seven-hour-old son in a yellow woolen baby blanket, Henry said, in a normal adult-to-adult tone but at lower volume, "This is Gabriella. She's my sister and your aunt."

Gab said, "Henry, where's Gwynneth?"

Addressing his son, Henry said, "Excuse me a sec, Gabriel." Then he said to Gab, "They rolled her down to radiology to get a sonogram. Radiology's in the basement here. That was an hour ago. Dr. Quinn wants to measure echogenic material in the uterine cavity. She said it's probably not a problem, but the amniotic sac ruptured early, and there was less uterine bleeding than usual during delivery. The doctor wants to check those out. They'll be back soon."

Gabriella nodded. "He's beautiful, Henry. He's dark, eh?"

Henry said to the baby. "You're one dark and beautiful lad, Gabe. Two hours ago, your face was redder, and your nose was flatter, but now you're just one beautiful baby."

Gabriella and Sergio had three children. Laura was light skinned. She looked Scandinavian. Lukas was as dark skinned as his father. Kevin, their youngest, was a swarthy-tawny hybrid.

Gab said, "And his eyes are open."

Henry looked over at his sister. "Gwynneth would ask you to wash your hands, please, in the sink there, and then, if you want, you can hold the baby. He's not even eight hours old."

As Gab slipped over to the sink, she said, "I called you from that excuse for a bus depot by the train station."

"I'm in airplane mode here so this gizmo doesn't awaken Gwynneth." He tilted his head toward his left front trouser pocket. "Or Gabriel, either. Did you see his full head of hair?"

Gab turned on the left faucet and waited for the water to get hot. She soaped, rinsed, and dried her hands. When she was finished, Henry got up from the recliner and handed the baby to her. She walked across the room to the window behind the recliner, humming to Gabriel.

"Can I look at his wrist?" she asked.

Henry blinked and then pointed to the recliner. "Why don't you put him here? You can unwrap him and look at the whole package.

And his name is on his wrist-band but you can ask me if you want. The print's small."

Gab looked at her brother and shook her headful of shoulder-length blond hair. She resumed humming the lullaby to the baby and said to Henry, "The hair is impressive. Have you seen the fingernails?"

"Yeah. When we counted his ten fingers and ten toes." He paused and then said, "Maybe all new parents say this, but he's already a miracle. We're lucky he's healthy. We're lucky Gwynneth had an easy time of it. She was a little scared about her water breaking. But still, just a few hours old, and he's a complete and unabridged miracle."

Gab kept humming to the baby.

A moment later, Henry said, "I want you to know we appreciate your dropping everything to be here with us and your nephew. I'm glad to see you. Gwynneth will be *ecstatic* to see you. We weren't sure when you'd be able to get away."

He stopped his verbal thank-you and changed the subject, asking, "Is that how you sang to Laura?"

"Yes," she answered, suspending her lilt for a moment. Then, turning her attention away from Henry, she said to Gabriel, "And to Lukas and to Kevin and now to you." She ended the lullaby with "the sweetest little baby in town."

They heard the soft chime of an elevator announcing its arrival on their floor. A moment later, a man about twice Conrad's size pushed Gwynneth and her bed into the room.

She saw Henry standing there but not the baby. Before she could react, he pointed behind him to Gab, holding Gabriel.

"Oh, Gab. *Gab.*" Gwynneth said, overjoyed to see her holding the baby.

The orderly swung Gwynneth's bed so its head met a wall of tubes and electrical connections. Then he repositioned two IV towers near the headboard.

Gab said, "Henry, take the baby." After the handoff, she leaned over the side of Gwynneth's bed. Without speaking, she rested her head on Gwynneth's shoulder and embraced the new mother with care, avoiding her stitches and tender loins. Gwynneth's arms rose and wrapped around Gab, holding her tightly in an intense and energetic hug.

A nurse announced her presence with her squeaky footwear on the room's clean floor. "I'm here to reinsert your IV drips and reconnect your monitors," she said. "It'll only take a minute."

Gab moved away from the bedside, watching the nurse's sure hands reinsert the drips into the ports on Gwynneth's arm. When the nurse reconnected the monitors, they chirped to announce they were on duty. Then, satisfied all the tubes were in place, the nurse looked at Gab and asked, "Need anything?"

Gab asked, "Me? Do *I* need anything?"

The nurse said, "There's bottled water at the nurse's station. And juices. Sandwiches in the refrigerator in the staff lounge just behind us. Help yourself to whatever you want. Ice cream is in the vending machines up on the sixth floor."

Gab thanked her in idiomatic Spanish. Surprised by the gringa's reply, the nurse blushed and smiled as she started out of the room.

Gwynneth also thanked the nurse, in a voice somewhat thick with a combination of fatigue and a residue of her epidural anesthetic. Then she said to Gab, "Everyone here's been good to me and the baby."

Gab asked, "Will they come for him and keep him in the nursery for the night?"

"Yes," Henry answered. "They keep all the infants overnight, but otherwise we can have him here as long as we want. At least I think that's what they told us. But we've only been here a few hours and don't know the drill."

"What about feeding?" Gab asked.

"I tried nursing him at four this afternoon," Gwynneth said. She sighed. "He didn't seem to get enough to eat, so we supplement my milk with the hospital's formula."

"Good idea," Gab said. "It's OK to relax and enjoy your time with your baby. If breastfeeding works, fine. If not, that's also fine."

Gwynneth lowered her head onto her pillow and sighed again.

Gab said, "Considering what you've been through, you look great."

Gwynneth bit her lip in appreciation for the remark. She said, "Thanks for all you've done, Gab, and for your love and support all these months. For being here now. So happy to see you here, holding Gabe. To see you and Henry holding him."

To give Gwynneth time to herself with Henry and the baby, Gab left the hospital. Following their directions, she walked down to the Whole Foods Market on South Street for zucchini, apples, crunchy peanut butter, a sourdough boulé, and a rotisserie chicken. She brought the groceries back to the Clinton Street house.

She took a shower, dressed, retrieved her overnight bag, and returned to the hospital. Gwynneth was propped up in her bed, holding Gabe and talking to him. She stopped talking when Gab knocked on the doorjamb to announce herself.

"I talked to Laura for months. When Sergio overheard me, he asked, 'Why are you talking to her if she can't understand a word you're saying?'"

Gwynneth was relieved to hear the story.

"I told him I wanted Laura to hear my voice. To hear the different cadences and tones of Spanish and English."

Gwynneth asked, "You spoke both at home?"

"Yes. Might've helped. No evidence it hurt anyone's language skills. They drive us crazy with other stuff."

Gwynneth laughed. "And when they drive you crazy?"

"You remember these days, when you loved them with abandon. Because their naked butts fit in the palm of your hand. They needed everything and relied on you to supply it. They listened and didn't talk back."

Gabe stirred as May rapped on the door four times with her familiar "Shave and a Haircut" cadence.

"Oh, May, come on in." Gwynneth said. "Meet Gabriella and little Gabe."

May strode into the room and put her coat and bag next to the recliner. She washed and dried her hands, and when Gab stood and extended her arm to greet her with a handshake, May slipped by it and gave her a tender but full embrace, which Gab returned. "I've heard about you for months, Gab. Glad to meet you in person."

Gabriella knew from Henry's description that May was tall, athletic, and gorgeous, but she was even more impressed to watch her put one knee on the hospital room floor and lean her head on Gwynneth's hip bone, away from her tender belly and the infant.

"I see you and the baby are well." May reached for Gwynneth's hand and gave it a firm squeeze. Their clasped hands shared the same coffee-color shade of deep brown. When she stood, she kept her eyes on Gwynneth, ignoring the bits of dust on the knee of her woolen pants.

"Where's Henry?" May asked.

Gwynneth said, "He's meeting my parents at the train station and getting them settled at Maria's."

Gab was surprised at May's attentiveness to them. After May's long flight from London and the ordeal of customs, she'd expected her to report on the trials of her long day, a seven-hour flight, the five-hour time difference, or the eleven-mile taxi ride into town. Yet after embracing Gab, May's earnest focus was on the baby and Gwynneth.

THIRTY-TWO

APRIL 10, 10:00 P.M.

Henry got home at ten o'clock Thursday night. As he sorted through his mail, Martin came down the hall from his apartment and asked, "How's everything?"

"I'm a little tired now, but April tenth has been a fabulous day, Martin. Gwynneth gave birth today around noon. She is healthy and tired and happy, and the baby is fine."

Martin smiled. "Congratulations on the healthy mother and child."

Henry sensed Martin had something else to say, so he took his time verifying that each piece of mail was junk. When he pitched them one at a time into the empty blue recycle bucket, each landed with a *thunk*. When he finished, he stood there holding one single piece of mail, a bank statement. He gazed at Martin, waiting.

Martin said, "What's the baby's name?"

Henry hesitated, stunned at the reality of hearing for the first time a question about his own son.

"Maybe that's none of my business, and I shouldn't have asked you."

Henry shook his head. "No. It's an honor to hear the question. And I'm glad you asked it, and it *is* your business. The baby's name is Gabriel. Gabriel Trevor Knudsen."

Martin nodded and smiled. "Gabriel. Strong angel in the Christian and Islamic traditions." He was quiet for a moment. "But it's late, so good night, Henry."

"Yeah, good night, Martin." But neither man moved away from the alcove toward hall or stairs.

Martin's look was stern as he asked, "It *is* late, and I'll let you go, but what did you say about the baby's name? That it *is* my business? Were those the words you used?"

"Those are close enough to what I said, yes."

"And? Do you want to say just a few words about —"

Henry was not exasperated, but in a calm tone, he said, "Martin, you've been cordial and supportive to me since the first day I rang your doorbell. You've been more a friend than just a landlord. When I came home mugged and confused —"

Martin broke in. "Yeah. I remember. I was concerned about you when you called me late that night."

"And you were patient with me all those months we disagreed about the guys who beat me that night and —"

Martin cut in again. "We're past that now." He was shaking his head, as if confused about why Henry was belaboring their differences.

Henry pressed on. "You've been kind and have watched out for Gwynneth when she visited me here. And we've both seen you in public in the company of Barbara Quinn. I'm sure you know she's Gwynneth's obstetrician."

Martin nodded.

Henry went on. "We've had more than just a casual landlord-and-tenant connection here in the last ten months."

Henry paused for a moment. Martin was still unsure where Henry was carrying the conversation, but he didn't tell Henry to get to the point. He waited.

"We were different when we met, and we have more sharp differences between us now."

Martin pulled back, his expression simulating surprise. He said, "Different? You and me? Mercy."

Henry smiled. "There's a good example of what I mean. We have accord on the gaps between us, and you treat them as unimportant whenever they come up. You look for a patch of common ground to stand on and salute one another. These differences…" He paused to consider what he was going to say. "These differences between us? I've seen smaller differences alienate and separate long-term friends. But it's just not happening between you and me."

Martin said, "*You're* one to talk. You still treat me with respect even though you think I'm a fascist police state booster."

"Ugh…and no, man. If I thought that about you —"

Martin interrupted. "Hold up," he said. "Hold up. That was hyperbole. OK? I believe in the rule of law. Some left-wingers think that makes me a —"

Henry shook his head and said, "Many people think I'm a libtard socialist do-gooder. Only the ones who stick around long enough to talk to me and listen to me know that isn't so. And…can I add?"

Martin nodded and waited.

"I don't discuss serious matters after sundown. By then my wits have left me, my energy's down, my listening's flawed. And I'm still here, delirious with joy over Gabe and Gwynneth, standing here on tired feet holding up tired legs, talking with you because I make exceptions for people who are important to me. You are one of those people."

Martin gazed at him with a look that conveyed his thanks and showed he was touched by Henry's heartfelt remarks.

Henry, in appreciation for Martin's nonverbal reply, said, "That's why I didn't tell you, 'Look, Martin, I've had a long day. Good night.' And why I'm still here, doing my little skit."

Martin smiled at his use of the word *skit*. He didn't think Henry was acting, but he did think he might not be finished. So they spent a few relaxed moments waiting for Henry's narration to resume or settle.

Martin broke the easy silence in the alcove. "Yeah, well, it's late, and we should both be on our way. But I appreciate what you've said."

Henry made two replies.

The first was spoken. "Right. Good night."

The second was to lean in as if to shake his hand, but instead he half-embraced their clasped hands, pressed his right chest to Martin's right chest, and touched the stockier man's broad back with his left hand. The gesture was a common intimacy between men who considered themselves close. Martin responded in kind.

After a second, they disengaged. Then, without further words, they went their separate ways, their friendship deeper and truer than when they'd first met in the foyer that night.

THIRTY-THREE

APRIL 11

At noon on Thursday, Andre Morneau and Dave Carmichael walked nine blocks to visit Gwynneth and the baby. The two men, who considered themselves cosmopolitan and who'd parented seven children between them, gawked at each other as they strode through the hospital lobby in their dark wool business suits.

Andre asked, "Who are we looking for here? Do we have a name we can give?"

Carmichael nodded as they approached the patient information desk. "Stanhope said to ask at patient information for Gwynneth Trevor."

Ten minutes later, they'd found her room. It was abuzz with the chatter of four women standing near Gwynneth, who lay in bed. As they entered, Carmichael greeted Maxine Palapye and May Kim.

Carmichael said, "Hi, Max." Then, turning to Andre, he said, "Maxine Palapye has been a friend of our family for...twenty years, is it, Max?"

Max said, "It's been about that, Dave."

"Max is the deputy general counsel at Scriptaphage."

Andre reached across the space between them. He and Max shook hands, the first of many handshakes and nods.

May welcomed the two men and introduced them to Gwynneth, Gab, Jasmine Lugo, and Sonia Trevor. Sonia looked happy to be holding her grandson.

May said, "Sonia is Gwynnie's mother." It was the first time Gab had heard Gwynneth called by anything other than her full given name.

Sonia was in her early fifties, darker skinned than her daughter, and a petite five feet two inches tall. She wore a turquoise-colored pantsuit and black flats and held Gabe with the ease of an experienced grandmother. She showed little interest in the others' small talk about where Henry and her own husband had gone to eat or the weak cell phone signal in the room or anything else. Her attention was riveted on Gabriel.

May added, "Jasmine works at Scriptaphage with Max and Gwynnie."

Carmichael waited for a break in the chatter and said to Gwynneth, "Well, we can't stay. We wanted to stop by to say hello and congratulate you." He did not move.

Andre said, "Glad to see everyone is well, especially you, Gwynneth, and the baby." He turned and started out of the room. Carmichael followed him. None of the women objected to their departure.

As they passed through the doorway into the hall, they met a dark-skinned black man in his late fifties and a younger white man. They nodded at one another.

The man gave his name. "I'm Martin Perez, Henry's friend. And this is my associate, Detective Ronald Sweeney, Pennsylvania State Police. We stopped by to visit Gwynneth and Henry and the baby." Martin and Sweeney wore creased khakis, white button-down dress shirts, and shined leather shoes.

Carmichael introduced himself and Andre. "We work with Henry. He's out of the office today." He tilted his head toward the doorway to Gwynneth's room and added, "We were told he's having lunch at Smokin' Betty's with Cedric Trevor, Gwynneth's father. But it looks as if they're comin' down the hall here."

Andre added, "Already a full house in there. Gonna get crowded now."

Martin and Ronald thanked them and went in to greet Gwynneth and the baby. Henry and Cedric Trevor followed the two police officers into Gwynneth's room.

When the four men entered, the room's atmosphere changed from cozy and animated to cramped and silent. Jasmine greeted Henry by name, and he returned the greeting, adding, "Jasmine and I are in a street seminary studying the Bible." Gwynneth and Max frowned and shrugged at one another. Neither had heard of that connection.

Then Gwynneth said, "Oh, Martin…come in, come *in.*"

Martin introduced Ronald Sweeney, who waved to the quiet assembly.

Happy to see Martin, Gwynneth stretched her arm to beckon him closer.

He edged toward her and gave her a gentle hug, mindful of stitches and the ordeal of childbirth, and then said, *sotto voce* and in Spanish, "*Que ambos sean muy felices toda su vida.*" It was an artful blessing with so many others present, not specifying who he meant when he wished *both* of them a happy life. Then, in English, he said, "We look forward to seeing you soon, dear. And we'll leave you to your family and friends."

Cedric Trevor was eager to leave the crowded premises, and, with a tilt of his head in Henry's direction, asked him to manage their escape. Henry complied, saying to Gwynneth, "We're going too, to show your father our new place."

The women were still as the four left the room.

After they left May asked, "And who is that?"

Gwynneth answered, "Martin is Henry's friend. He was just the landlord ten months ago, but —"

May cut in. "You told me about the landlord. He's your obstetrician's friend. Who's the younger guy?"

The women oohed at May's question, but even as Sonia's eyes shone the brightest, she said, "*¿No es un poco viejo para ti?*"

May said, "OK. He's a little older. But did you see his carriage? His vitality?"

Max shook her head and said, "*Lekgoa*, eh?"

May glared at her and said, "He's white in Tswana and in English, Max. No one missed that."

Gab said, "It's OK for a man to look alive, May."

They laughed as loving sisters might tease, but Max and Gab moved closer to May to embrace her. Gwynneth reached out her hand to add her support. May appreciated the gestures.

Gwynneth said, "May. If you want to meet him, we can make that happen over tea or dinner after the baby comes home. Soon."

Late that afternoon, Max went home. At six, May and Sonia walked back to Maria's house on Clinton Street, made a dinner from the chicken and zucchini Gab had bought, and turned in, May in her own bed, Sonia and Cedric in Gwynneth's.

Gab and Gwynneth spent the early evening talking to the baby and undressing him. With a smile and feigned disgust, Gab waved her hand in front of her nose as if to disperse the foul smell of the baby's soiled diaper. After wrapping him in a kimono but not putting his arms into its sleeves, she handed the infant to his mother.

As Gwynneth watched, Gab used a pitcher to put an inch of warm water in a small plastic tub the hospital had supplied. She set the tub on Gwynneth's bed and unwrapped the baby. When she lowered Gabe into the tub, he seemed to enjoy the warm water and Gab's cooing. And while they were glad to free his butt and genitalia of the remains of his emptied bowel, they saw he was happier when they took him out of his makeshift bath and dried him by wrapping him in a thick towel.

Gab dressed the baby in a clean diaper. As she swaddled him, she said to Gabe, "Your little butt goes right in the center, between these folds. Then we remove the cover of this adhesive tab and fasten it in front. We repeat with the tab on this side and fasten that one in front. Now you're ready to roll. Snug, but not tight." Holding an index and middle finger between the diaper and Gabe's protruding belly, she took care not to jostle the bloody stub of his umbilical cord. "In a couple of days, you'll be an expert."

Gwynneth heard and cherished every word.

At ten o'clock, an aide put Gabe into a rolling bassinet and took him to the nursery. Gwynneth and Gab slept.

THIRTY-FOUR
APRIL 14

Early on Monday afternoon, Sweeney and Martin Perez cruised up Germantown Avenue. At the wheel, Sweeney did his best to avoid the roadway's trolley tracks.

Martin said, "Acme in the next block. Want to check out the deli?"

As he stopped for the traffic light at Sedgwick, Sweeny said, "Not hungry." Then he added, "You know every Acme in Pennsylvania?"

Martin ignored the question. He looked across Germantown Avenue and said, "Turn in here. That's Gerhardt and three of his buddies."

"Where?" said Sweeney.

"End of the parking lot, by the hill."

Sweeney turned into the lot and parked near the store, far from where Heinrich Gerhardt stood with three young men in front of two cars. All four were dressed in dungarees and short-sleeved T-shirts. Gerhardt's friends were heavyset, their arms muscular and their bellies hanging well beyond their chests. All were drinking from longnecks. Two were smoking filtered cigarettes.

"Looking for some privacy there for their little party, where the edge of the lot forms a horseshoe and a little hill in back of them," said Sweeney.

Martin said, "Could serve as a corral, too."

"Do we want to see if they're our hit-and-run squad?"

"We can ask for identification. Shouldn't be drinking in public."

"We are two. They are four."

Martin tilted his head toward the four men. "Let's go."

Sweeney drove to where the four men stood drinking and talking and stopped in front of the two cars, pinning them in their parking places.

They bolted from their car. Martin said, "Gentlemen. We got a report of some youngsters drinking in public. You know anything about that?"

The startled men neither moved nor answered Martin.

"Pennsylvania State Police here," said Sweeney, holding up his badge. Then, sheathing the ID in his coat pocket, he asked, "May we see some identification?"

The four turned to one another, caucusing, not responding to Sweeney's request.

Martin said, "We can run you over to the barracks for identification if you'd rather not be outdoors."

Gerhardt sneered at the cops. "You can't roust us. We haven't done anything —"

"You are drinking in public," Sweeney said. "You are resisting the lawful request of a police officer. You can be detained if that's —"

The shortest man in the quartet made a rude response. "Get cursed lost."

"Have it your way," Martin said. "You are all under arrest."

Sweeney got everyone's attention when he pulled his Taurus cannon from its holster and released the safety. Seeking to cool the situation, Martin said, "It's drinking in public. Can we settle it without getting excited?"

When the four resumed their caucus, Sweeney surprised Gerhardt, handcuffing him and steering him into the back seat of the police vehicle. As he did, Gerhardt hollered, "The safety is off the cursed weasel's Taurus, Billy."

Martin slipped into the cruiser and spoke into the radio. "Requesting backup." He gave the address and their location, adding, "No light, no siren."

Three minutes later, backup officers arrived in a state police cruiser and, recognizing the unmarked cruiser's antenna, parked next to it. Martin identified himself and summarized the situation.

The backup officers frisked and cuffed the three others and secured them in the police cars.

Martin asked, "Follow us to Belmont Avenue?" They agreed, and the two vehicles drove the five miles to the barracks.

THIRTY-FIVE

SEPTEMBER 11

After Labor Day, the *Philadelphia Inquirer* reported that the merged boards of AmeRxOne and Scriptaphage had replaced an interim CEO and named Ed Spurgeon as Scriptaphage's new CEO, effective September 15.

At their chapter early on September 11, Max told Gwynneth, "Short item. Ed Spurgeon is dropping by at ten this morning."

Gwynneth nodded and waited.

"Melinda Hawthorne, his chief of staff at Scriptaphage, knows a few key officers here, including the outgoing interim CEO. She's been in touch with them. They've talked about your slick resolution of the Norman Hughes dilemma. And not a peep that you're a working mother. So Melinda Hawthorne suggested Ed reach out to you in September, before his arrival as the new CEO. He's not gonna interrogate you today. He's not here to forge a blood alliance. He wants to say hello and thank you. That's it."

Gwynneth said, "Thanks for the briefing. Does he want *anything* from us today?"

"He wants nothing from *us*. He's here to see *you*."

Gwynneth frowned. Her expression asked for amplification.

"OK. You don't see it?"

Gwynneth kept her gaze on Max.

"How you managed the Norman Hughes issue. Any nitwit can fire someone. And some can also scare the daylights out of the survivors. The trick is to do it the way you sacked Norman Hughes.

It was long overdue. The inertia was a big hurdle. You cleared it. His sense of entitlement was potent. Laches were in play. You were new and untested. He'd gotten away with blustering to cover his incompetence for so long he thought he was safe. You *erased* him."

When she took a breath, Gwynneth broke in. "OK, Max," she said without emotion, "you're making a speech here."

Max nodded in agreement. "I'm wrapping up. The whole company benefited from his firing. Costs in Hughes's division are down thirty percent. And your approach was brilliant. All business. No talk of political correctness. You did your cursed homework. Which you —"

Gwynneth interrupted. "Jasmine Lugo did all the —"

Max cut in to override the interruption but did not raise her voice. "No. Jasmine did what she was *told*. All this is why Spurgeon wants to meet you."

Gwynneth nodded and asked, "When did you say he's coming?"

"Ten. You have two hours."

"You've been involved in this kind of thing before?"

"A merger? Yes. But at lower levels, where all we had was rumors for weeks and then a done deal. I've never seen one unfold right in front of me."

She paused, then said, "Another thing. We just found out Natalia Petrovic will be in charge of managing details of the merger. She's thirty-five, forty. Got her MBA at Xavier University. She's done at least one other merger, but we don't know much about her."

Gwynneth repeated the name. "Natalia Petrovic."

"Right. And they'll be here at ten."

"Natalia and Ed?"

"And maybe Melinda."

"Thanks, Max," Gwynneth said.

After Max left, Gwynneth called Stanhope. "His visit is a surprise. Any thoughts about how to manage it?" she asked.

"Yes. If he crows about your accomplishments, point to your team. And remember, he's coming by to greet you in person…and maybe to salute you, too. Don't raise any heavy issues. Don't ask him how many Norman Hugheses he's carrying at the old Scriptaphage. Be cordial, not contentious. Let him do the talking."

At ten, Max sent a text from outside Gwynneth's office. "They're here. Ten seconds."

Gwynneth put her computer to sleep. As she stood to greet the visitors, Max rapped on the doorjamb.

"Good morning," Gwynneth said.

"Good morning. I'm Natalia Petrovic."

Natalia was not petite and at five feet four inches was almost as tall as Gwynneth. She wore a comfortable-looking dark-gray pantsuit and red leather flats. A jade necklace complemented a brilliant emerald she wore in a ring on the middle finger of her left hand.

"Let me introduce Ed Spurgeon," she said.

Spurgeon was a wiry man of fifty-five or sixty. His thinning gray hair was almost white and contrasted with his horn-rimmed glasses. He wore an inky dark-blue suit, pale yellow shirt, and orange-and-black striped tie. The odor of excessive cologne he brought into the room was not nauseating to Gwynneth, but it was not pleasant.

The two women shook hands. Ed Spurgeon nodded as Gwynneth shook hands with him. Then, her open palm gesturing to the sofa and chairs around her small table, she offered them seats. They accepted. Ed sat himself on the low sofa. Gwynneth and Natalia sat in adjacent chairs across from him.

As she had in her meeting with Norman Hughes, Gwynneth sat and waited for an overture from the new CEO. Ed Spurgeon did not speak.

Gwynneth turned in her chair to face Natalia and, using a reference to one of the local commuter routes, asked, "We're a little off the Main Line here. Any difficulty finding us?"

"No," said Natalia. "Max gave us directions."

Gwynneth nodded and smiled, then turned back to Ed Spurgeon.

Ed sat up straight on the sofa and said, "We can stay just a few minutes, Dr. Trevor." He paused, waiting for Gwynneth to correct him and ask him to call her by her first name. She nodded and let him continue.

"We're in the middle of an exciting merger, as you know. A major challenge in executing a merger of two large firms is building on our strengths and eliminating redundancies. We can add significant value to a new firm."

Gwynneth nodded at him and at Natalia as well. She noticed that Natalia looked a little bored. *Maybe she's heard this rap a few times*, Gwynneth mused.

"Most redundancies occur in so-called overhead centers. Fewer occur in operations such as yours — risk assessment and monitoring clinical trials."

Gwynneth, suppressing a frown and pout, did not point out overlap existed in operations in the two merging firms. She kept eye contact with Ed and sat, ready for his follow-up.

"During mergers, we rely on trusted incumbents in both firms to help us with identifying superfluous staff," he said. "Standard metrics can help but don't always distinguish the high-value employees from the ones we want to outplace. Some incumbents have suggested you'd be a valuable help to us in that process," he concluded, sitting back and awaiting a response.

Gwynneth tried to ignore his clichés and said, "That's reassuring to hear." She paused, waiting for Ed Spurgeon to continue.

Ed said, "Your performance in this directorate has been outstanding and has drawn the attention of many."

Gwynneth, mindful of Stanhope's counsel, did not scold him for dousing himself with cologne, but said, "That's kind of you to say about our team."

Ed leaned forward. "We want you to know we look forward to working with you one-on-one," he said.

Gwynneth mused on whether she'd detected a faint whiff of sexual innuendo. She decided she was overreacting, but in response to her calm gaze, it was Ed who looked away first.

Imagining they were seconds away from ending their chat, he followed up with a cursory query. "Did you have any questions for us?"

"No," she said. "I appreciate your visit."

Ed had not expected her brief answer and was confounded by it. He said, "Well, we're eager to keep our firm lean and alert to opportunities for sustaining our profitable —"

Gwynneth broke in to say, "You may have heard we've cut one poor performer here." Her statement was not a question. It seemed to take him by surprise. He nodded.

She added, "There's more of that to be done."

Ed responded to her comment with a frown. His expression suggested that he preferred the role of giving the bold summaries to underlings, whose proper role was to heed his comments. And Gwynneth, thinking she might've overstepped the bounds of Stanhope's counsel to let him do the talking, said nothing further.

Ed gave his own wrap-up. "Good. We'll be interested in discussing those matters in the near future."

Then he stood and said to Natalia, "Shall we?" And to Gwynneth, "We thank you for your time. I am glad to have met you and had a chance to talk to you."

A few minutes after they left, Max looked in but started to leave when she saw Gwynneth on the telephone. Standing beside her desk, Gwynneth motioned her to stay.

"I'm just trying to reach Carmen Stanhope," she said.

Max nodded and stood on the other side of the desk.

Into the phone, Gwynneth said, "Hi. Max is here in the office. I called to tell you about my session with Ed Spurgeon."

Max heard Gwynneth recap the visit, then ask into the phone, "Any thoughts?"

Stanhope's reply must've been brief.

"Appreciate your ideas earlier this morning," Gwynneth said. "Talk to you soon."

THIRTY-SIX
SEPTEMBER 18–22

On Thursday, September 18, Gwynneth stopped by CEO Ed Spurgeon's executive suite. Belinda Hawthorne, the chief of staff, was chatting with Natalia Petrovic, who beckoned Gwynneth to join them. Before she sat, Gwynneth set her time sheet on Belinda's desk.

"All well in the monitoring directorate?"

Gwynneth nodded. "Yes. Just wanted to remind you I'm taking off a few hours tomorrow."

"I remember the date," Belinda said. "Long weekend?"

"Going to the Barnes in Merion for a guided tour of the arboretum."

"Isn't that closed?"

"Not the arboretum. Max'll drive us. And we'll spend time in the medicinal plant garden."

At noon on Friday, Max drove her gray Nissan Juke out of the parking garage on Market Street. By twelve fifteen, they were standing in a shady parking spot opposite the arboretum's greenhouse.

They used Gwynneth's family membership card and a guest pass to enter. After strolling among the medicinal plants, they spent a half hour on the guided tour. As they left the arboretum, Gwynneth spoke for a few minutes into her cell phone, then said to Max, "Take us over the Schuylkill on Roosevelt Avenue and down Broad Street. We can stop at Temple for a bit."

Gwynneth directed them to street parking on Montgomery Avenue. Minutes later, they were sitting with Dr. Ernesto Castillo.

"Thanks for squeezing us in here on a Friday afternoon," she said.

"Glad to visit any former student of Hildegard Zimmer," he said.

"I wanted to be sure you knew we're aware of some of your clinical research on multiple myeloma. Participants have life expectancy of less than six months —"

Dr. Castillo cut in and said, "They're difficult times for most patients and their families."

"Can you account for the high levels of customer and family satisfaction with their treatment here? These are people suffering the worst physical and emotional —"

Dr. Castillo interrupted. "Yes. They are. And you know, when I first saw that, I thought our data collection was flawed. Could they really feel good about us? Their dear ones were *dying*. But they did, and it was humbling when we discovered the reasons families loved us even though they were heartbroken. You want to guess?"

Max said, "In some clinical trials, participant families compliment the nurse practitioners more than the doctors."

Castillo said, "That was part of it. But the biggest factors were two-dollar valet parking and orderlies who wheeled the participants in from curbside. We got those ideas last year."

"Ideas?" asked Gwynneth.

"Someone who works for Dr. George Cramer conducted a site visit in March 2013. He saw participants waiting in line in the cold entryway and lobby off Montgomery Avenue. He also noticed the parking tower was half empty, and asked us about valet parking. He must've talked to his boss about it, because someone in Dr. Cramer's office called us and asked if we'd be interested in offering valet parking for three months. We tried it, and it was popular, so we've kept it."

"Is it expensive?" Max asked.

Castillo shook his head. "No. It isn't much. Back then, AmeRxOne authorized twenty thousand dollars to cover start-up costs, and Scriptaphage will support it through 2015. We asked other clinical centers about it. Only a few offer valet parking. And here, community groups who've criticized us in the past called to thank us for hiring locals to park the cars. A radio station broadcast a segment on it. We got so much good publicity we hired the valets full-time and stopped collecting the two dollars."

After a pause, Castillo shook his head. "We want patients in clinical trials to recognize our medical and scientific brilliance. But the families most appreciated valet parking and orderlies who helped with wheelchairs."

Gwynneth thanked him again for his time. The visit ended.

In the car, Gwynneth asked Max to drop her at the office. At Scriptaphage, Gwynneth went straight to Cramer's office. He was not pleased to see her.

"Just a quick drop-by here at four on a Friday afternoon, George. We stopped at Temple's school of science and technology today —"

He interrupted her. "Looking for some dirt to slander me?"

She shook her head. "No, George, I —"

"You don't just barge in here anytime you want to sow your chaos. You can take your cursed female self outta here right *now*."

"As you wish, George. I came here to pay you a compliment about —"

He cut in again. "I can live without any of that from you. Do I have to ask you again to take your cursed body part out of here?"

She turned away and left his office.

At the execs' meeting Monday morning, in his summary presentation George finished with a cryptic note. "Just want to report it's disconcerting to be invaded by trespassers who have problems heeding civil boundaries."

The CFO, Tim Shekel, asked him to amplify. George Cramer lambasted Gwynneth for ambushing him in his office three days earlier. Shekel frowned at her.

"Is your frown a question?" Gwynneth asked. "Are you asking me for a response?"

"Yes," he said.

"I stopped by to pay a compliment —"

George interrupted her, "That's total cursed nonsense. And a lie."

"It was a courtesy visit to —"

"From a cursed *liar*," George snapped.

It was tense in the conference room. Seventeen other executives were at sea about how to respond to the exchange.

In Gwynneth's direction, Shekel said, "Can you say something about the compliment?"

"She's nothing but a token incompetent who had no *business* coming into —"

Gwynneth picked up her cell phone and slammed its flat back on the conference table. Its sharp sound had the impact of a gunshot. Everyone was hushed by it, even George Cramer.

She activated the cell phone and pushed two buttons. All nineteen sets of ears heard a recording of her voice: "Just a quick drop-by here at four on a Friday afternoon, George. We stopped at Temple's —"

George roared at the sound, "She recorded me without my cursed permission, and I'll —"

Shekel said, "George, you can sue her for that, but first we're going to hear the rest of this." He turned to her and said, "Dr. Trevor, restart that recording. And Dr. Cramer, while she cues that up, you may be quiet, or you may be excused."

"You think you can throw me *out* —"

"You may be excused, Dr. Cramer, or be quiet. What's it going to be?"

Marvin Felderman leaned over toward George and spoke to him. George gave Marvin and Tim menacing looks but was still.

Gwynneth played the thirty-second recording of her attempt to pay a compliment and Cramer's crude rejections.

Scriptaphage's executives sitting around the conference table were stunned. The men looked at each other or the tabletop and winced at George's vulgarities. The women stared at one another and at Shekel. George sat in open defiance and without remorse at the damning audio clip, glaring at what he regarded as three pieces of vapid abstract artwork hanging on the conference room wall.

When the recording ended, a canopy of silence descended on the conference room. Shekel, challenging her but determined to sound impartial, asked, "What was your compliment?"

Gwynneth said, "After a site visit to Temple last year, one of George Cramer's researchers suggested valet parking and wheelchair help for participants in a clinical trial. Patients and their families are happy with those services."

Shekel was dumbfounded at the story and disappointed that he hadn't heard it.

He exhaled, then said, "This meeting is adjourned." He got up from his chair, shook his head, and left the conference room.

Marvin spoke to George Cramer, whose emotional fury and humiliation contorted his countenance and projected the image of an immature soul in turmoil. He was not mollified by Marvin's remarks.

After a few uneasy moments, fifteen Scriptaphage execs followed Shekel out of the conference room, leaving George Cramer, Bob Peterson, and Marvin Felderman in its gloomy quiet.

THIRTY-SEVEN

OCTOBER 10

At seven thirty on Friday morning, Henry wheeled his son's stroller up the entrance ramp into the drop-off area of the Quaker Daycare Center, a preschool program Gabe, now six months old, had begun attending on October 1. Maya Khoury, head of the school, greeted them.

Gabe had awakened when Henry unlatched the car seat and lifted it out of the stroller. Nadine Cadmus, Gabe's teacher, took the child and his car seat from Henry, who pushed the empty stroller into an alcove jammed with a dozen others. Giselle and Esperanza, twin three-year-olds who stood beside Maya, ran to Nadine's side and said, "*Hola*, Gabe." In reply, Gabe kicked at the sides of his car seat and squealed at the girls.

"See you at six," Henry said to Maya and Nadine.

Henry walked five blocks to his office from Gabe's campus at Race and Fifteenth Streets. He greeted and spoke for a few minutes with Carmen Stanhope about their progress on work they were doing for the Broad Street Bank.

Stanhope asked about his Lauder program. "Still thinking the Chinese is doable?"

"Yes," he said. "It's working fine."

"And the baby?"

"Gabe?" Henry blinked. "He's preverbal. Hasn't said a word in any —"

Stanhope laughed. "I know he's not in the Chinese language program. I meant his schedule."

"Hard to say. It's his eighth day in childcare outside the home," Henry said. Gwynneth had used two of her three months of maternity leave from Scriptaphage and returned to work in mid-June.

Stanhope nodded. "I was an emotional wreck when I put our oldest in day care. He was happy there, but I couldn't go back and leave him the second day. We just waited for all three kids to be in elementary school before I went to Temple and then to work."

Henry waited to see if Stanhope had more to say about day care for one's children. When she didn't elaborate, he said, "Quaker schools get high ratings. They pay their teachers well, and at QDC, kids are infatuated with Gabe and talk to him every day. That didn't happen when we were managing his day care at home with a doula, a nanny, and Gwynneth's cousins."

Stanhope said, "Right. She mentioned that too. Hope day care works out for everybody. And the Lauder isn't overwhelming you?"

"No. The eight-week immersion in Beijing helped. And you—"

Stanhope was taken aback. "Me?"

He waited. When she said no more, he said, "Lauder teaches fluency in business and cultural language. But you've also taught us key business and cultural principles. The facts are always friendly. Show up early. Come prepared for meetings. Listen. Those impress clients more than speaking three languages."

Stanhope nodded and said, "Thanks for saying that, Henry."

"And," he said, then hesitated, letting Stanhope know he had more to say. "And during our work in Africa, we're in contact with Chinese project managers. They're financing and building roads and bridges and ports. It's a big advantage to speak to the bankers and engineers in their own language. But the only reason I'm there, in Gabarone and Durban and Maputo —"

She interrupted again. "OK, Henry. I got it. Here in the eastern time zone, it's comin' up on eight o'clock. Time to get our morning underway."

"Just one more quick point?"

Stanhope nodded. "Go ahead."

"Gwynneth isn't teaching biochemistry and in a lab fifty hours a week. She's a senior manager at a pharmaceutical company and studying in the business school at Drexel. You were the key in creating the pharma option —"

Stanhope cut in. "OK, Henry. Thanks. Let's get at it here."

Henry smiled and said, "Right," then strode off.

Michael Larson heard him approaching and caught up with him outside his office.

"Hey, Michael."

Henry smiled and waited. Sometimes when Michael came into the office this early, he wanted to talk.

Michael asked, "Anything in your Gospel about impressing the boss? Or chasing bonus money?"

Henry's smile melted from his countenance. He sighed and said, "There's some. But what's in there hasn't helped me."

Michael waited a few seconds for Henry to continue, then asked, "What *is* in there?"

Henry took another breath "The parables of the talents. One in Matthew 25 and one in Luke 19. They've vexed me for years."

"Glad to hear I'm not the only one put off by the parable of the talents."

Henry made eye contact and nodded to show his respect for the comment.

As the two young men stood in the early morning quiet of the ACI offices, Michael posed a question that Henry had asked him in somewhat different form and context the year before. "So? What are you gonna do?" Then, after a brief pause, Michael added a bold follow up to make the question sharper and less abstract. "You and Gwynneth have one baby in child care and another on the way. You gonna give up your careers and life here and raise your children in poverty?"

Henry nodded, admitting that Michael's question was apt. During more than a year of his tattoo practice he'd considered many career and lifestyle options. Few of his fellow citizens enjoyed his family's good health and financial prosperity. It was clear to him that his and Gwynneth's careers benefited from high status as well as a continued upward trajectory. It was less clear whether his pathway conflicted with his covenant to live life according to the Gospel.

He paused, not wanting to explain how he'd felt for months that a part of him was being reborn, as a chrysalis, relentlessly and naturally. But unlike a metamorphosing pupa with no idea of what lies ahead, he knew, despite the uncertainties, he was committed to be with Gwynneth, with two or more children, in Philadelphia, struggling to live his life according to the Gospel. It was exhilarating, not scary, to see how his drawings took form at the point of his compressed charcoal pencils. He said to Michael, "We're wrestling with some of the issues you raise. But right now, I confess, I do not know what I'm gonna do."

That afternoon, Carmichael and Andre conducted their customary Friday review of business prospects.

Andre said, "Stanhope has put two new proposals out there. One's to a brokerage, and one's to a bank. If either leads to a contract —"

Carmichael interrupted. "We're gonna need two or three new associates. Stanhope doesn't spend hours on proposals unless she's sure prospects will buy what she's selling."

"Stanhope follows trends in a few industries and when she sees potential clients, she avoids small talk. She discusses how to move them into the vanguard—"

Carmichael cut in again. "She learned that practice from you. And it's why she's successful." After a pause, he added, "You think she might decide to go out on her own? Could we lose her?"

Andre shrugged. "Maybe."

"Stanhope and Henry are bringing in millions in new work. If she goes and Henry follows her out the door? They'd be hard to replace."

Andre said, "Yeah, it'd be a loss if they go. But I think we'll be all right."

"Yeah," Carmichael said. "Agreed. We'll be all right."

www.ingramcontent.com/pod-product-compliance
Lightning Source LLC
Chambersburg PA
CBHW020549020726
47494CB00006B/1996